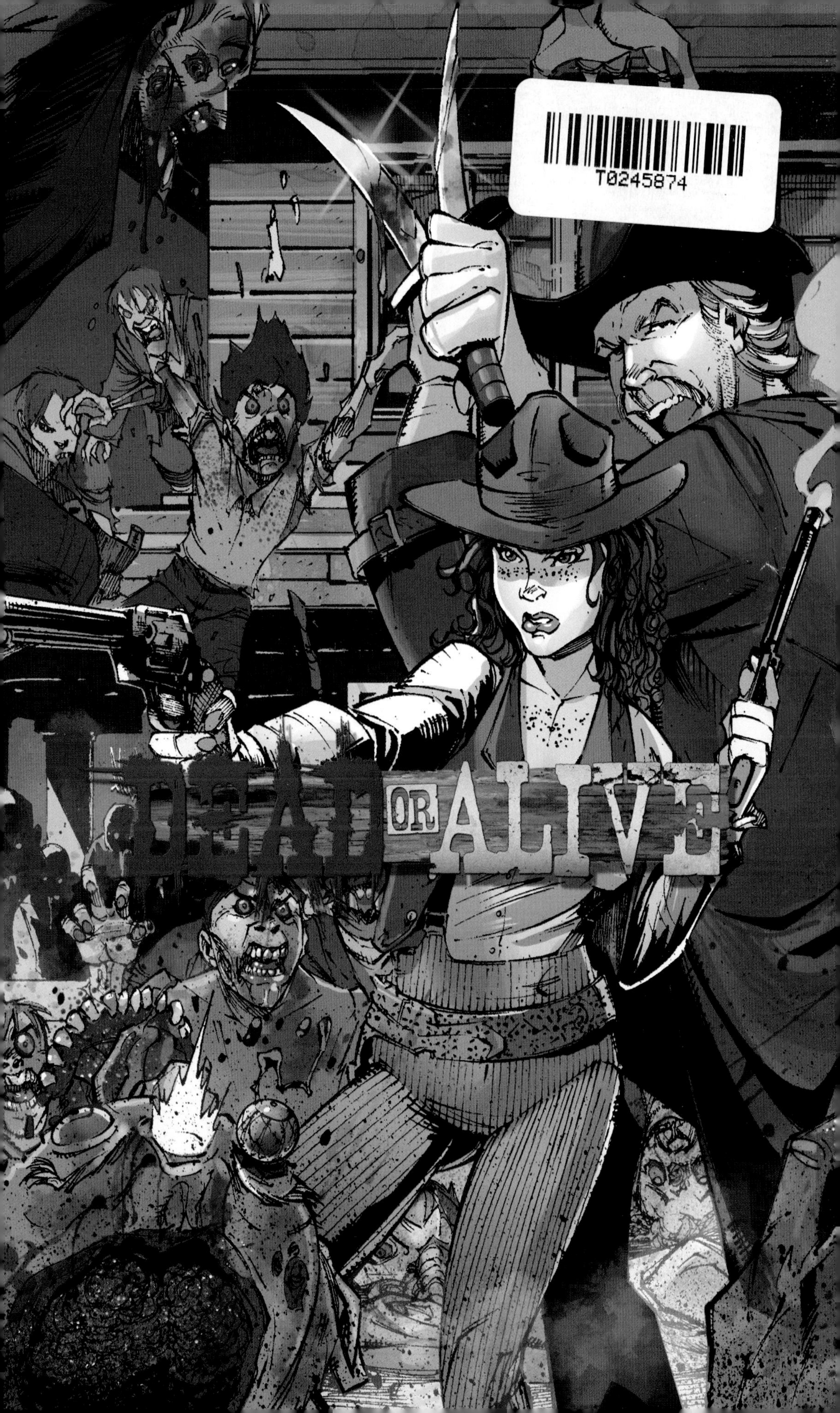
DEAD OR ALIVE

publishers
PAUL ENS, JOSHUA STARNES and SCOTT CHITWOOD

DEAD OR ALIVE

This volume collects DEAD OR ALIVE #1 through #4 of the comic-book series originally printed by Red 5 Comics.

Published by
RED 5 COMICS
27103 Kelsey Woods Court, Cypress, Texas 77433

www.red5comics.com

To find a comics shop in your area, call the Comic Shop Locator Service toll-free at 1-888-266-4226

First edition:
ISBN-13: 978-1-954167-14-8

Printed in South Korea.

DEAD OR ALIVE

SCRIPT
SCOTT CHITWOOD

ART
ALFONSO RUIZ

COLORS
GARY HENDERSON
IVAN PLASCENCIA

LETTERS
TROY PETERI

COVER ART
MATT BUSCH
ALFONSO RUIZ

RED 5 COMICS

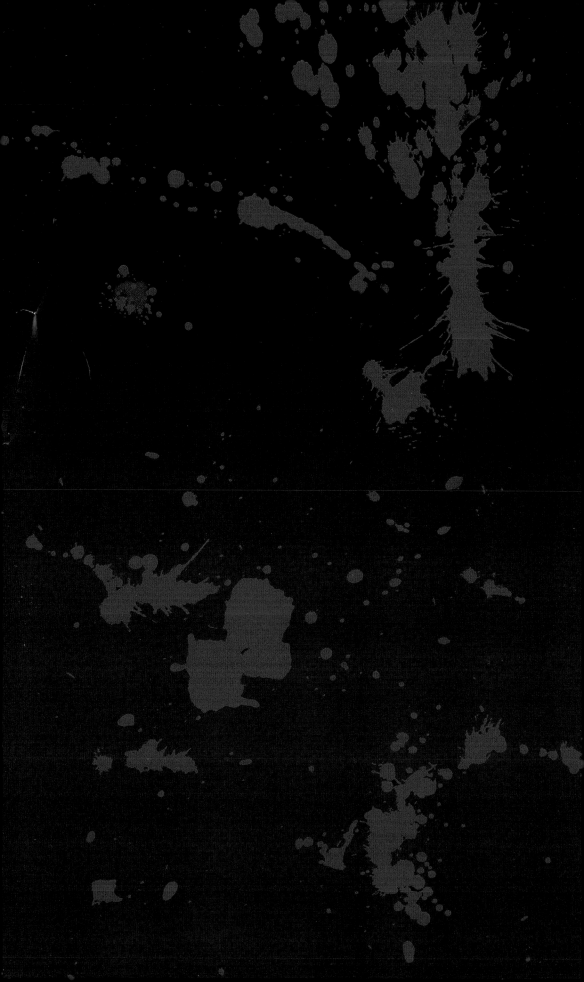

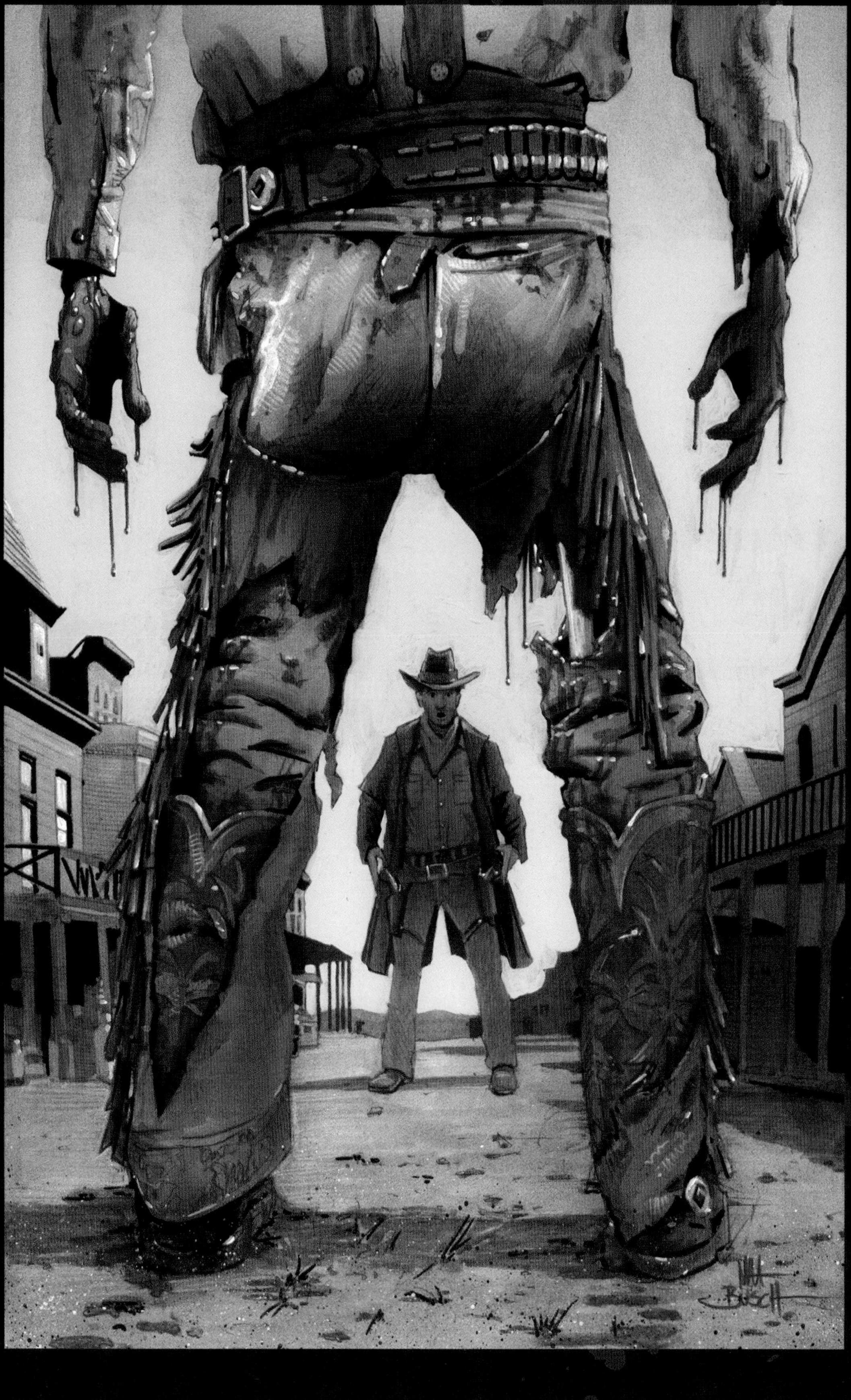

In 1873, John Moss was prospecting in Montezuma County, Colorado when he entered a canyon and discovered an incredible Native American city built among the cliffs. Originally constructed by the Ancestral Pueblo (or Anasazi) around the 12th century, the city in Mesa Verde was long since abandoned. Buildings with 150 rooms, large religious constructions called kivas, and impressive towers were mysteriously left untouched for centuries. The rooms of the buildings were filled with basic household objects, food, and tools as if they were all abandoned by the Ancestral Pueblo the day they disappeared.

"Anasazi" is the Navajo word for "ancient enemy".

The cause of their sudden disappearance around 1275 A.D. has never been explained.

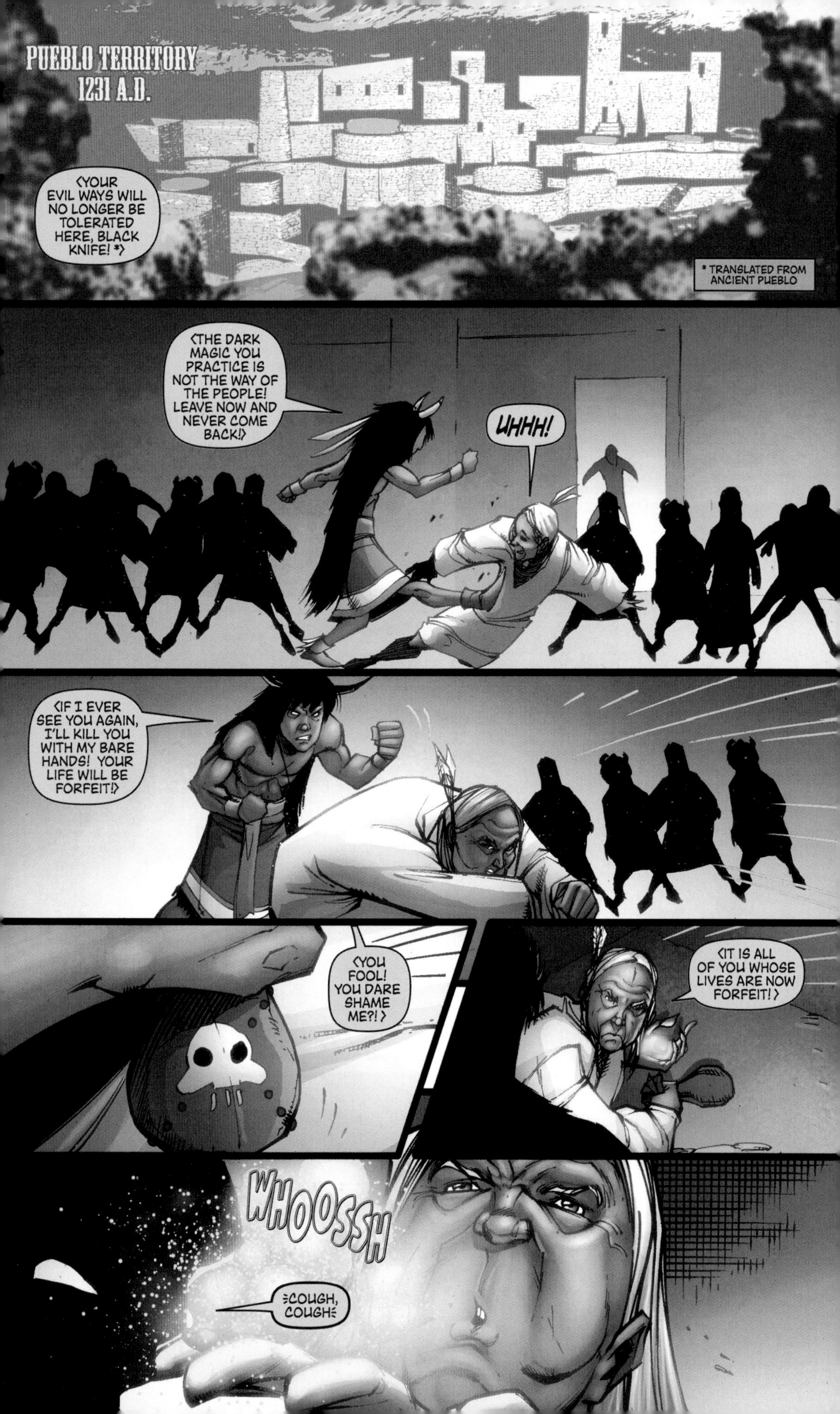
PUEBLO TERRITORY 1231 A.D.
<YOUR EVIL WAYS WILL NO LONGER BE TOLERATED HERE, BLACK KNIFE! *>
* TRANSLATED FROM ANCIENT PUEBLO
<THE DARK MAGIC YOU PRACTICE IS NOT THE WAY OF THE PEOPLE! LEAVE NOW AND NEVER COME BACK!>
UHHH!
<IF I EVER SEE YOU AGAIN, I'LL KILL YOU WITH MY BARE HANDS! YOUR LIFE WILL BE FORFEIT!>
<YOU FOOL! YOU DARE SHAME ME?!>
<IT IS ALL OF YOU WHOSE LIVES ARE NOW FORFEIT!>
WHOOSSH
COUGH, COUGH

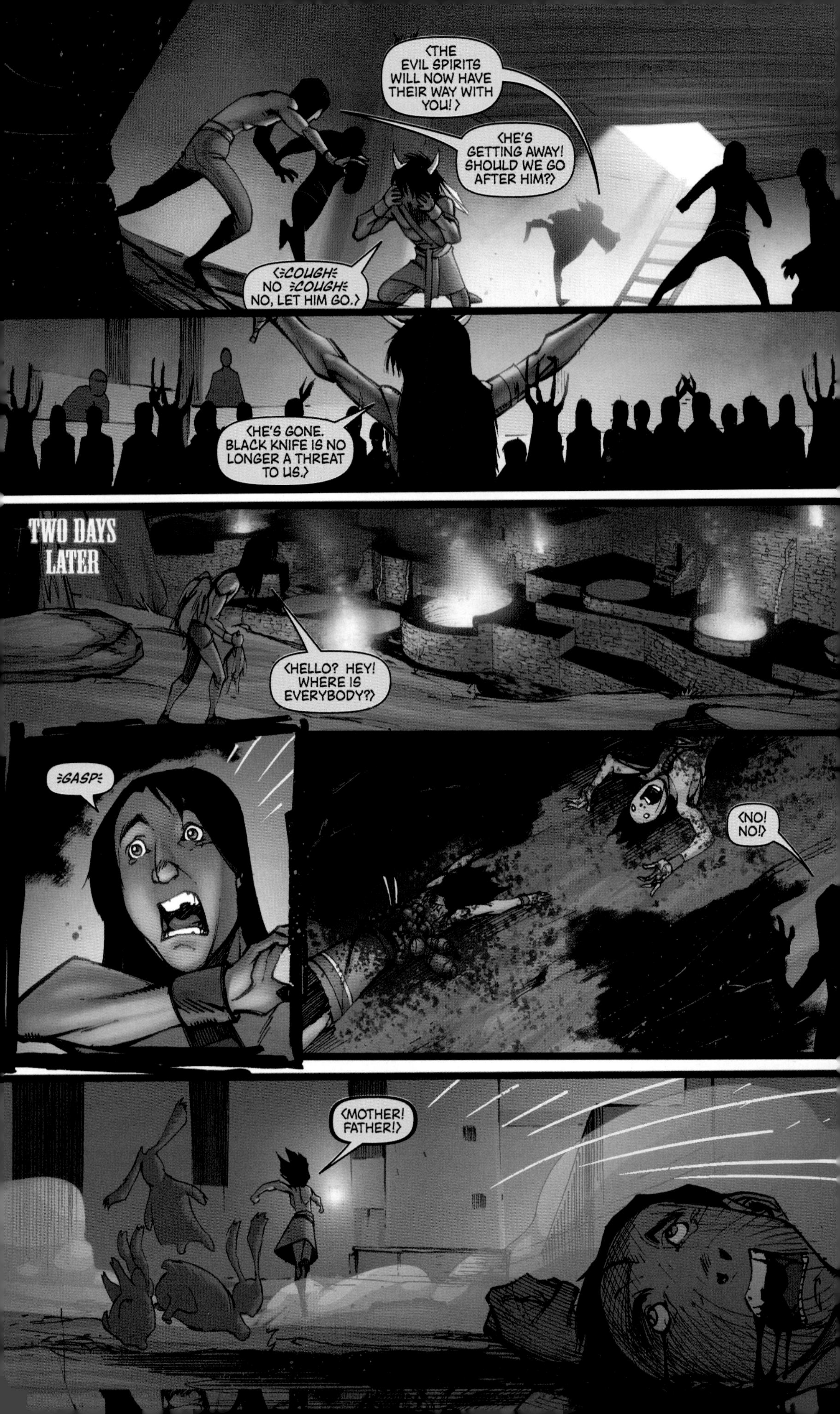
‹THE EVIL SPIRITS WILL NOW HAVE THEIR WAY WITH YOU!›
‹HE'S GETTING AWAY! SHOULD WE GO AFTER HIM?›
‹≡COUGH≡ NO ≡COUGH≡ NO, LET HIM GO.›
‹HE'S GONE. BLACK KNIFE IS NO LONGER A THREAT TO US.›
TWO DAYS LATER
‹HELLO? HEY! WHERE IS EVERYBODY?›
≡GASP≡
‹NO! NO!›
‹MOTHER! FATHER!›

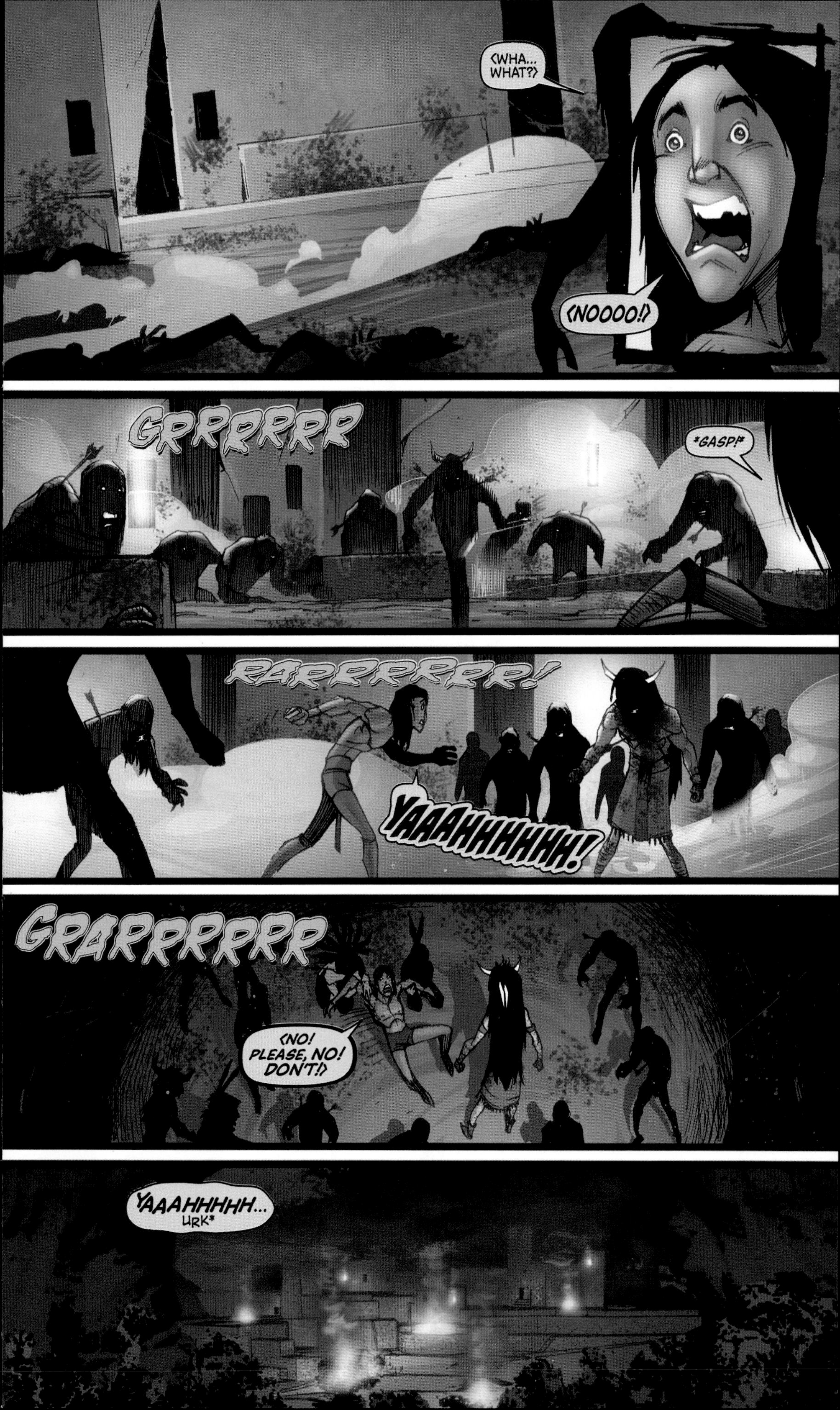

<WHA... WHAT?>
<NOOOO!>
GRRRRRR
GASP!
RARRRRRRR!
YAAAHHHHHH!
GRARRRRRR
<NO! PLEASE, NO! DON'T!>
YAAAHHHHH... URK*

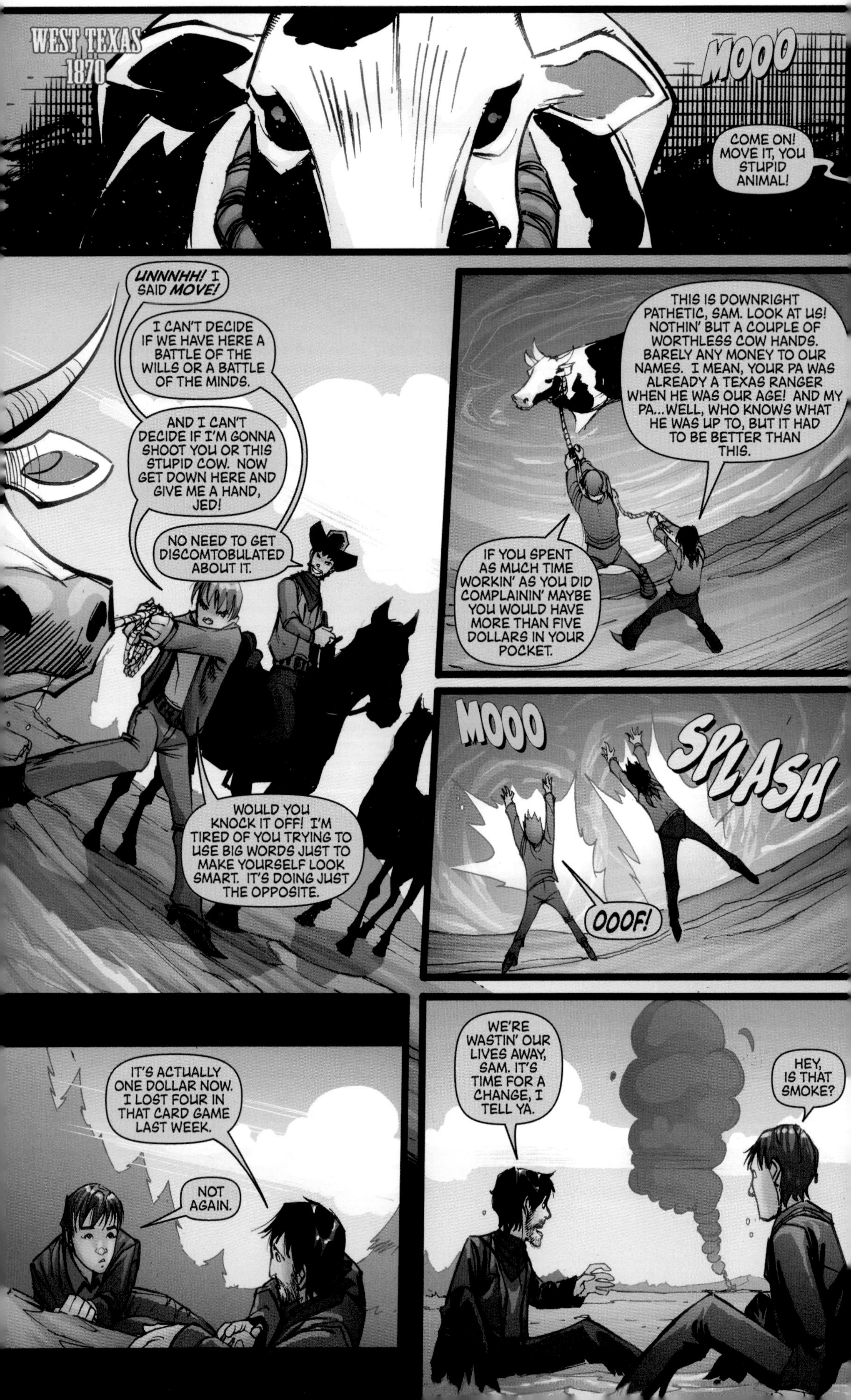
WEST TEXAS
1870
MOOO
COME ON! MOVE IT, YOU STUPID ANIMAL!
UNNNHH! I SAID MOVE!
I CAN'T DECIDE IF WE HAVE HERE A BATTLE OF THE WILLS OR A BATTLE OF THE MINDS.
AND I CAN'T DECIDE IF I'M GONNA SHOOT YOU OR THIS STUPID COW. NOW GET DOWN HERE AND GIVE ME A HAND, JED!
NO NEED TO GET DISCOMTOBULATED ABOUT IT.
WOULD YOU KNOCK IT OFF! I'M TIRED OF YOU TRYING TO USE BIG WORDS JUST TO MAKE YOURSELF LOOK SMART. IT'S DOING JUST THE OPPOSITE.
THIS IS DOWNRIGHT PATHETIC, SAM. LOOK AT US! NOTHIN' BUT A COUPLE OF WORTHLESS COW HANDS. BARELY ANY MONEY TO OUR NAMES. I MEAN, YOUR PA WAS ALREADY A TEXAS RANGER WHEN HE WAS OUR AGE! AND MY PA...WELL, WHO KNOWS WHAT HE WAS UP TO, BUT IT HAD TO BE BETTER THAN THIS.
IF YOU SPENT AS MUCH TIME WORKIN' AS YOU DID COMPLAININ' MAYBE YOU WOULD HAVE MORE THAN FIVE DOLLARS IN YOUR POCKET.
MOOO
SPLASH
OOOF!
IT'S ACTUALLY ONE DOLLAR NOW. I LOST FOUR IN THAT CARD GAME LAST WEEK.
NOT AGAIN.
WE'RE WASTIN' OUR LIVES AWAY, SAM. IT'S TIME FOR A CHANGE, I TELL YA.
HEY, IS THAT SMOKE?

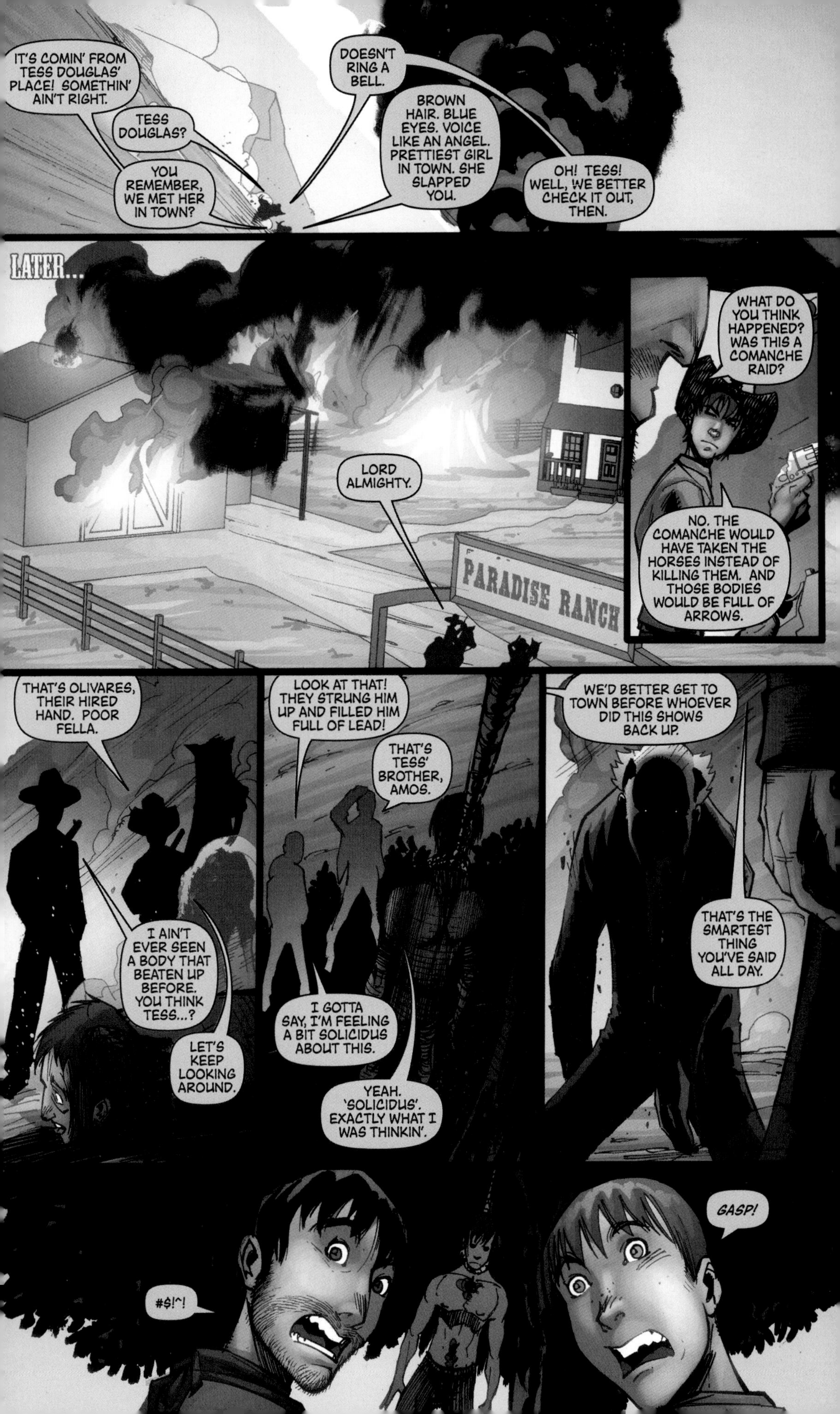
IT'S COMIN' FROM TESS DOUGLAS' PLACE! SOMETHIN' AIN'T RIGHT.
TESS DOUGLAS?
YOU REMEMBER, WE MET HER IN TOWN?
DOESN'T RING A BELL.
BROWN HAIR. BLUE EYES. VOICE LIKE AN ANGEL. PRETTIEST GIRL IN TOWN. SHE SLAPPED YOU.
OH! TESS! WELL, WE BETTER CHECK IT OUT, THEN.
LATER...
LORD ALMIGHTY.
PARADISE RANCH
WHAT DO YOU THINK HAPPENED? WAS THIS A COMANCHE RAID?
NO. THE COMANCHE WOULD HAVE TAKEN THE HORSES INSTEAD OF KILLING THEM. AND THOSE BODIES WOULD BE FULL OF ARROWS.
THAT'S OLIVARES, THEIR HIRED HAND. POOR FELLA.
I AIN'T EVER SEEN A BODY THAT BEATEN UP BEFORE. YOU THINK TESS...?
LET'S KEEP LOOKING AROUND.
LOOK AT THAT! THEY STRUNG HIM UP AND FILLED HIM FULL OF LEAD!
THAT'S TESS' BROTHER, AMOS.
I GOTTA SAY, I'M FEELING A BIT SOLICIDUS ABOUT THIS.
YEAH. 'SOLICIDUS'. EXACTLY WHAT I WAS THINKIN'.
WE'D BETTER GET TO TOWN BEFORE WHOEVER DID THIS SHOWS BACK UP.
THAT'S THE SMARTEST THING YOU'VE SAID ALL DAY.
GASP!
#$!^!

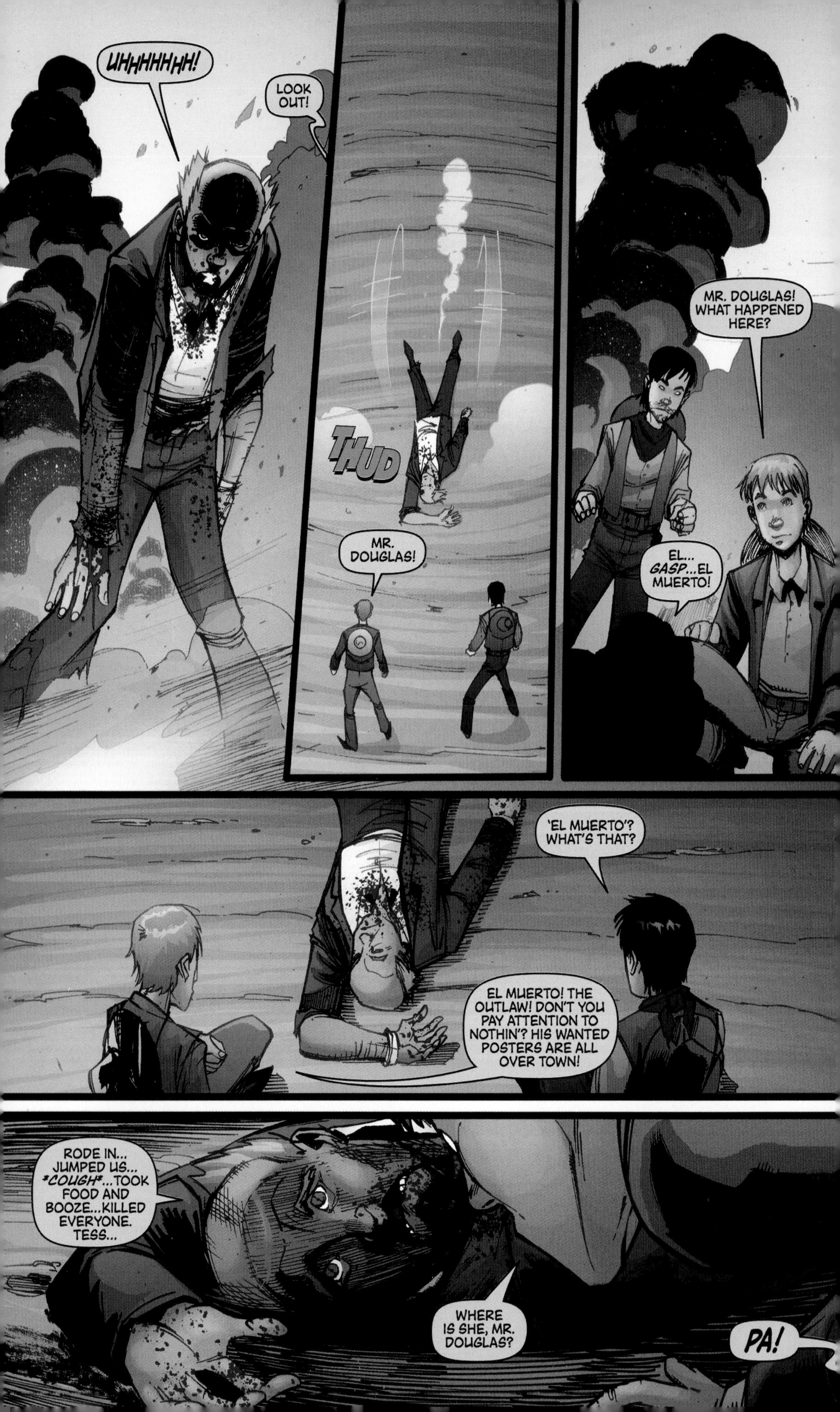
UHHHHHHH!
LOOK OUT!
THUD
MR. DOUGLAS!
MR. DOUGLAS! WHAT HAPPENED HERE?
EL... GASP...EL MUERTO!
'EL MUERTO'? WHAT'S THAT?
EL MUERTO! THE OUTLAW! DON'T YOU PAY ATTENTION TO NOTHIN'? HIS WANTED POSTERS ARE ALL OVER TOWN!
RODE IN... JUMPED US... *COUGH*...TOOK FOOD AND BOOZE...KILLED EVERYONE. TESS...
WHERE IS SHE, MR. DOUGLAS?
PA!

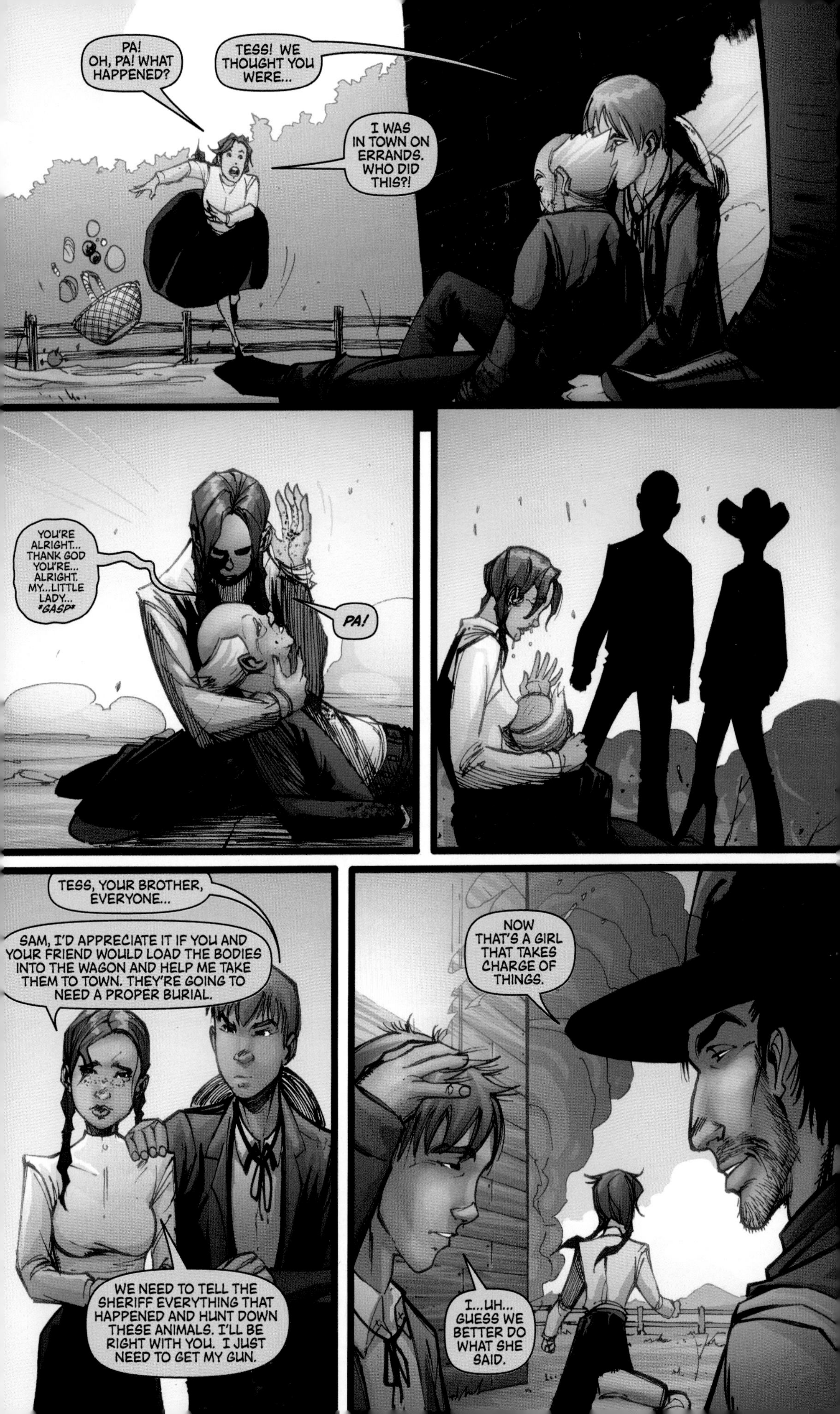
PA! OH, PA! WHAT HAPPENED?
TESS! WE THOUGHT YOU WERE...
I WAS IN TOWN ON ERRANDS. WHO DID THIS?!
YOU'RE ALRIGHT... THANK GOD YOU'RE... ALRIGHT. MY...LITTLE LADY... *GASP*
PA!
TESS, YOUR BROTHER, EVERYONE...
SAM, I'D APPRECIATE IT IF YOU AND YOUR FRIEND WOULD LOAD THE BODIES INTO THE WAGON AND HELP ME TAKE THEM TO TOWN. THEY'RE GOING TO NEED A PROPER BURIAL.
WE NEED TO TELL THE SHERIFF EVERYTHING THAT HAPPENED AND HUNT DOWN THESE ANIMALS. I'LL BE RIGHT WITH YOU. I JUST NEED TO GET MY GUN.
NOW THAT'S A GIRL THAT TAKES CHARGE OF THINGS.
I...UH... GUESS WE BETTER DO WHAT SHE SAID.

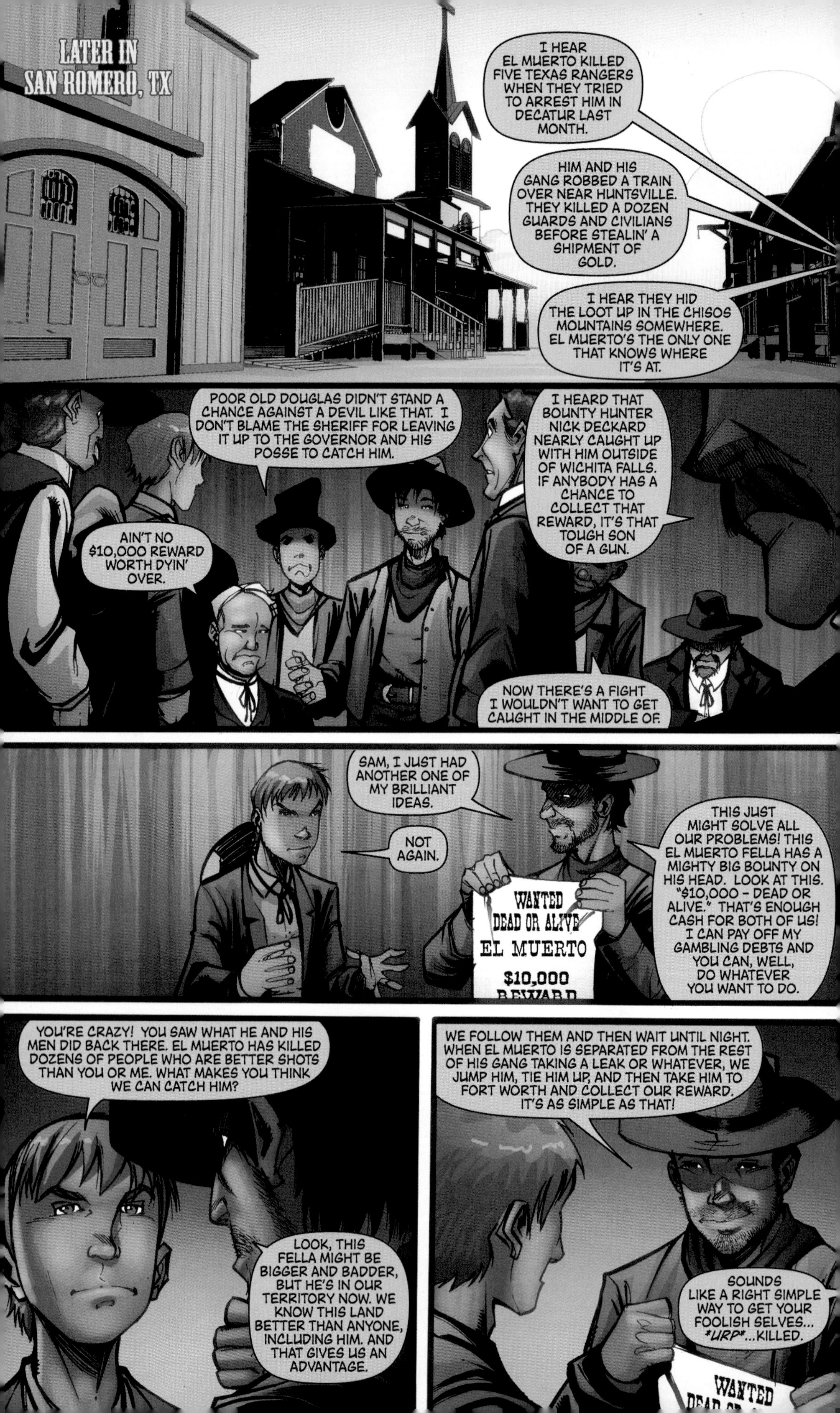
LATER IN SAN ROMERO, TX
I HEAR EL MUERTO KILLED FIVE TEXAS RANGERS WHEN THEY TRIED TO ARREST HIM IN DECATUR LAST MONTH.
HIM AND HIS GANG ROBBED A TRAIN OVER NEAR HUNTSVILLE. THEY KILLED A DOZEN GUARDS AND CIVILIANS BEFORE STEALIN' A SHIPMENT OF GOLD.
I HEAR THEY HID THE LOOT UP IN THE CHISOS MOUNTAINS SOMEWHERE. EL MUERTO'S THE ONLY ONE THAT KNOWS WHERE IT'S AT.
POOR OLD DOUGLAS DIDN'T STAND A CHANCE AGAINST A DEVIL LIKE THAT. I DON'T BLAME THE SHERIFF FOR LEAVING IT UP TO THE GOVERNOR AND HIS POSSE TO CATCH HIM.
AIN'T NO $10,000 REWARD WORTH DYIN' OVER.
I HEARD THAT BOUNTY HUNTER NICK DECKARD NEARLY CAUGHT UP WITH HIM OUTSIDE OF WICHITA FALLS. IF ANYBODY HAS A CHANCE TO COLLECT THAT REWARD, IT'S THAT TOUGH SON OF A GUN.
NOW THERE'S A FIGHT I WOULDN'T WANT TO GET CAUGHT IN THE MIDDLE OF.
SAM, I JUST HAD ANOTHER ONE OF MY BRILLIANT IDEAS.
NOT AGAIN.
THIS JUST MIGHT SOLVE ALL OUR PROBLEMS! THIS EL MUERTO FELLA HAS A MIGHTY BIG BOUNTY ON HIS HEAD. LOOK AT THIS. "$10,000 – DEAD OR ALIVE." THAT'S ENOUGH CASH FOR BOTH OF US! I CAN PAY OFF MY GAMBLING DEBTS AND YOU CAN, WELL, DO WHATEVER YOU WANT TO DO.
WANTED DEAD OR ALIVE
EL MUERTO
$10,000
YOU'RE CRAZY! YOU SAW WHAT HE AND HIS MEN DID BACK THERE. EL MUERTO HAS KILLED DOZENS OF PEOPLE WHO ARE BETTER SHOTS THAN YOU OR ME. WHAT MAKES YOU THINK WE CAN CATCH HIM?
LOOK, THIS FELLA MIGHT BE BIGGER AND BADDER, BUT HE'S IN OUR TERRITORY NOW. WE KNOW THIS LAND BETTER THAN ANYONE, INCLUDING HIM. AND THAT GIVES US AN ADVANTAGE.
WE FOLLOW THEM AND THEN WAIT UNTIL NIGHT. WHEN EL MUERTO IS SEPARATED FROM THE REST OF HIS GANG TAKING A LEAK OR WHATEVER, WE JUMP HIM, TIE HIM UP, AND THEN TAKE HIM TO FORT WORTH AND COLLECT OUR REWARD. IT'S AS SIMPLE AS THAT!
SOUNDS LIKE A RIGHT SIMPLE WAY TO GET YOUR FOOLISH SELVES... *URP*...KILLED.
WANTED

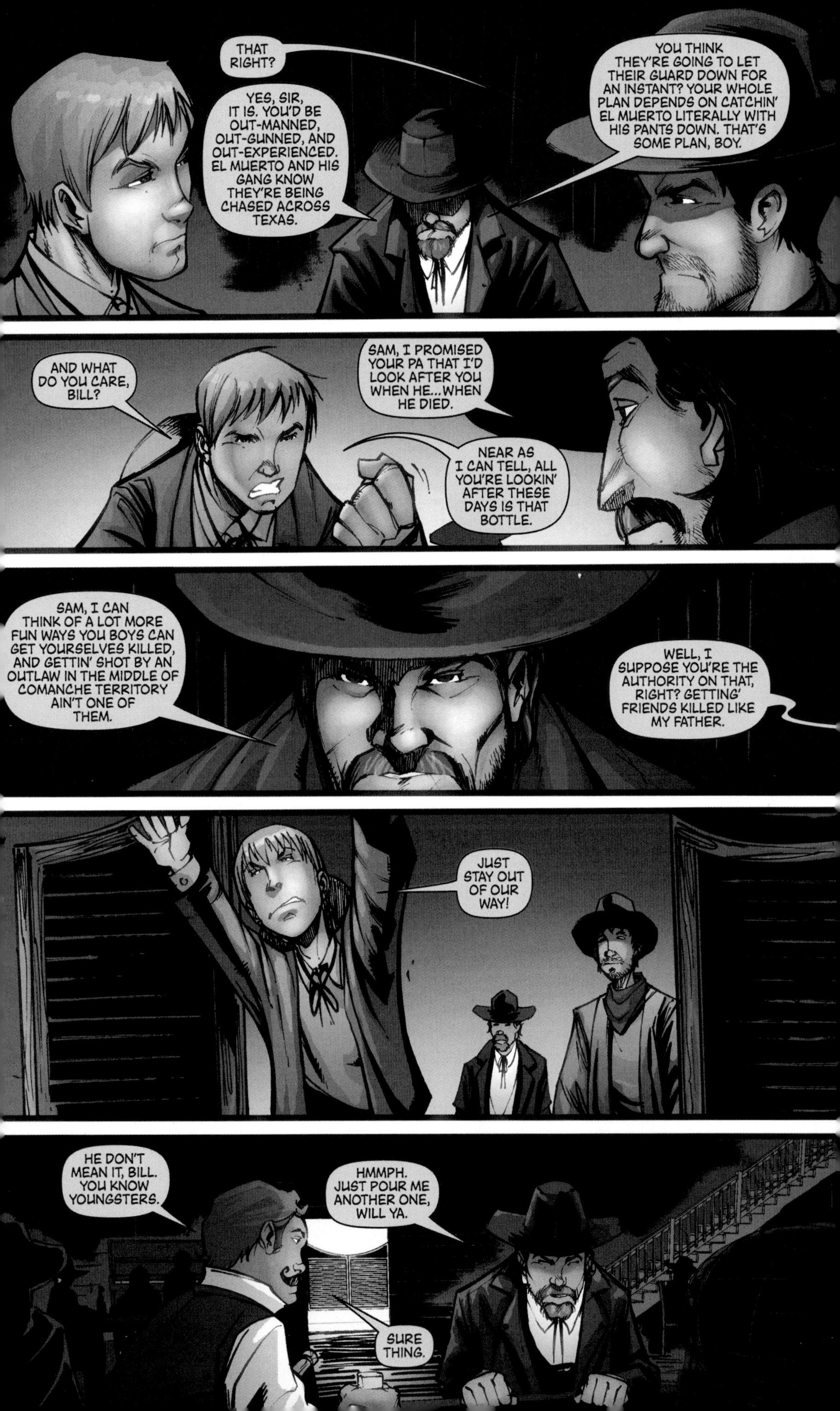
THAT RIGHT?
YES, SIR, IT IS. YOU'D BE OUT-MANNED, OUT-GUNNED, AND OUT-EXPERIENCED. EL MUERTO AND HIS GANG KNOW THEY'RE BEING CHASED ACROSS TEXAS.
YOU THINK THEY'RE GOING TO LET THEIR GUARD DOWN FOR AN INSTANT? YOUR WHOLE PLAN DEPENDS ON CATCHIN' EL MUERTO LITERALLY WITH HIS PANTS DOWN. THAT'S SOME PLAN, BOY.
AND WHAT DO YOU CARE, BILL?
SAM, I PROMISED YOUR PA THAT I'D LOOK AFTER YOU WHEN HE...WHEN HE DIED.
NEAR AS I CAN TELL, ALL YOU'RE LOOKIN' AFTER THESE DAYS IS THAT BOTTLE.
SAM, I CAN THINK OF A LOT MORE FUN WAYS YOU BOYS CAN GET YOURSELVES KILLED, AND GETTIN' SHOT BY AN OUTLAW IN THE MIDDLE OF COMANCHE TERRITORY AIN'T ONE OF THEM.
WELL, I SUPPOSE YOU'RE THE AUTHORITY ON THAT, RIGHT? GETTING' FRIENDS KILLED LIKE MY FATHER.
JUST STAY OUT OF OUR WAY!
HE DON'T MEAN IT, BILL. YOU KNOW YOUNGSTERS.
HMMPH. JUST POUR ME ANOTHER ONE, WILL YA.
SURE THING.

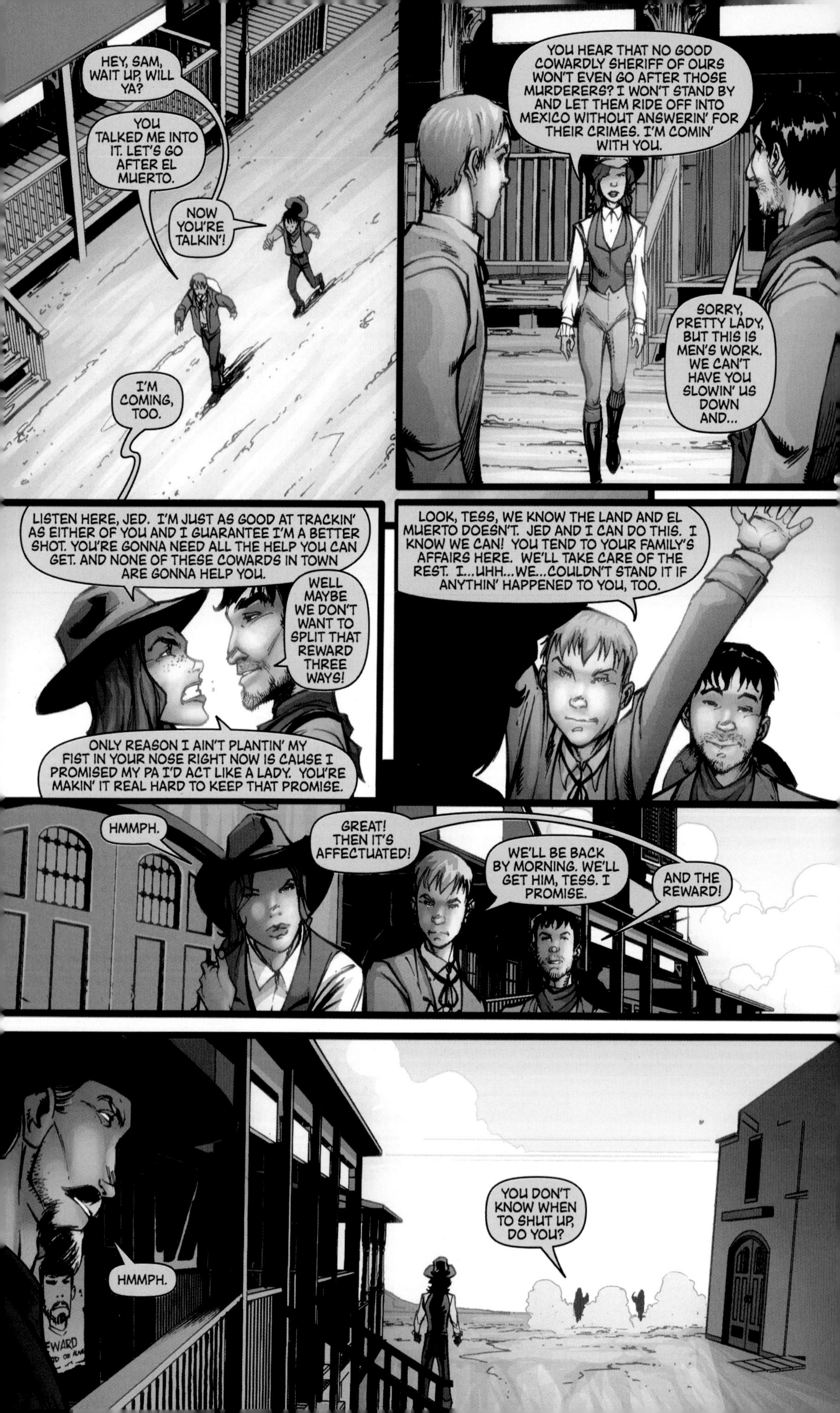
HEY, SAM, WAIT UP, WILL YA?
YOU TALKED ME INTO IT. LET'S GO AFTER EL MUERTO.
NOW YOU'RE TALKIN'!
I'M COMING, TOO.
YOU HEAR THAT NO GOOD COWARDLY SHERIFF OF OURS WON'T EVEN GO AFTER THOSE MURDERERS? I WON'T STAND BY AND LET THEM RIDE OFF INTO MEXICO WITHOUT ANSWERIN' FOR THEIR CRIMES. I'M COMIN' WITH YOU.
SORRY, PRETTY LADY, BUT THIS IS MEN'S WORK. WE CAN'T HAVE YOU SLOWIN' US DOWN AND...
LISTEN HERE, JED. I'M JUST AS GOOD AT TRACKIN' AS EITHER OF YOU AND I GUARANTEE I'M A BETTER SHOT. YOU'RE GONNA NEED ALL THE HELP YOU CAN GET. AND NONE OF THESE COWARDS IN TOWN ARE GONNA HELP YOU.
WELL MAYBE WE DON'T WANT TO SPLIT THAT REWARD THREE WAYS!
ONLY REASON I AIN'T PLANTIN' MY FIST IN YOUR NOSE RIGHT NOW IS CAUSE I PROMISED MY PA I'D ACT LIKE A LADY. YOU'RE MAKIN' IT REAL HARD TO KEEP THAT PROMISE.
LOOK, TESS, WE KNOW THE LAND AND EL MUERTO DOESN'T. JED AND I CAN DO THIS. I KNOW WE CAN! YOU TEND TO YOUR FAMILY'S AFFAIRS HERE. WE'LL TAKE CARE OF THE REST. I...UHH...WE...COULDN'T STAND IT IF ANYTHIN' HAPPENED TO YOU, TOO.
HMMPH.
GREAT! THEN IT'S AFFECTUATED!
WE'LL BE BACK BY MORNING. WE'LL GET HIM, TESS. I PROMISE.
AND THE REWARD!
HMMPH.
YOU DON'T KNOW WHEN TO SHUT UP, DO YOU?

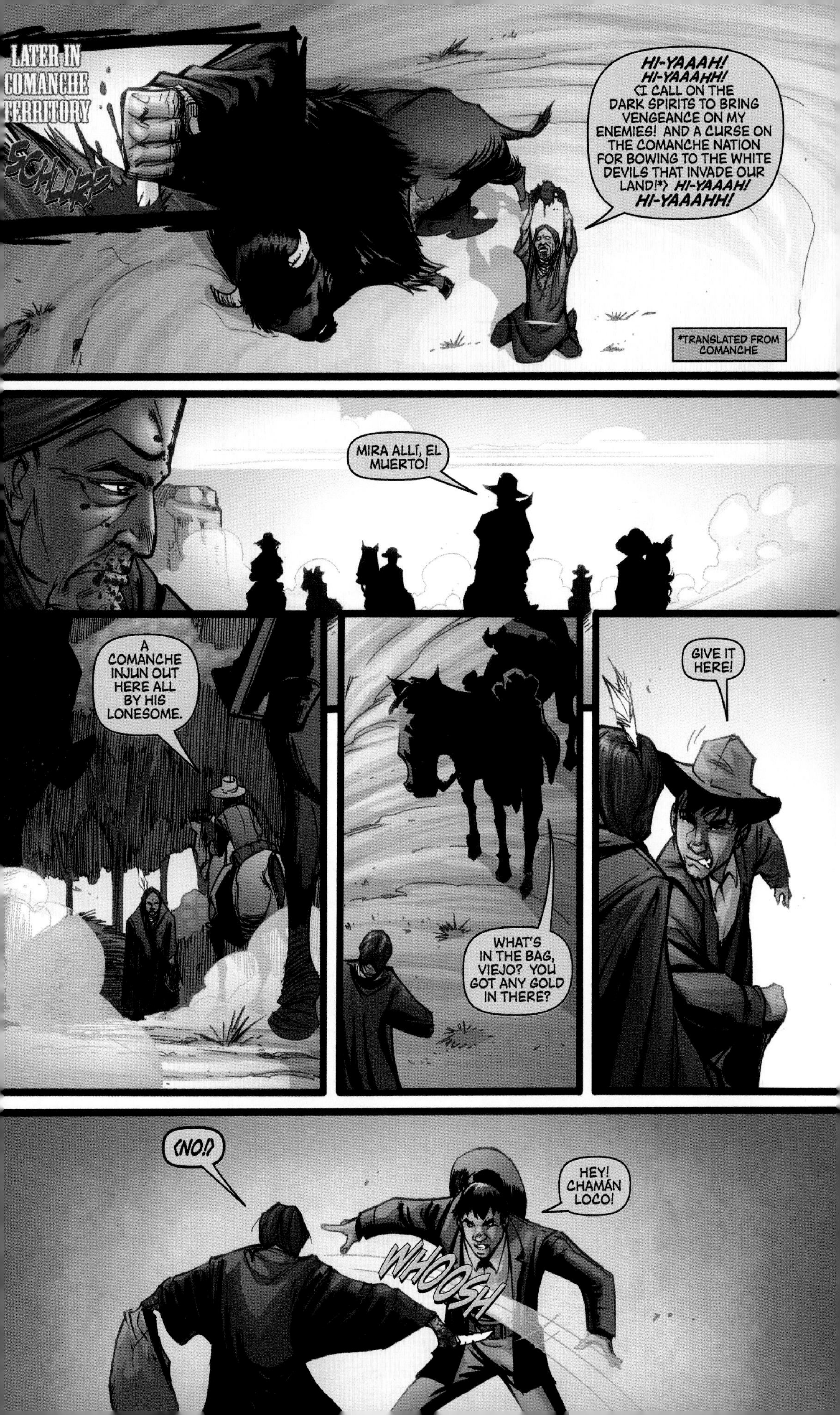
LATER IN COMANCHE TERRITORY
SCHLURP
HI-YAAAH! HI-YAAAHH! ‹I CALL ON THE DARK SPIRITS TO BRING VENGEANCE ON MY ENEMIES! AND A CURSE ON THE COMANCHE NATION FOR BOWING TO THE WHITE DEVILS THAT INVADE OUR LAND!*› HI-YAAAH! HI-YAAAHH!
*TRANSLATED FROM COMANCHE
MIRA ALLÍ, EL MUERTO!
A COMANCHE INJUN OUT HERE ALL BY HIS LONESOME.
WHAT'S IN THE BAG, VIEJO? YOU GOT ANY GOLD IN THERE?
GIVE IT HERE!
‹NO!›
HEY! CHAMÁN LOCO!
WHOOSH

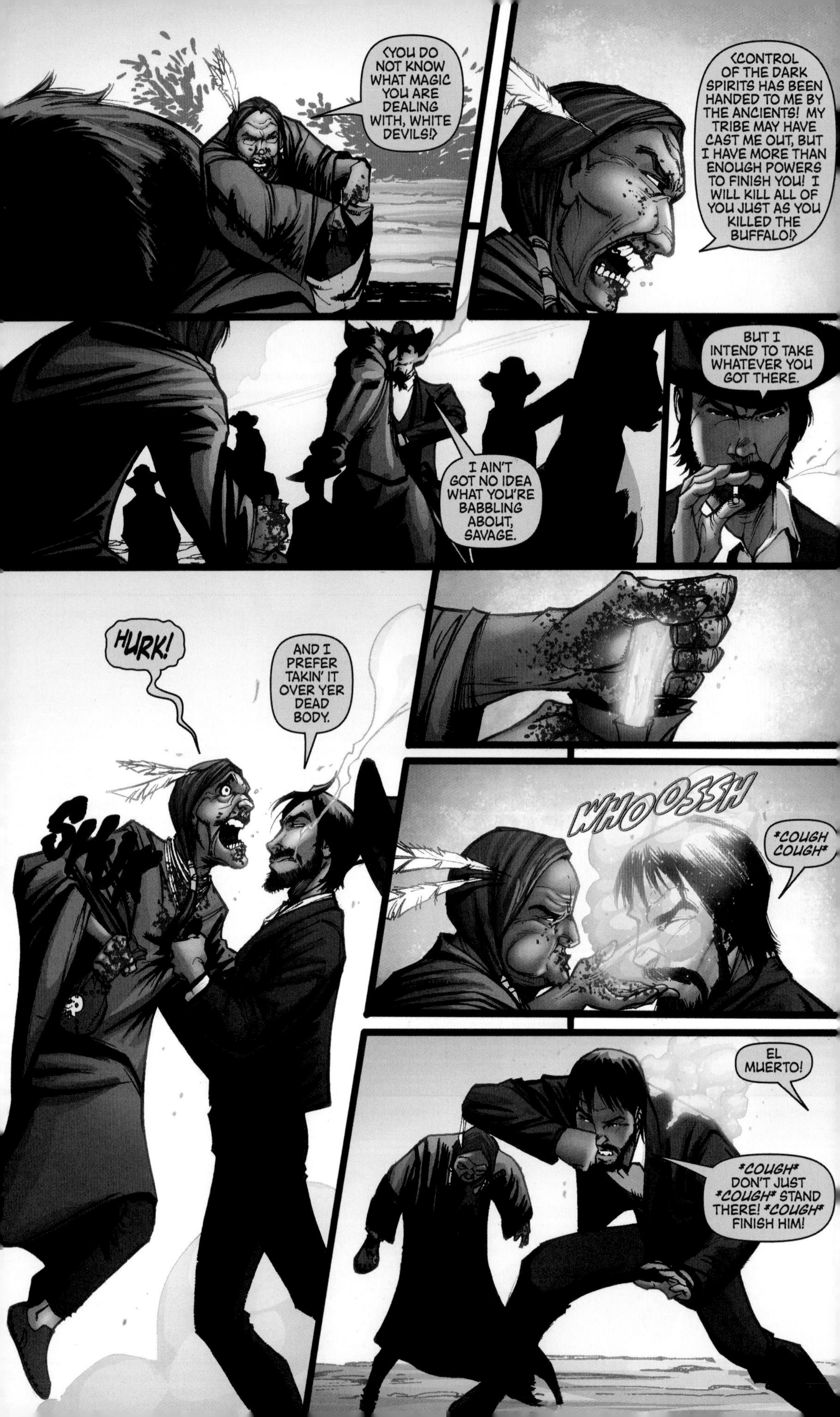
<YOU DO NOT KNOW WHAT MAGIC YOU ARE DEALING WITH, WHITE DEVILS!>
<CONTROL OF THE DARK SPIRITS HAS BEEN HANDED TO ME BY THE ANCIENTS! MY TRIBE MAY HAVE CAST ME OUT, BUT I HAVE MORE THAN ENOUGH POWERS TO FINISH YOU! I WILL KILL ALL OF YOU JUST AS YOU KILLED THE BUFFALO!>
I AIN'T GOT NO IDEA WHAT YOU'RE BABBLING ABOUT, SAVAGE.
BUT I INTEND TO TAKE WHATEVER YOU GOT THERE.
AND I PREFER TAKIN' IT OVER YER DEAD BODY.
HURK!
WHOOSSH
COUGH COUGH
EL MUERTO!
COUGH DON'T JUST *COUGH* STAND THERE! *COUGH* FINISH HIM!

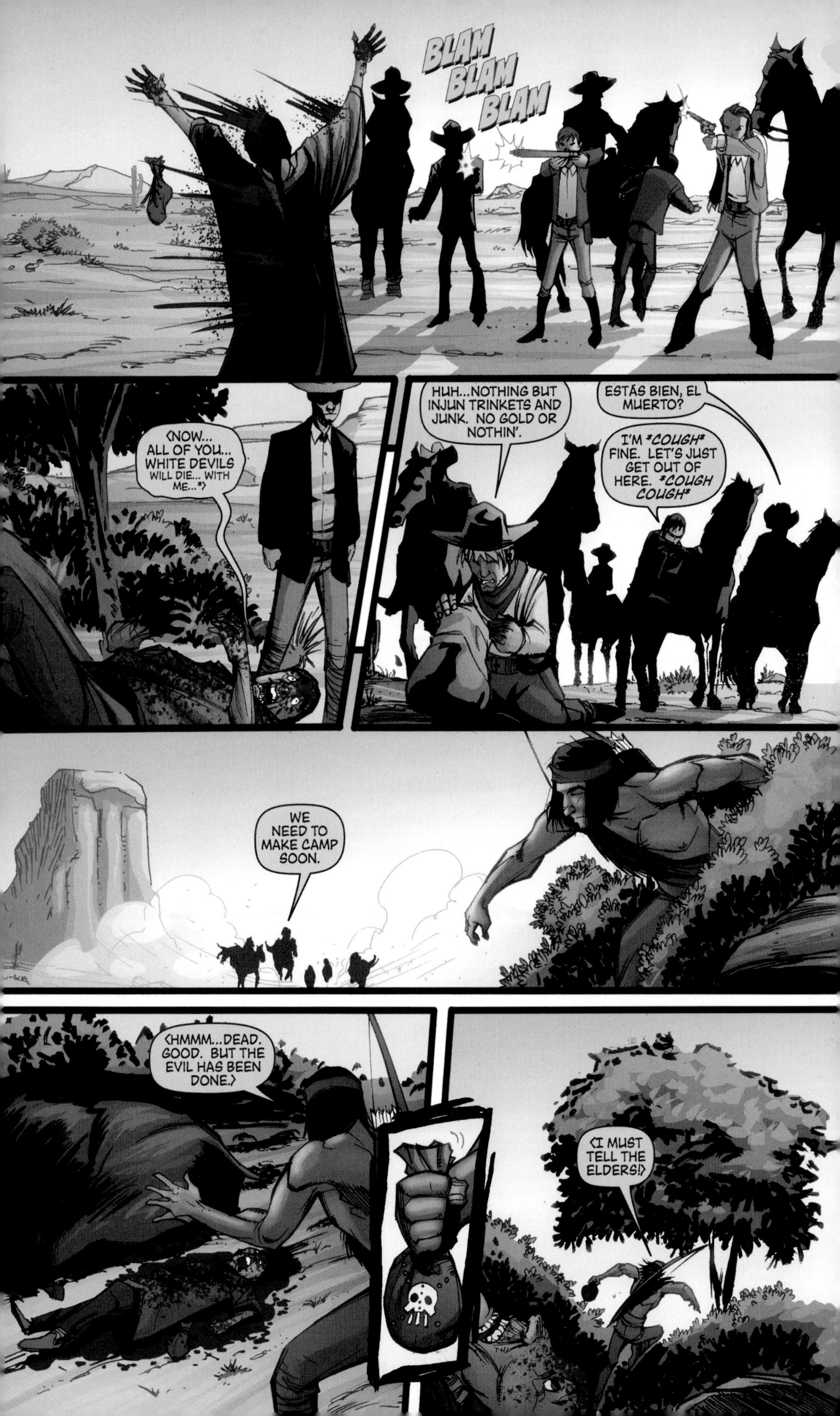
BLAM
BLAM
BLAM
<NOW... ALL OF YOU... WHITE DEVILS WILL DIE... WITH ME...*>
HUH...NOTHING BUT INJUN TRINKETS AND JUNK. NO GOLD OR NOTHIN'.
ESTÁS BIEN, EL MUERTO?
I'M *COUGH* FINE. LET'S JUST GET OUT OF HERE. *COUGH COUGH*
WE NEED TO MAKE CAMP SOON.
<HMMM...DEAD. GOOD. BUT THE EVIL HAS BEEN DONE.>
<I MUST TELL THE ELDERS!>

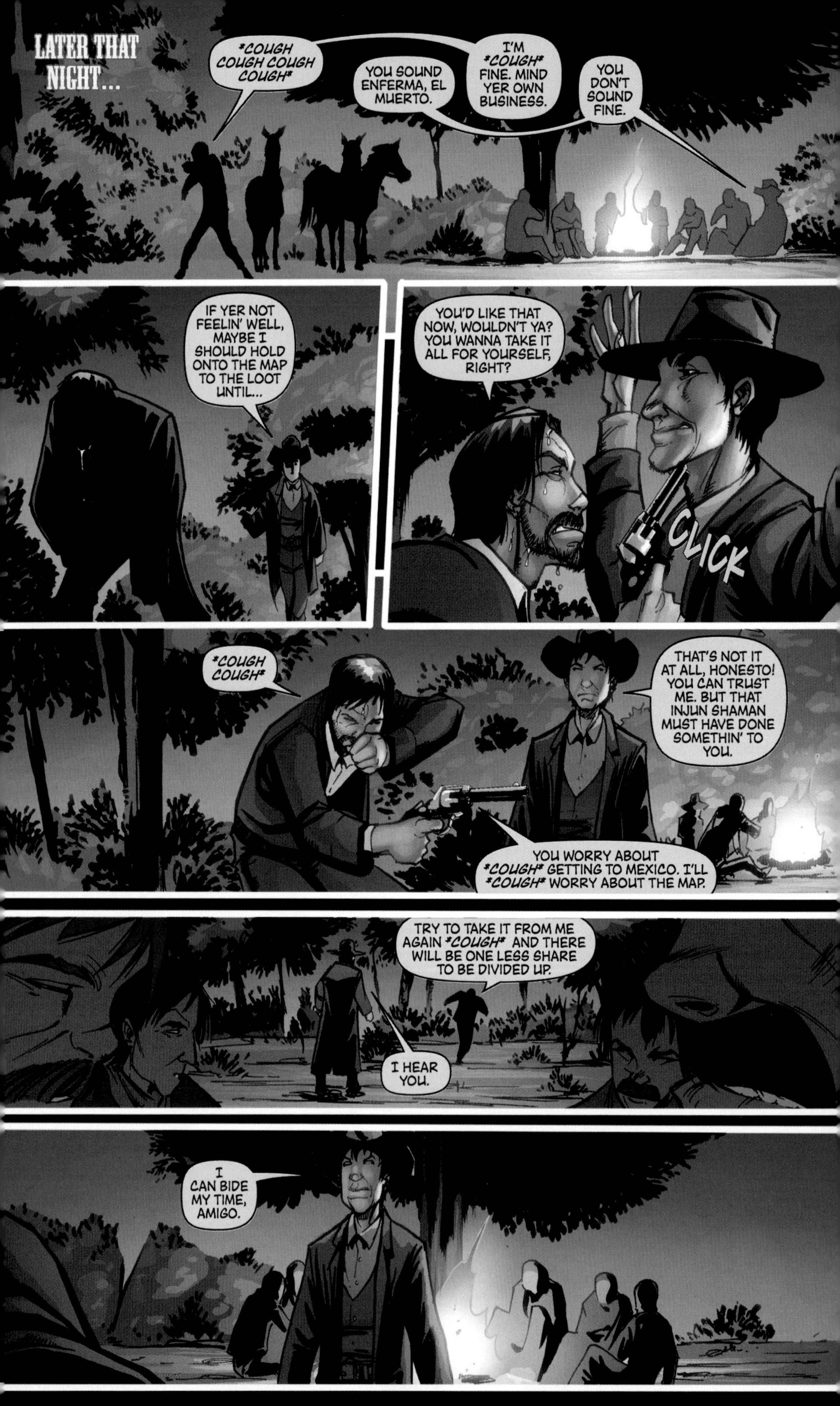
LATER THAT NIGHT...
COUGH COUGH COUGH COUGH
YOU SOUND ENFERMA, EL MUERTO.
I'M *COUGH* FINE. MIND YER OWN BUSINESS.
YOU DON'T SOUND FINE.
IF YER NOT FEELIN' WELL, MAYBE I SHOULD HOLD ONTO THE MAP TO THE LOOT UNTIL...
YOU'D LIKE THAT NOW, WOULDN'T YA? YOU WANNA TAKE IT ALL FOR YOURSELF, RIGHT?
CLICK
COUGH COUGH
THAT'S NOT IT AT ALL, HONESTO! YOU CAN TRUST ME. BUT THAT INJUN SHAMAN MUST HAVE DONE SOMETHIN' TO YOU.
YOU WORRY ABOUT *COUGH* GETTING TO MEXICO. I'LL *COUGH* WORRY ABOUT THE MAP.
TRY TO TAKE IT FROM ME AGAIN *COUGH* AND THERE WILL BE ONE LESS SHARE TO BE DIVIDED UP.
I HEAR YOU.
I CAN BIDE MY TIME, AMIGO.

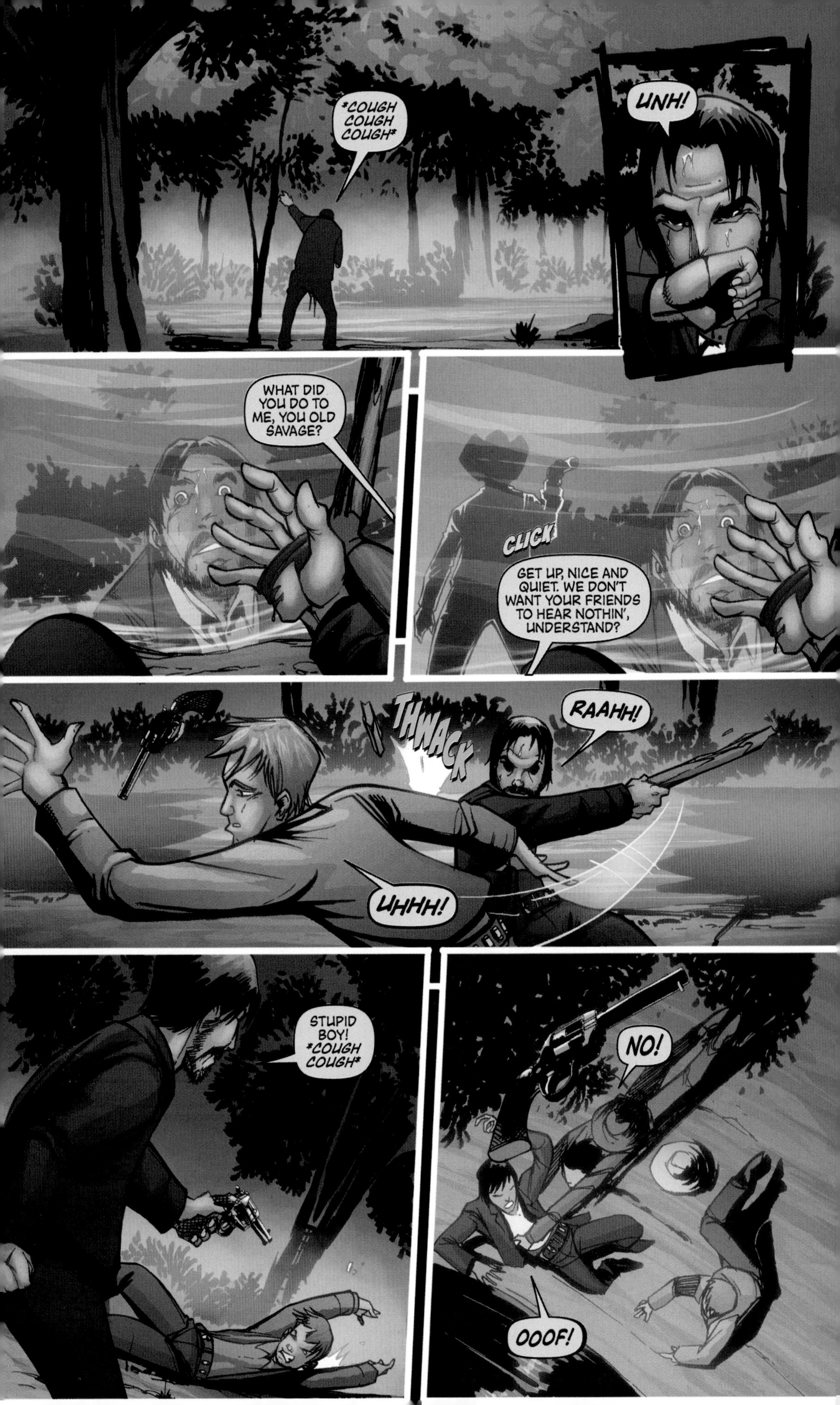
COUGH COUGH COUGH
UNH!
WHAT DID YOU DO TO ME, YOU OLD SAVAGE?
CLICK
GET UP, NICE AND QUIET. WE DON'T WANT YOUR FRIENDS TO HEAR NOTHIN', UNDERSTAND?
THWACK
RAAHH!
UHHH!
STUPID BOY! *COUGH COUGH*
NO!
OOOF!

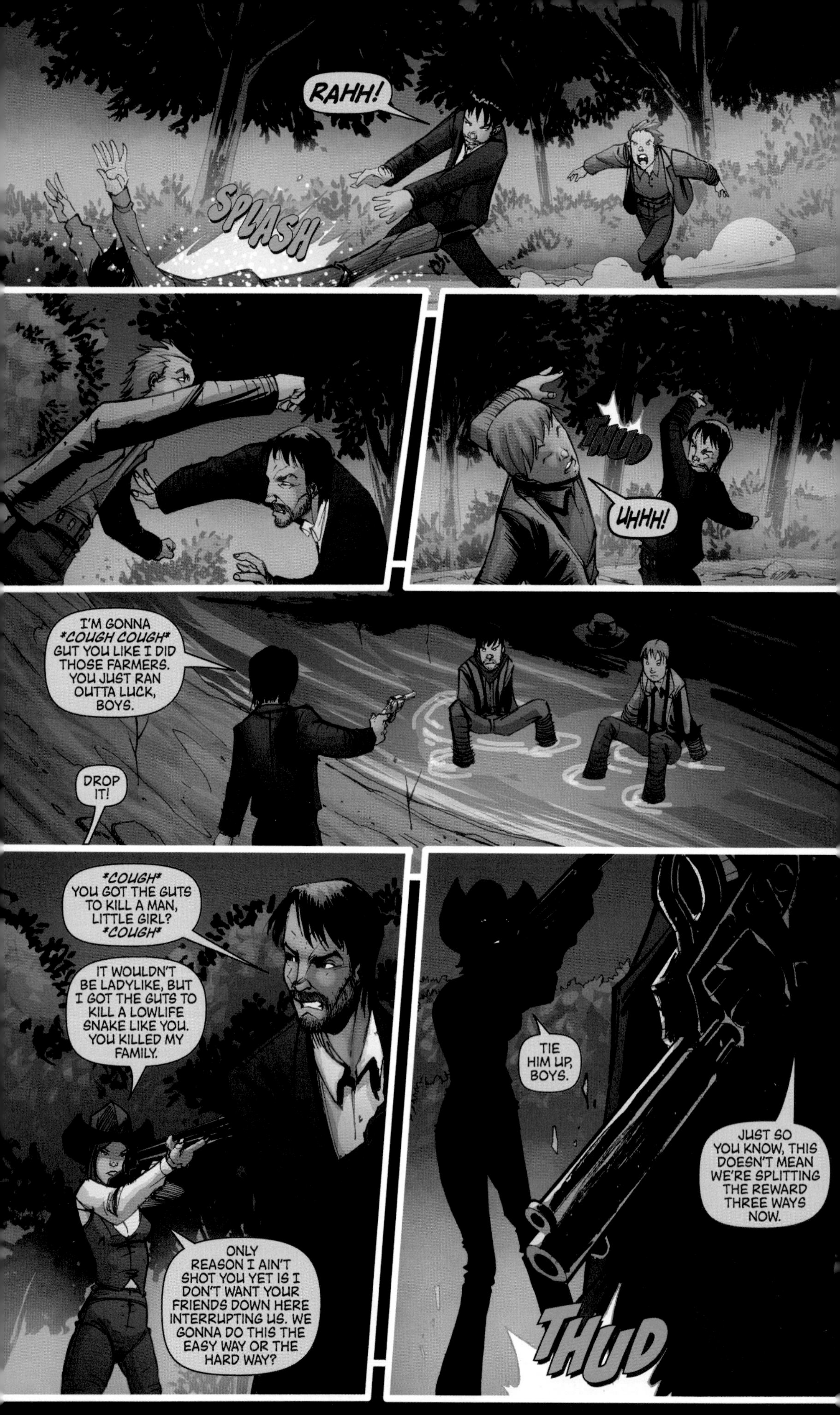
RAHH!
SPLASH
THUD
UHHH!
I'M GONNA *COUGH COUGH* GUT YOU LIKE I DID THOSE FARMERS. YOU JUST RAN OUTTA LUCK, BOYS.
DROP IT!
COUGH YOU GOT THE GUTS TO KILL A MAN, LITTLE GIRL? *COUGH*
IT WOULDN'T BE LADYLIKE, BUT I GOT THE GUTS TO KILL A LOWLIFE SNAKE LIKE YOU. YOU KILLED MY FAMILY.
ONLY REASON I AIN'T SHOT YOU YET IS I DON'T WANT YOUR FRIENDS DOWN HERE INTERRUPTING US. WE GONNA DO THIS THE EASY WAY OR THE HARD WAY?
THUD
TIE HIM UP, BOYS.
JUST SO YOU KNOW, THIS DOESN'T MEAN WE'RE SPLITTING THE REWARD THREE WAYS NOW.

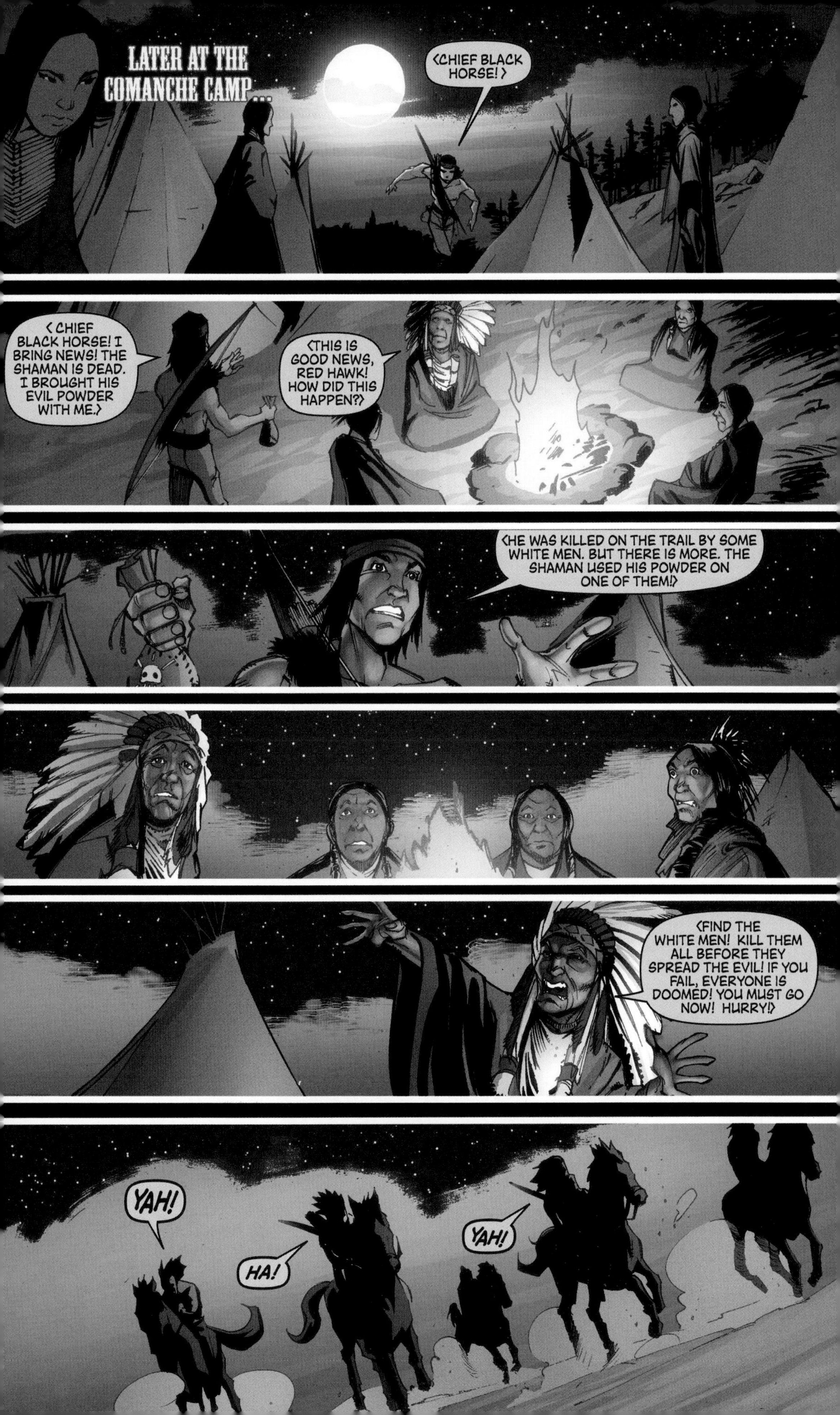
LATER AT THE COMANCHE CAMP...
<CHIEF BLACK HORSE!>
<CHIEF BLACK HORSE! I BRING NEWS! THE SHAMAN IS DEAD. I BROUGHT HIS EVIL POWDER WITH ME.>
<THIS IS GOOD NEWS, RED HAWK! HOW DID THIS HAPPEN?>
<HE WAS KILLED ON THE TRAIL BY SOME WHITE MEN. BUT THERE IS MORE. THE SHAMAN USED HIS POWDER ON ONE OF THEM!>
<FIND THE WHITE MEN! KILL THEM ALL BEFORE THEY SPREAD THE EVIL! IF YOU FAIL, EVERYONE IS DOOMED! YOU MUST GO NOW! HURRY!>
YAH!
HA!
YAH!

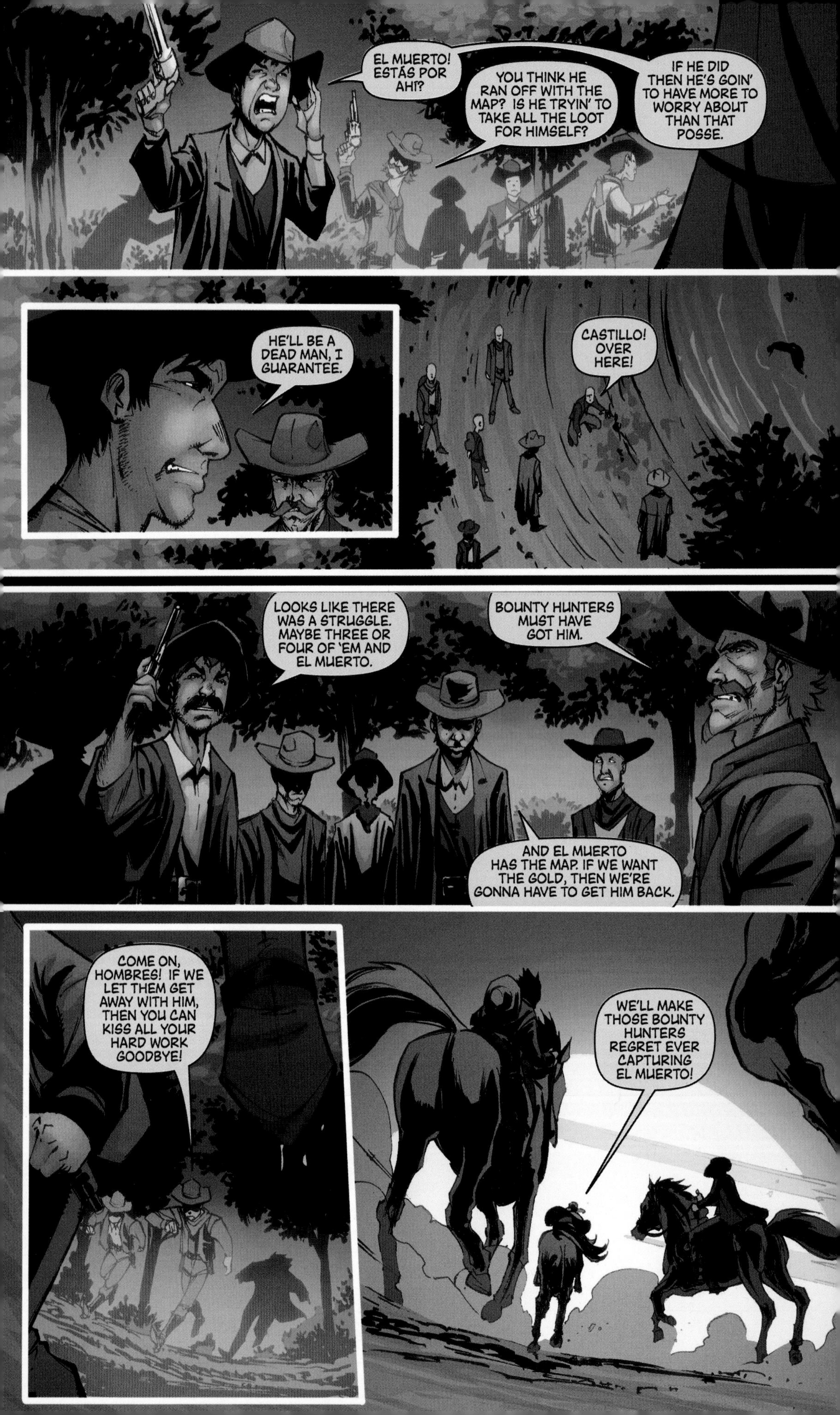
EL MUERTO! ESTÁS POR AHI?
YOU THINK HE RAN OFF WITH THE MAP? IS HE TRYIN' TO TAKE ALL THE LOOT FOR HIMSELF?
IF HE DID THEN HE'S GOIN' TO HAVE MORE TO WORRY ABOUT THAN THAT POSSE.
HE'LL BE A DEAD MAN, I GUARANTEE.
CASTILLO! OVER HERE!
LOOKS LIKE THERE WAS A STRUGGLE. MAYBE THREE OR FOUR OF 'EM AND EL MUERTO.
BOUNTY HUNTERS MUST HAVE GOT HIM.
AND EL MUERTO HAS THE MAP. IF WE WANT THE GOLD, THEN WE'RE GONNA HAVE TO GET HIM BACK.
COME ON, HOMBRES! IF WE LET THEM GET AWAY WITH HIM, THEN YOU CAN KISS ALL YOUR HARD WORK GOODBYE!
WE'LL MAKE THOSE BOUNTY HUNTERS REGRET EVER CAPTURING EL MUERTO!

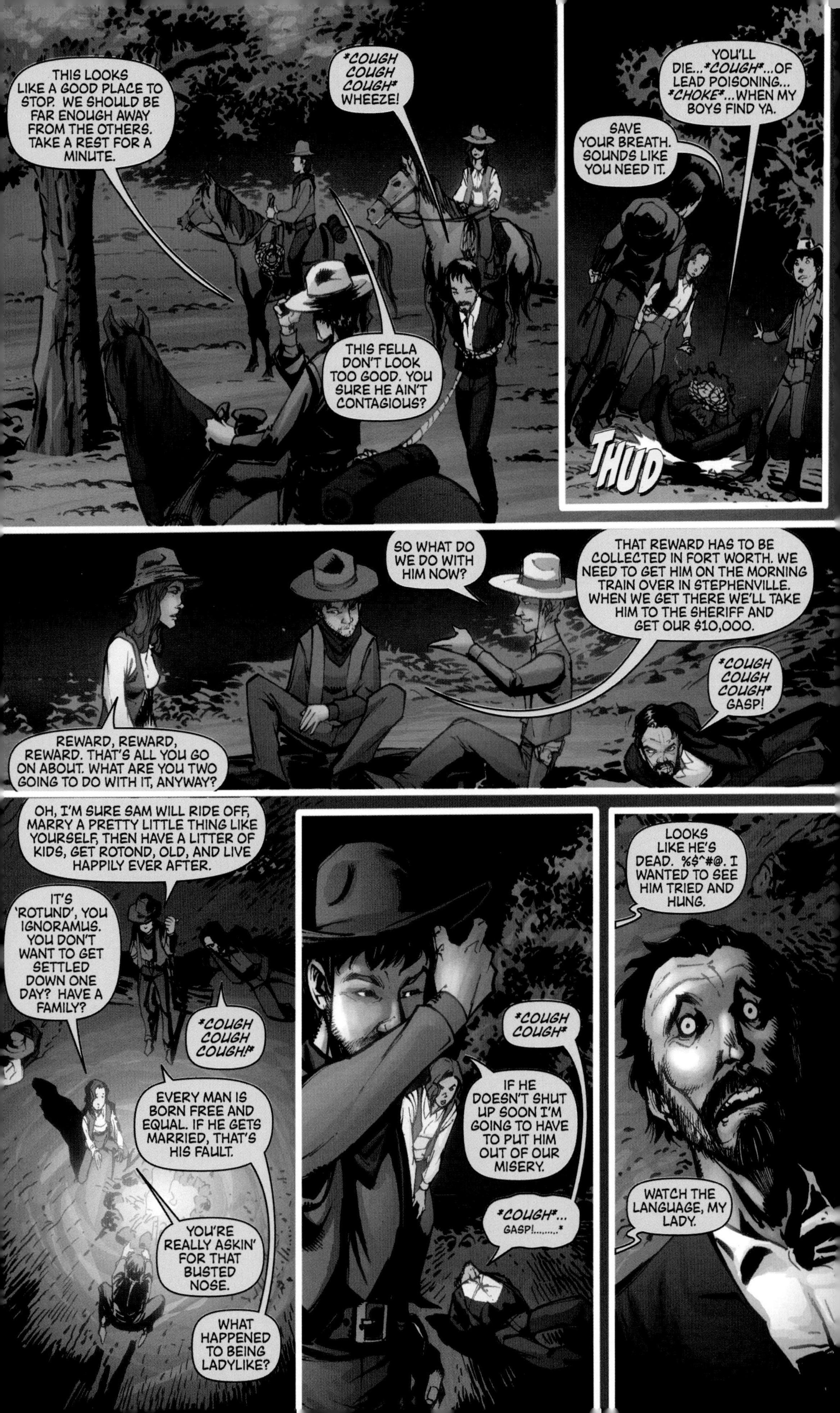
THIS LOOKS LIKE A GOOD PLACE TO STOP. WE SHOULD BE FAR ENOUGH AWAY FROM THE OTHERS. TAKE A REST FOR A MINUTE.
COUGH COUGH COUGH WHEEZE!
THIS FELLA DON'T LOOK TOO GOOD. YOU SURE HE AIN'T CONTAGIOUS?
YOU'LL DIE...*COUGH*...OF LEAD POISONING... *CHOKE*...WHEN MY BOYS FIND YA.
SAVE YOUR BREATH. SOUNDS LIKE YOU NEED IT.
THUD
SO WHAT DO WE DO WITH HIM NOW?
THAT REWARD HAS TO BE COLLECTED IN FORT WORTH. WE NEED TO GET HIM ON THE MORNING TRAIN OVER IN STEPHENVILLE. WHEN WE GET THERE WE'LL TAKE HIM TO THE SHERIFF AND GET OUR $10,000.
COUGH COUGH COUGH GASP!
REWARD, REWARD, REWARD. THAT'S ALL YOU GO ON ABOUT. WHAT ARE YOU TWO GOING TO DO WITH IT, ANYWAY?
OH, I'M SURE SAM WILL RIDE OFF, MARRY A PRETTY LITTLE THING LIKE YOURSELF, THEN HAVE A LITTER OF KIDS, GET ROTOND, OLD, AND LIVE HAPPILY EVER AFTER.
IT'S 'ROTUND', YOU IGNORAMUS. YOU DON'T WANT TO GET SETTLED DOWN ONE DAY? HAVE A FAMILY?
COUGH COUGH COUGH!
EVERY MAN IS BORN FREE AND EQUAL. IF HE GETS MARRIED, THAT'S HIS FAULT.
YOU'RE REALLY ASKIN' FOR THAT BUSTED NOSE.
WHAT HAPPENED TO BEING LADYLIKE?
COUGH COUGH
IF HE DOESN'T SHUT UP SOON I'M GOING TO HAVE TO PUT HIM OUT OF OUR MISERY.
COUGH... GASP!........*
LOOKS LIKE HE'S DEAD. %$^#@. I WANTED TO SEE HIM TRIED AND HUNG.
WATCH THE LANGUAGE, MY LADY.

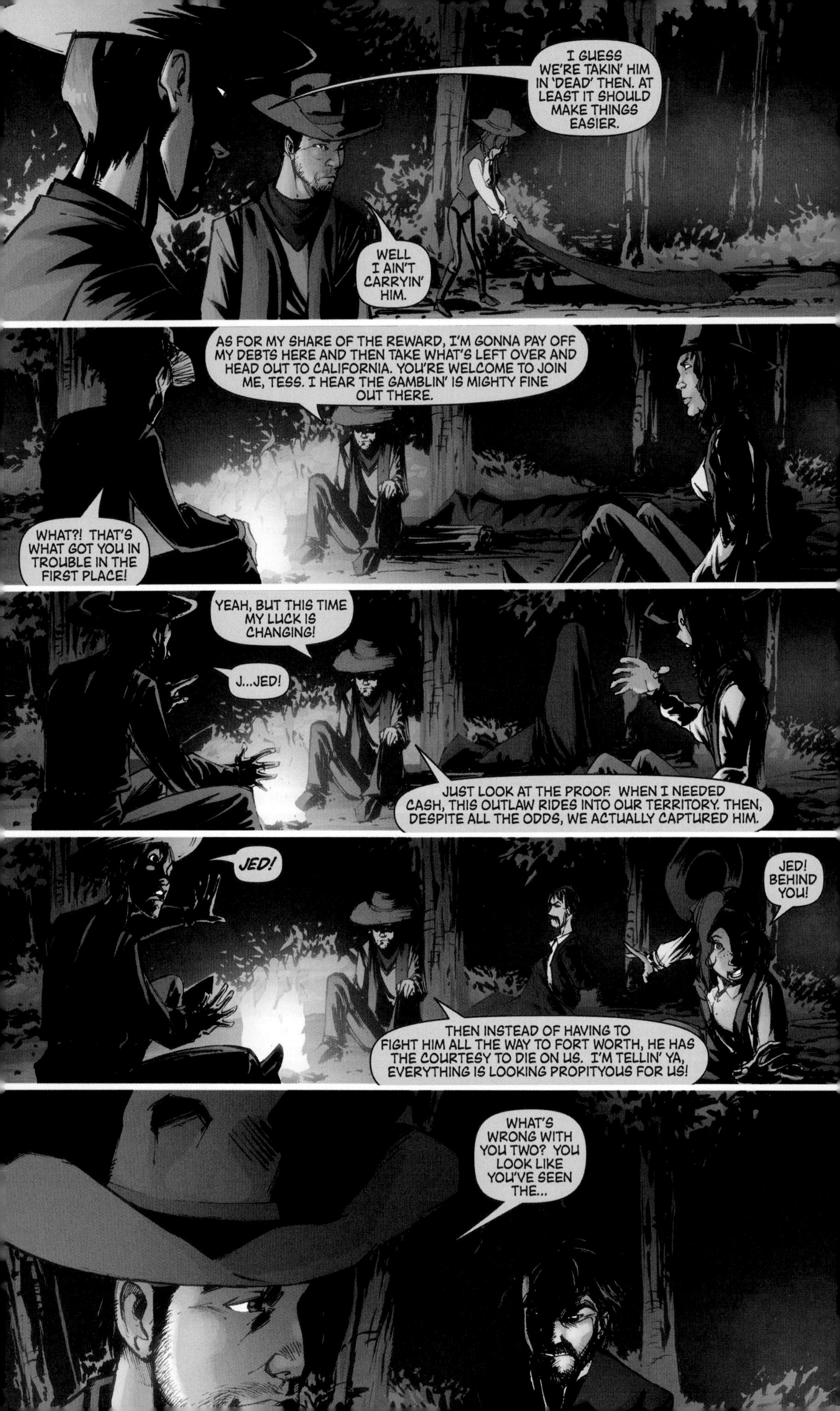
I GUESS WE'RE TAKIN' HIM IN 'DEAD' THEN. AT LEAST IT SHOULD MAKE THINGS EASIER.
WELL I AIN'T CARRYIN' HIM.
AS FOR MY SHARE OF THE REWARD, I'M GONNA PAY OFF MY DEBTS HERE AND THEN TAKE WHAT'S LEFT OVER AND HEAD OUT TO CALIFORNIA. YOU'RE WELCOME TO JOIN ME, TESS. I HEAR THE GAMBLIN' IS MIGHTY FINE OUT THERE.
WHAT?! THAT'S WHAT GOT YOU IN TROUBLE IN THE FIRST PLACE!
YEAH, BUT THIS TIME MY LUCK IS CHANGING!
J...JED!
JUST LOOK AT THE PROOF. WHEN I NEEDED CASH, THIS OUTLAW RIDES INTO OUR TERRITORY. THEN, DESPITE ALL THE ODDS, WE ACTUALLY CAPTURED HIM.
JED!
JED! BEHIND YOU!
THEN INSTEAD OF HAVING TO FIGHT HIM ALL THE WAY TO FORT WORTH, HE HAS THE COURTESY TO DIE ON US. I'M TELLIN' YA, EVERYTHING IS LOOKING PROPITYOUS FOR US!
WHAT'S WRONG WITH YOU TWO? YOU LOOK LIKE YOU'VE SEEN THE...

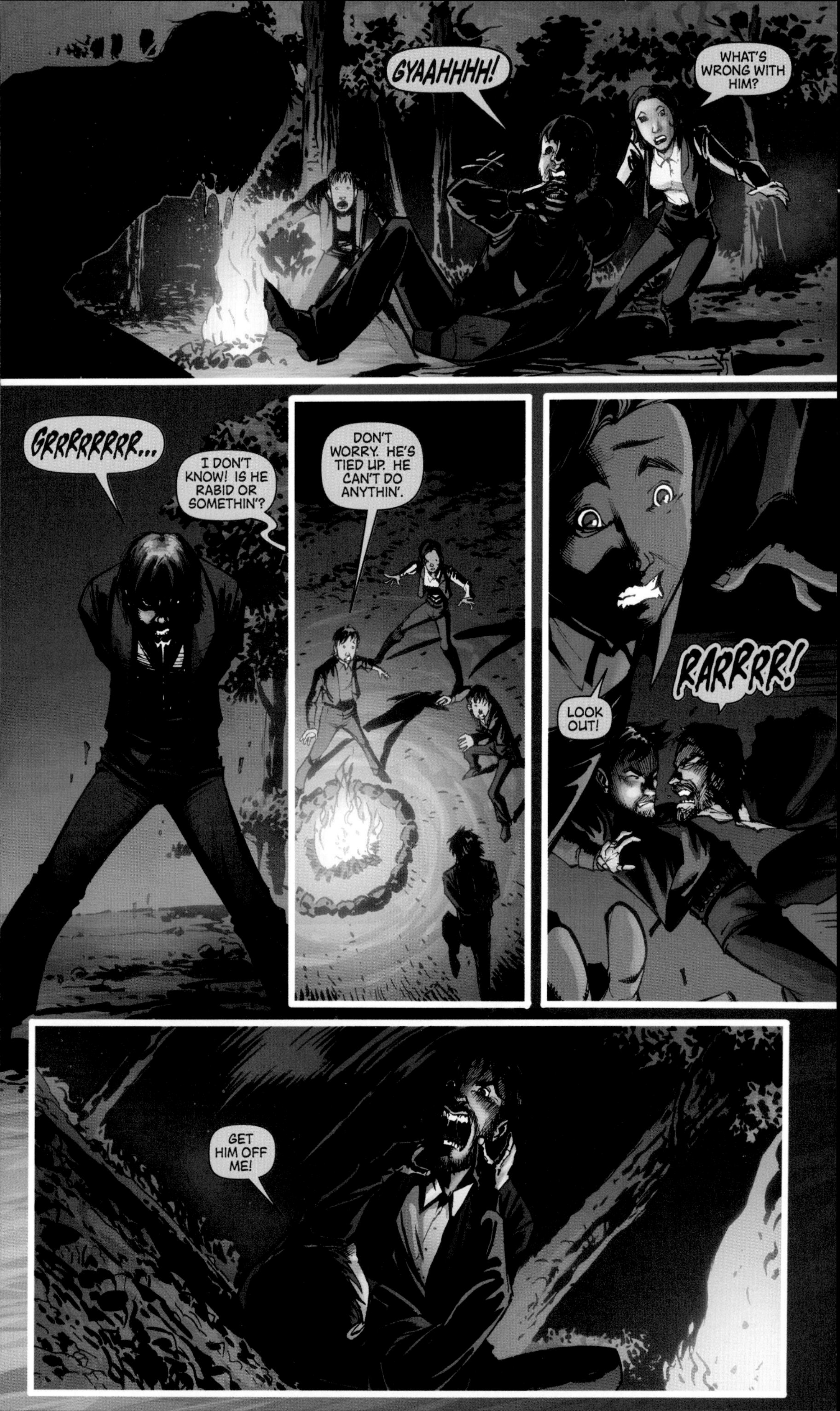
GYAAHHHH!
WHAT'S WRONG WITH HIM?
GRRRRRRRR...
I DON'T KNOW! IS HE RABID OR SOMETHIN'?
DON'T WORRY. HE'S TIED UP. HE CAN'T DO ANYTHIN'.
RARRRR!
LOOK OUT!
GET HIM OFF ME!

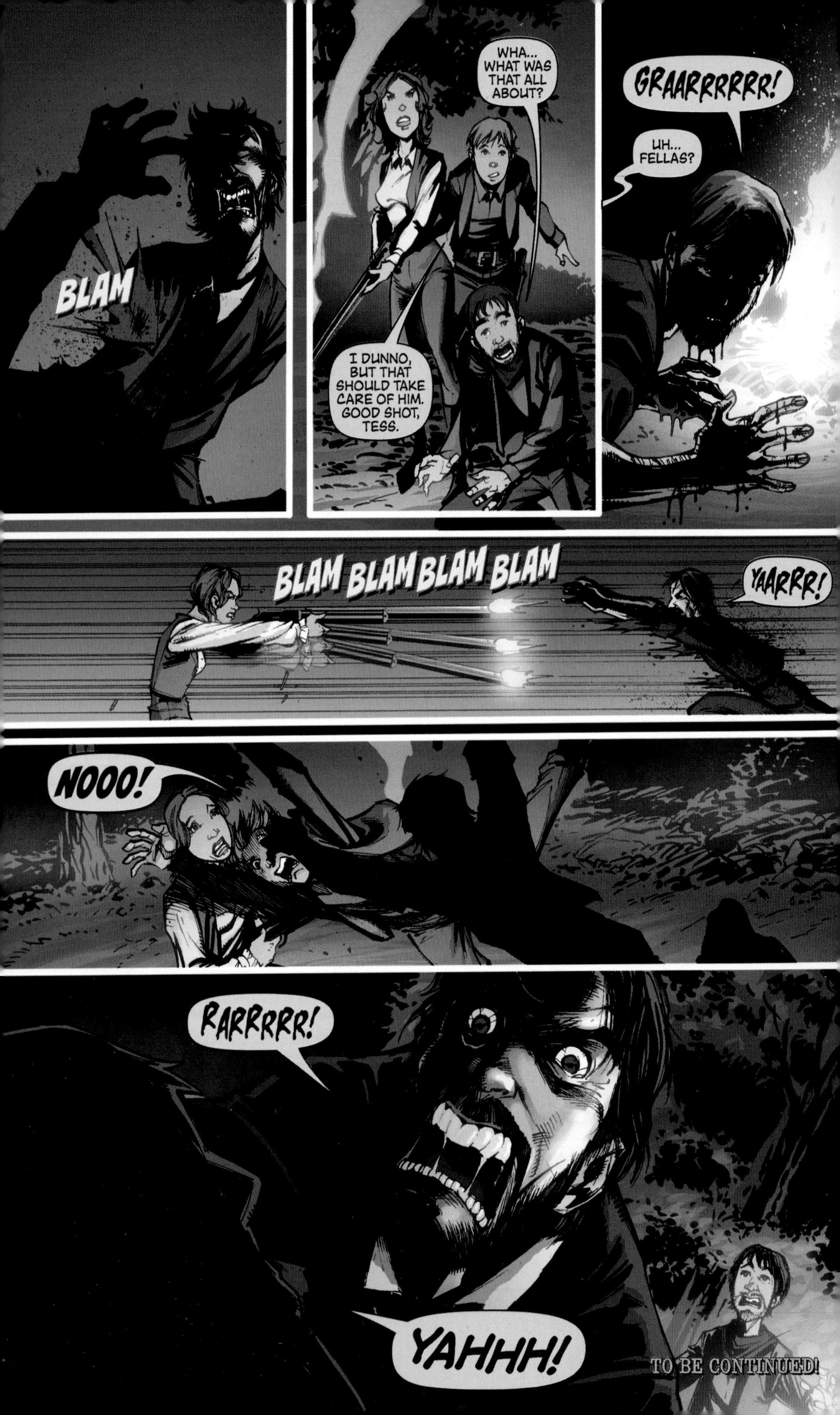
BLAM
WHA... WHAT WAS THAT ALL ABOUT?
I DUNNO, BUT THAT SHOULD TAKE CARE OF HIM. GOOD SHOT, TESS.
GRAARRRRRR!
UH... FELLAS?
BLAM BLAM BLAM BLAM
YAARRR!
NOOO!
RARRRRR!
YAHHH!
TO BE CONTINUED!

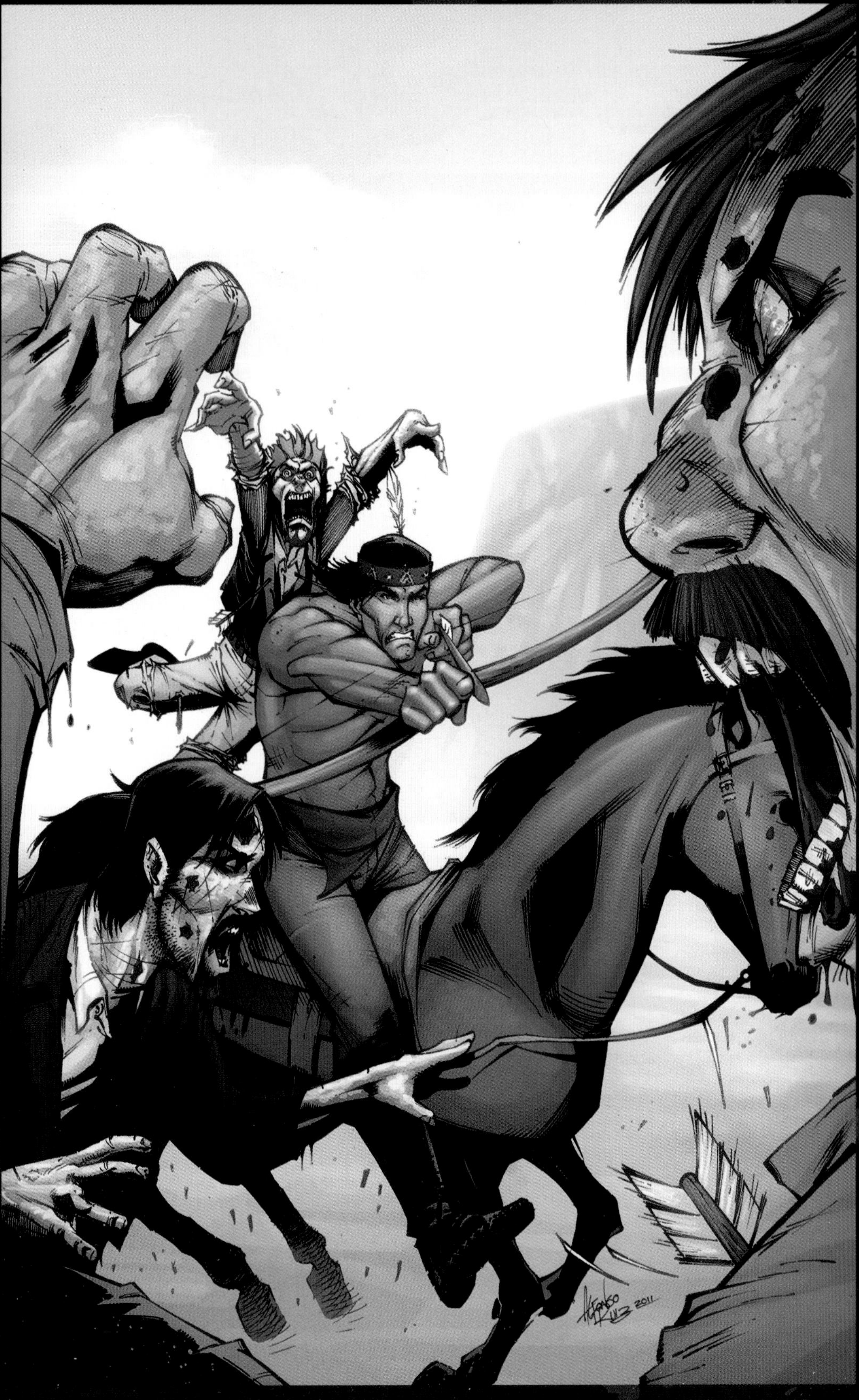

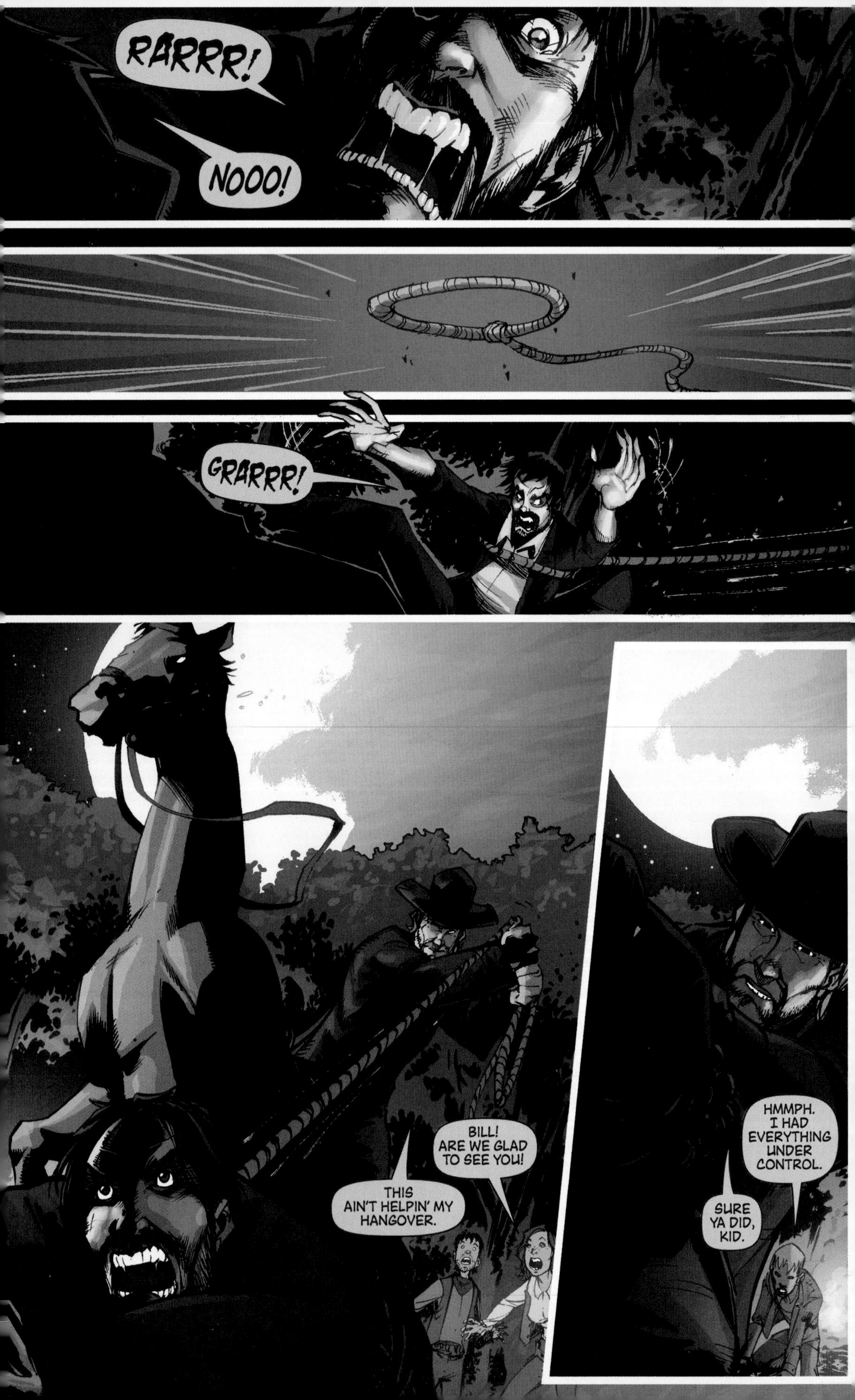
RARRR!
NOOO!
GRARRR!
BILL! ARE WE GLAD TO SEE YOU!
THIS AIN'T HELPIN' MY HANGOVER.
HMMPH. I HAD EVERYTHING UNDER CONTROL.
SURE YA DID, KID.

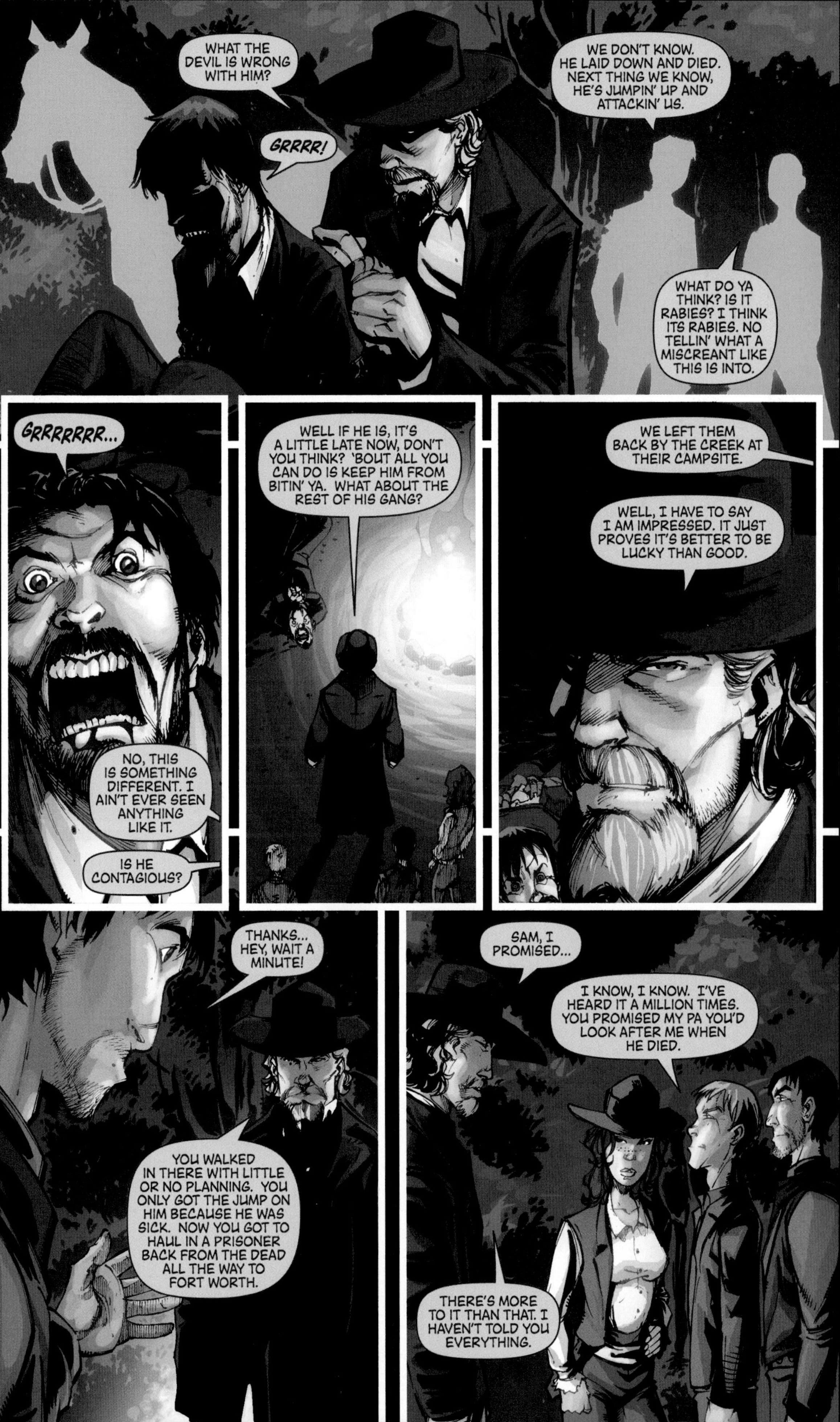

WHAT THE DEVIL IS WRONG WITH HIM?
GRRRR!
WE DON'T KNOW. HE LAID DOWN AND DIED. NEXT THING WE KNOW, HE'S JUMPIN' UP AND ATTACKIN' US.
WHAT DO YA THINK? IS IT RABIES? I THINK ITS RABIES. NO TELLIN' WHAT A MISCREANT LIKE THIS IS INTO.
GRRRRRRR...
NO, THIS IS SOMETHING DIFFERENT. I AIN'T EVER SEEN ANYTHING LIKE IT.
IS HE CONTAGIOUS?
WELL IF HE IS, IT'S A LITTLE LATE NOW, DON'T YOU THINK? 'BOUT ALL YOU CAN DO IS KEEP HIM FROM BITIN' YA. WHAT ABOUT THE REST OF HIS GANG?
WE LEFT THEM BACK BY THE CREEK AT THEIR CAMPSITE.
WELL, I HAVE TO SAY I AM IMPRESSED. IT JUST PROVES IT'S BETTER TO BE LUCKY THAN GOOD.
THANKS... HEY, WAIT A MINUTE!
YOU WALKED IN THERE WITH LITTLE OR NO PLANNING. YOU ONLY GOT THE JUMP ON HIM BECAUSE HE WAS SICK. NOW YOU GOT TO HAUL IN A PRISONER BACK FROM THE DEAD ALL THE WAY TO FORT WORTH.
SAM, I PROMISED...
I KNOW, I KNOW. I'VE HEARD IT A MILLION TIMES. YOU PROMISED MY PA YOU'D LOOK AFTER ME WHEN HE DIED.
THERE'S MORE TO IT THAN THAT. I HAVEN'T TOLD YOU EVERYTHING.

YOU KNOW YOUR PA AND I WERE BOTH TEXAS RANGERS. WE WERE PROTECTING THE LOCALS FROM COMANCHE RAIDS WHEN YOU WERE LITTLE. ONE DAY WE WERE CHASING DOWN A WAR PARTY AS THEY WENT INTO A CANYON.

YOUR FATHER AND THE OTHER RANGERS WANTED TO HOLD BACK. THEY THOUGHT WE MIGHT BE WALKING INTO A TRAP. I PUSHED THEM FORWARD AND RACED IN.

YOUR PA AND THE OTHERS WERE RIGHT. THE COMANCHE WARRIORS HAD US PINNED.

THEY KILLED EVERYONE. AS YOUR PA LAY DYIN', HE MADE ME PROMISE TO LOOK AFTER YOU IF I MADE IT OUT ALIVE. AND THAT'S WHAT I DID.

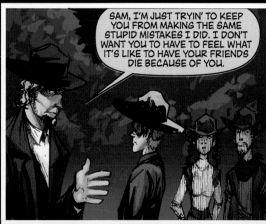

SAM, I'M JUST TRYIN' TO KEEP YOU FROM MAKING THE SAME STUPID MISTAKES I DID. I DON'T WANT YOU TO HAVE TO FEEL WHAT IT'S LIKE TO HAVE YOUR FRIENDS DIE BECAUSE OF YOU.

YOU SHOULD WALK AWAY FROM THIS BEFORE SOMEBODY GETS KILLED.

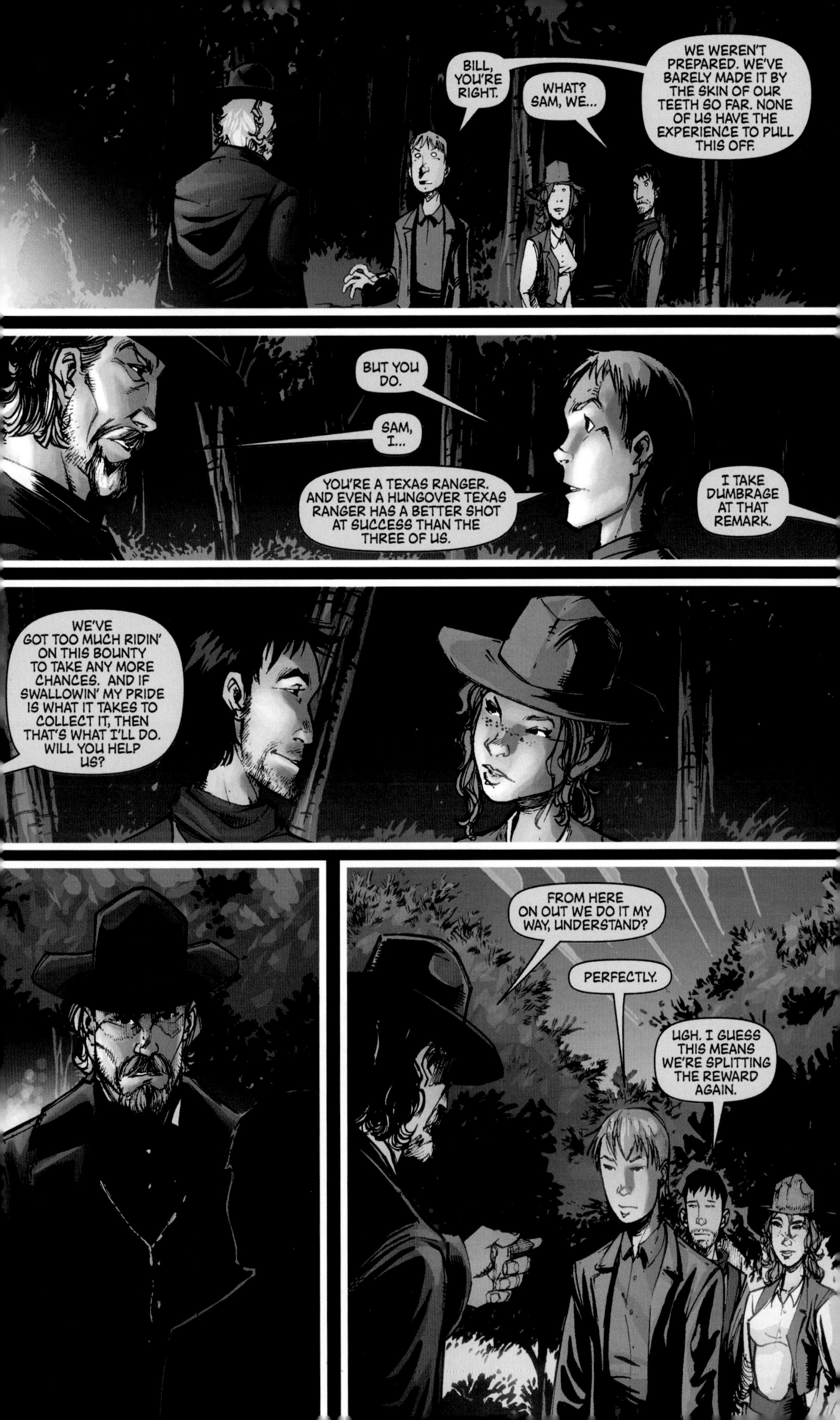
BILL, YOU'RE RIGHT.
WHAT? SAM, WE...
WE WEREN'T PREPARED. WE'VE BARELY MADE IT BY THE SKIN OF OUR TEETH SO FAR. NONE OF US HAVE THE EXPERIENCE TO PULL THIS OFF.
BUT YOU DO.
SAM, I...
YOU'RE A TEXAS RANGER. AND EVEN A HUNGOVER TEXAS RANGER HAS A BETTER SHOT AT SUCCESS THAN THE THREE OF US.
I TAKE DUMBRAGE AT THAT REMARK.
WE'VE GOT TOO MUCH RIDIN' ON THIS BOUNTY TO TAKE ANY MORE CHANCES. AND IF SWALLOWIN' MY PRIDE IS WHAT IT TAKES TO COLLECT IT, THEN THAT'S WHAT I'LL DO. WILL YOU HELP US?
FROM HERE ON OUT WE DO IT MY WAY, UNDERSTAND?
PERFECTLY.
UGH. I GUESS THIS MEANS WE'RE SPLITTING THE REWARD AGAIN.

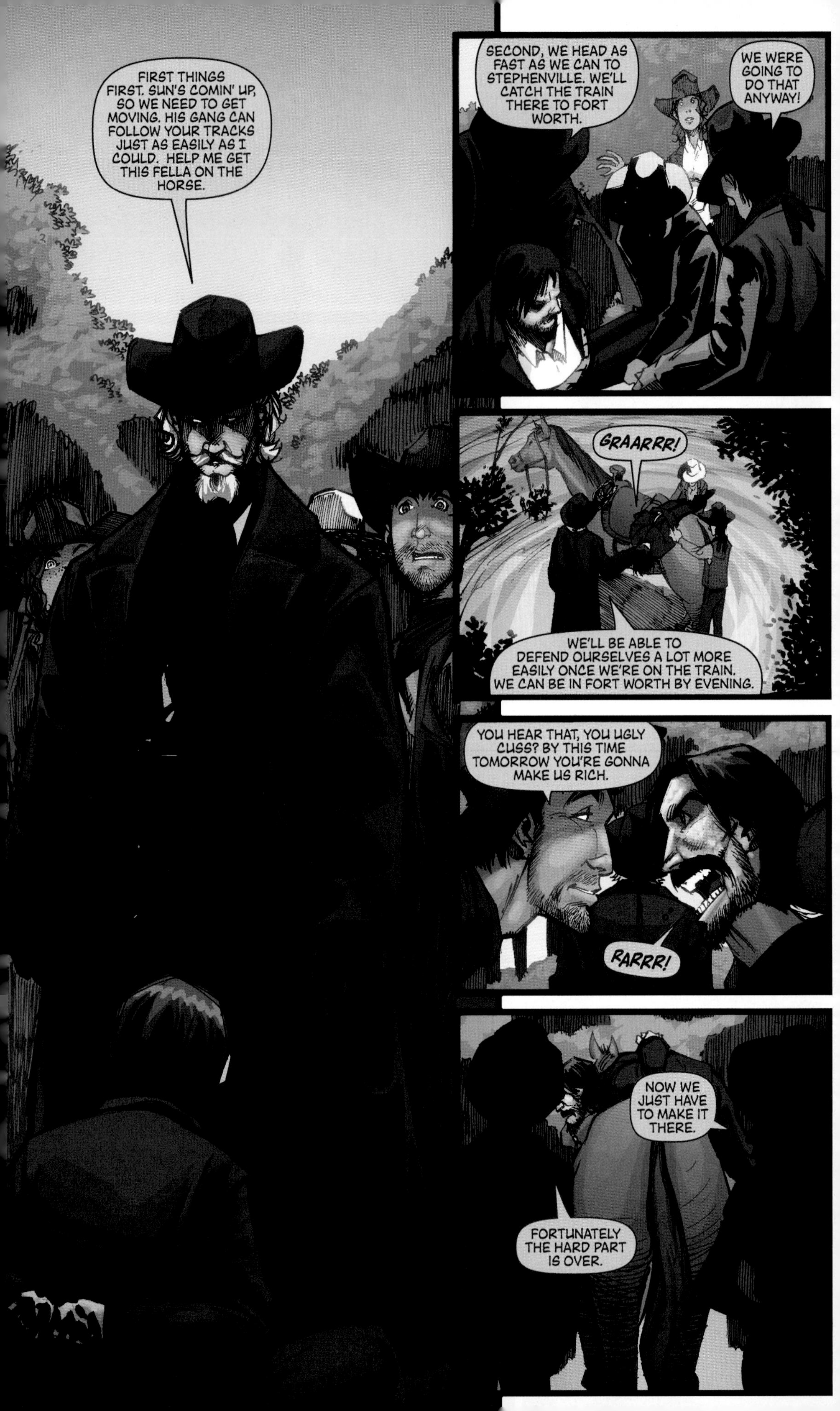
FIRST THINGS FIRST. SUN'S COMIN' UP, SO WE NEED TO GET MOVING. HIS GANG CAN FOLLOW YOUR TRACKS JUST AS EASILY AS I COULD. HELP ME GET THIS FELLA ON THE HORSE.
SECOND, WE HEAD AS FAST AS WE CAN TO STEPHENVILLE. WE'LL CATCH THE TRAIN THERE TO FORT WORTH.
WE WERE GOING TO DO THAT ANYWAY!
GRAARRR!
WE'LL BE ABLE TO DEFEND OURSELVES A LOT MORE EASILY ONCE WE'RE ON THE TRAIN. WE CAN BE IN FORT WORTH BY EVENING.
YOU HEAR THAT, YOU UGLY CUSS? BY THIS TIME TOMORROW YOU'RE GONNA MAKE US RICH.
RARRR!
NOW WE JUST HAVE TO MAKE IT THERE.
FORTUNATELY THE HARD PART IS OVER.

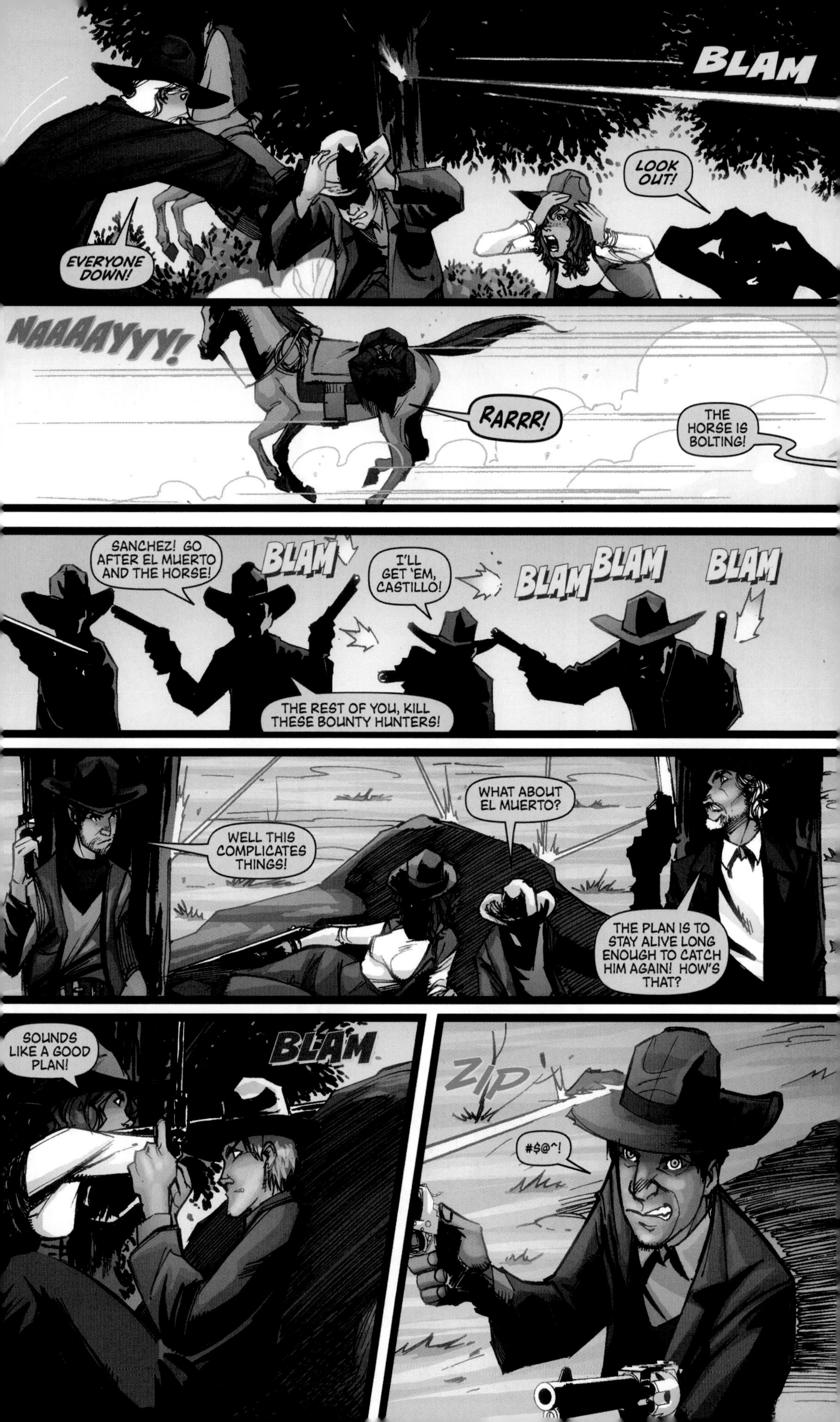

BLAM
EVERYONE DOWN!
LOOK OUT!
NAAAAYYY!
RARRR!
THE HORSE IS BOLTING!
SANCHEZ! GO AFTER EL MUERTO AND THE HORSE!
BLAM
I'LL GET 'EM, CASTILLO!
BLAM BLAM
BLAM
THE REST OF YOU, KILL THESE BOUNTY HUNTERS!
WELL THIS COMPLICATES THINGS!
WHAT ABOUT EL MUERTO?
THE PLAN IS TO STAY ALIVE LONG ENOUGH TO CATCH HIM AGAIN! HOW'S THAT?
SOUNDS LIKE A GOOD PLAN!
BLAM
ZIP
#$@^!

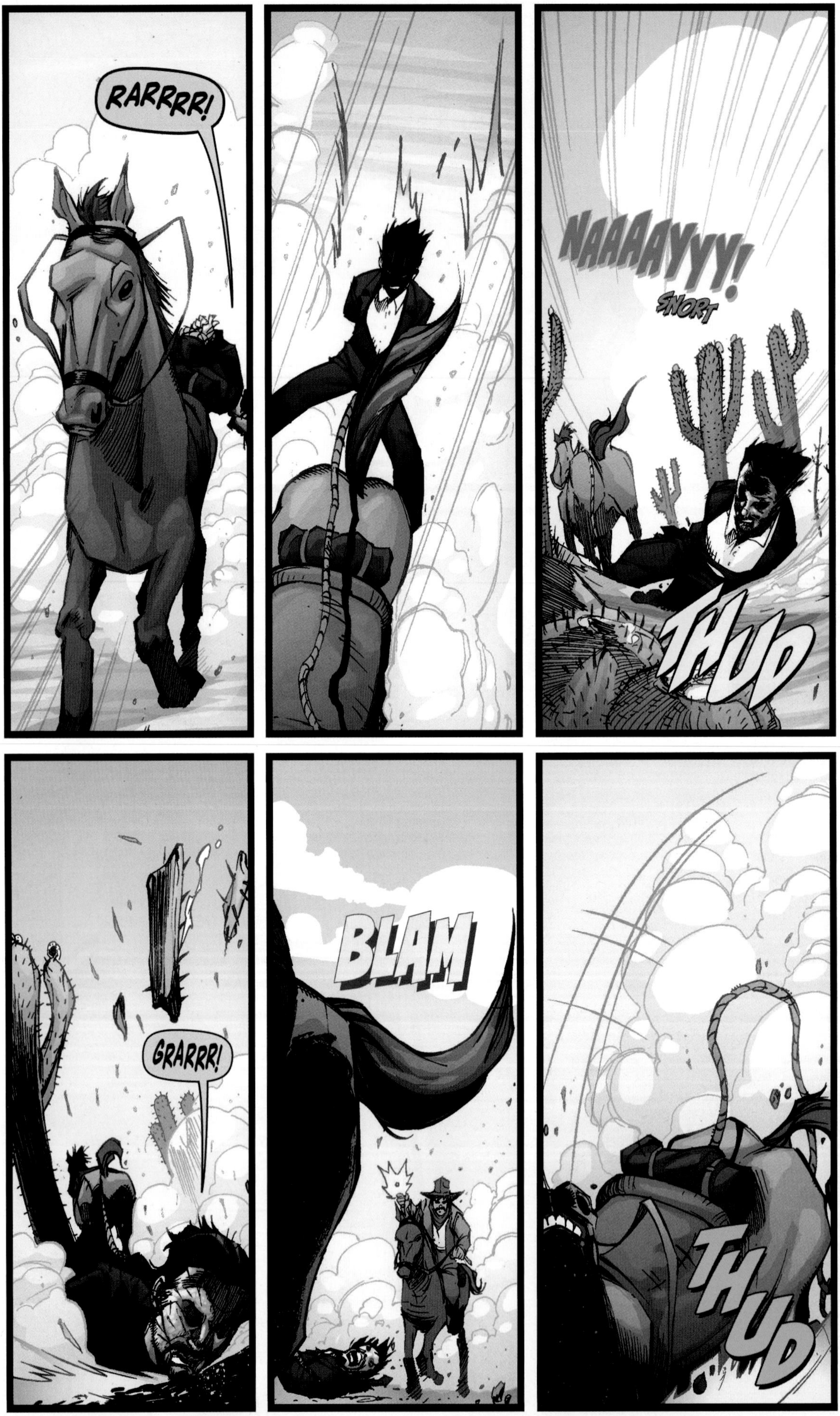
RARRRR!
NAAAAYYY!
SNORT
THUD
GRARRR!
BLAM
THUD

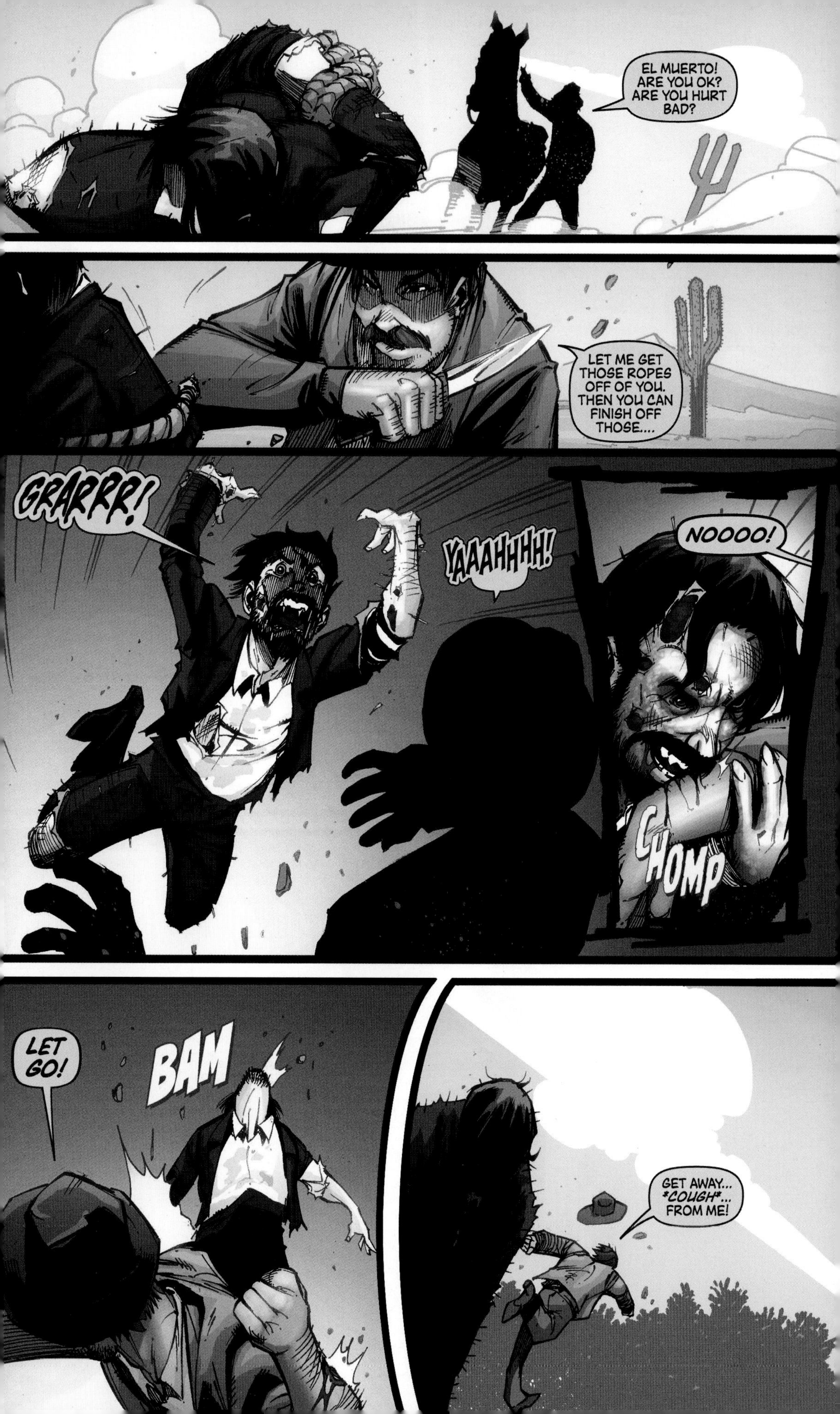
EL MUERTO! ARE YOU OK? ARE YOU HURT BAD?
LET ME GET THOSE ROPES OFF OF YOU. THEN YOU CAN FINISH OFF THOSE....
GRARRR!
YAAAHHHH!
NOOOO!
CHOMP
LET GO!
BAM
GET AWAY... *COUGH*... FROM ME!

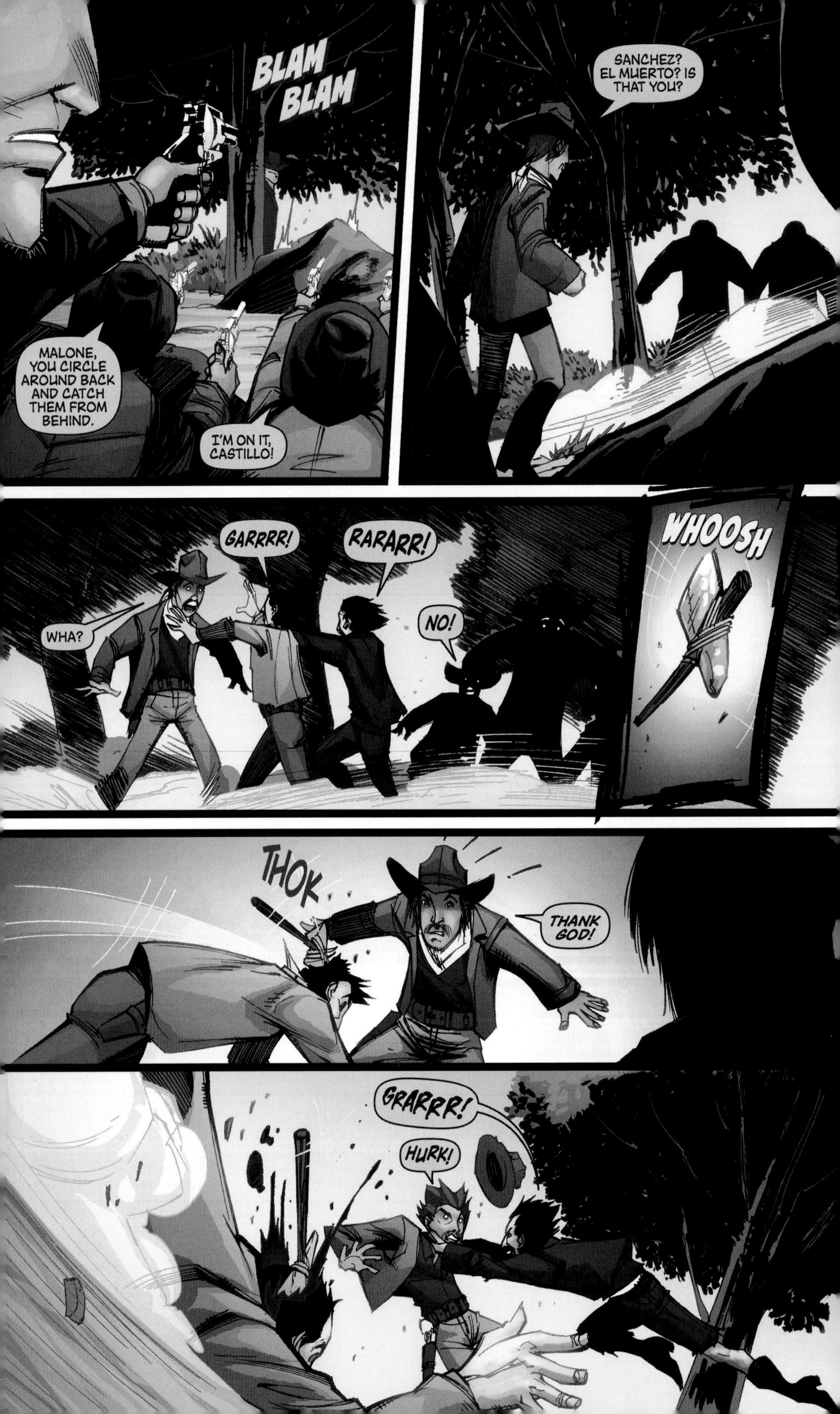
BLAM
BLAM
MALONE, YOU CIRCLE AROUND BACK AND CATCH THEM FROM BEHIND.
I'M ON IT, CASTILLO!
SANCHEZ? EL MUERTO? IS THAT YOU?
GARRRR!
RARARR!
WHA?
NO!
WHOOSH
THOK
THANK GOD!
GRARRR!
HURK!

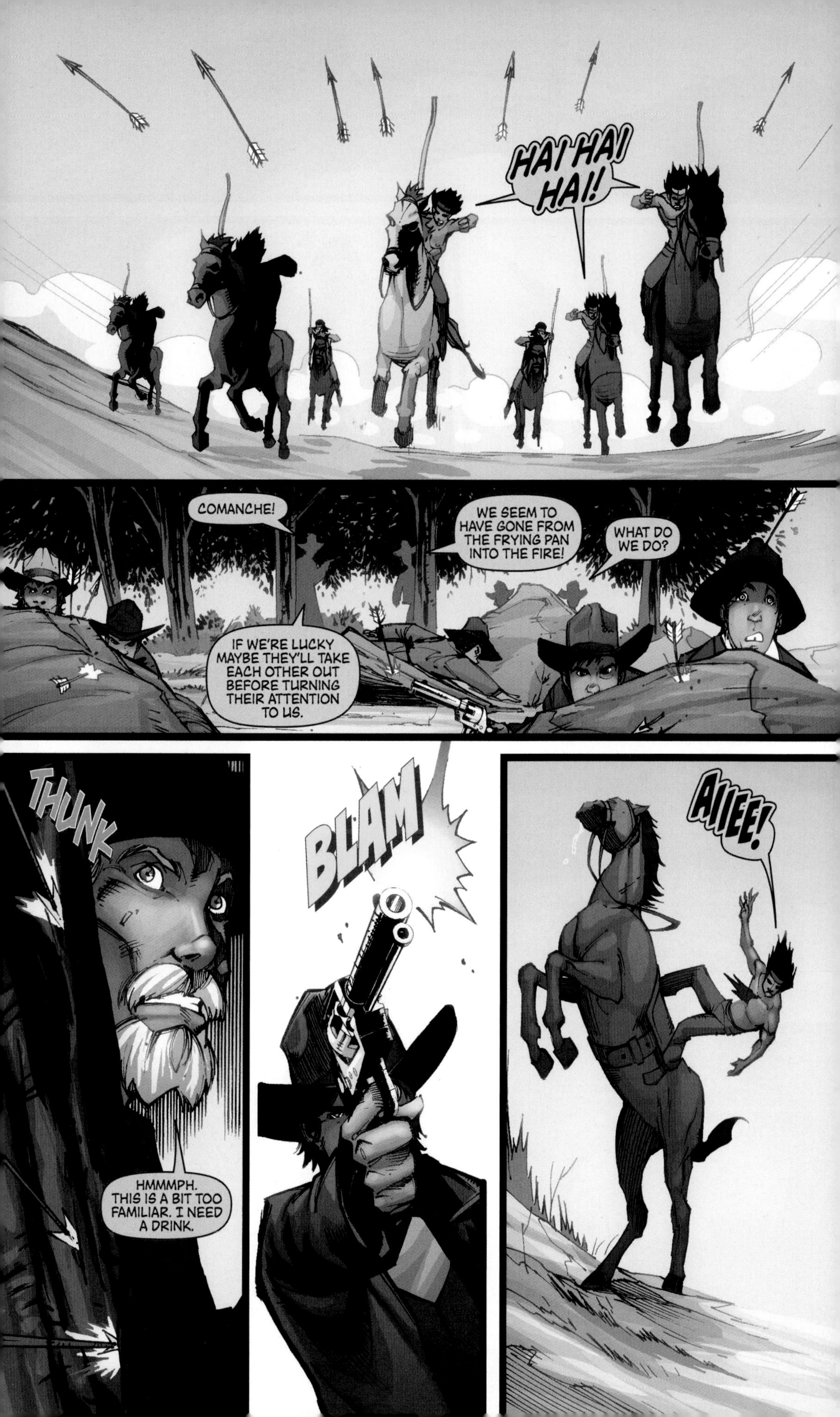
HAI HAI HAI!
COMANCHE!
WE SEEM TO HAVE GONE FROM THE FRYING PAN INTO THE FIRE!
WHAT DO WE DO?
IF WE'RE LUCKY MAYBE THEY'LL TAKE EACH OTHER OUT BEFORE TURNING THEIR ATTENTION TO US.
THUNK
HMMMPH. THIS IS A BIT TOO FAMILIAR. I NEED A DRINK.
BLAM
AIIEE!

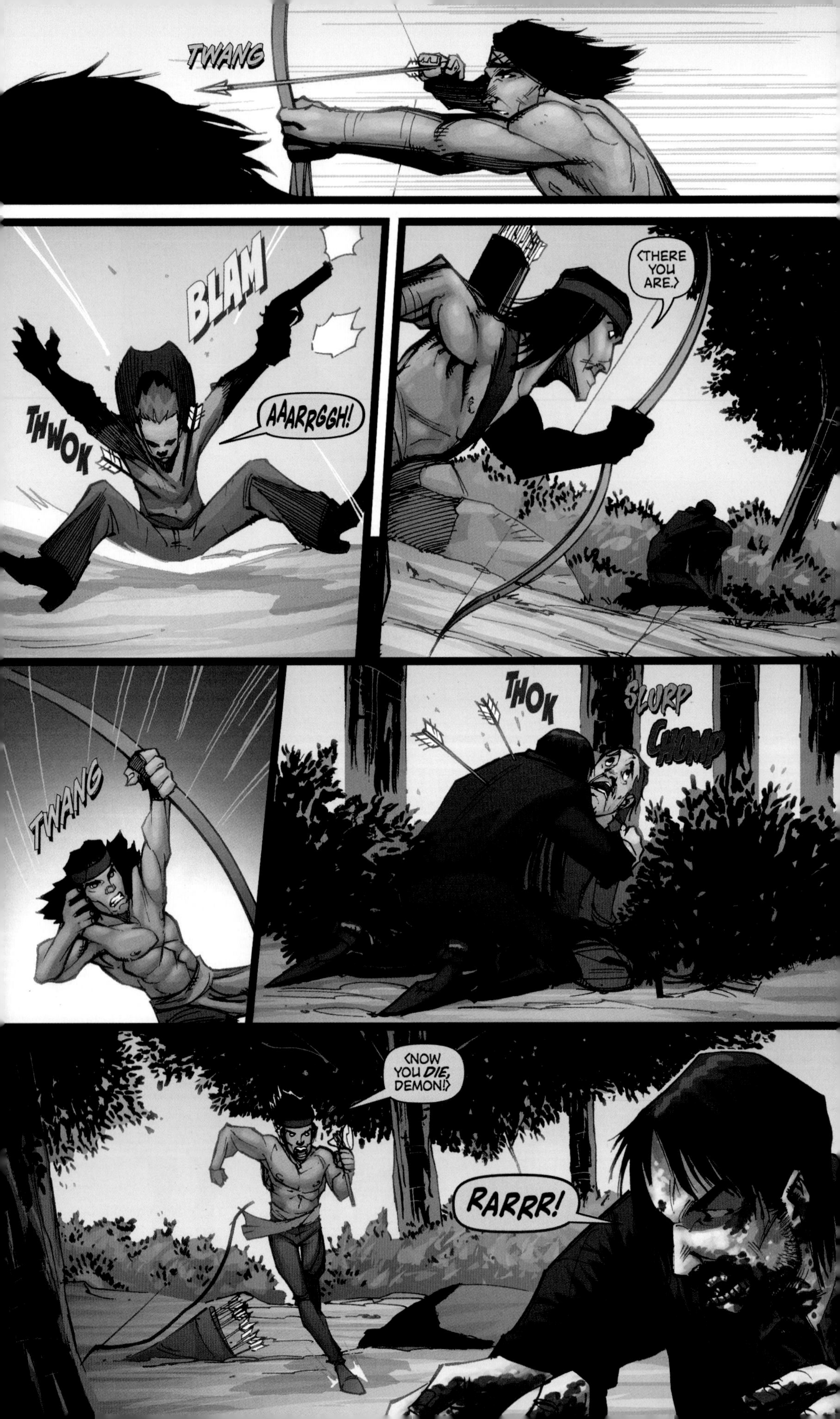

TWANG
BLAM
THWOK
AAARRGGH!
<THERE YOU ARE.>
TWANG
THOK
SLURP
CHOMP
<NOW YOU DIE, DEMON!>
RARRR!

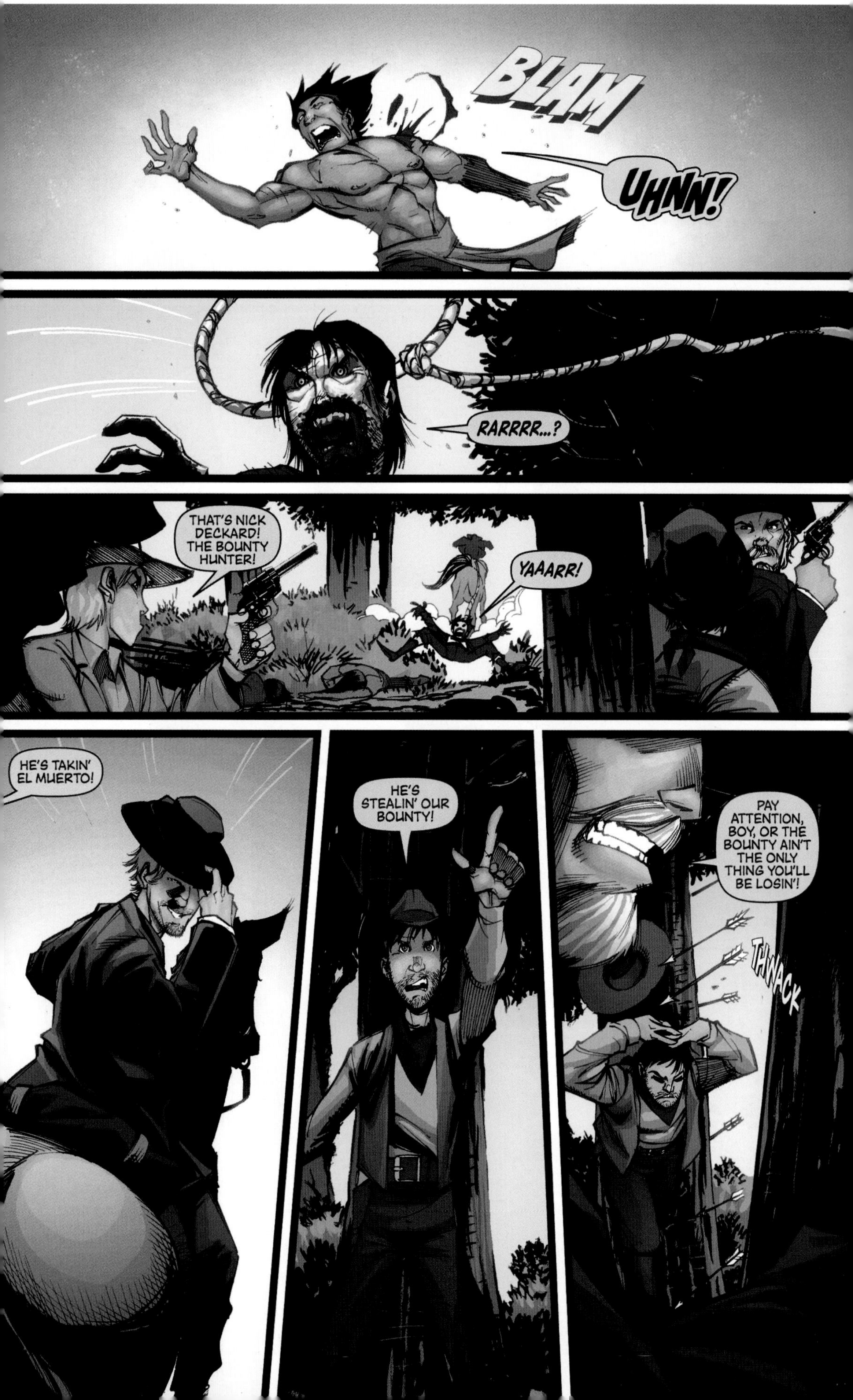
BLAM
UHNN!
RARRRR...?
THAT'S NICK DECKARD! THE BOUNTY HUNTER!
YAAARR!
HE'S TAKIN' EL MUERTO!
HE'S STEALIN' OUR BOUNTY!
PAY ATTENTION, BOY, OR THE BOUNTY AIN'T THE ONLY THING YOU'LL BE LOSIN'!
THWACK

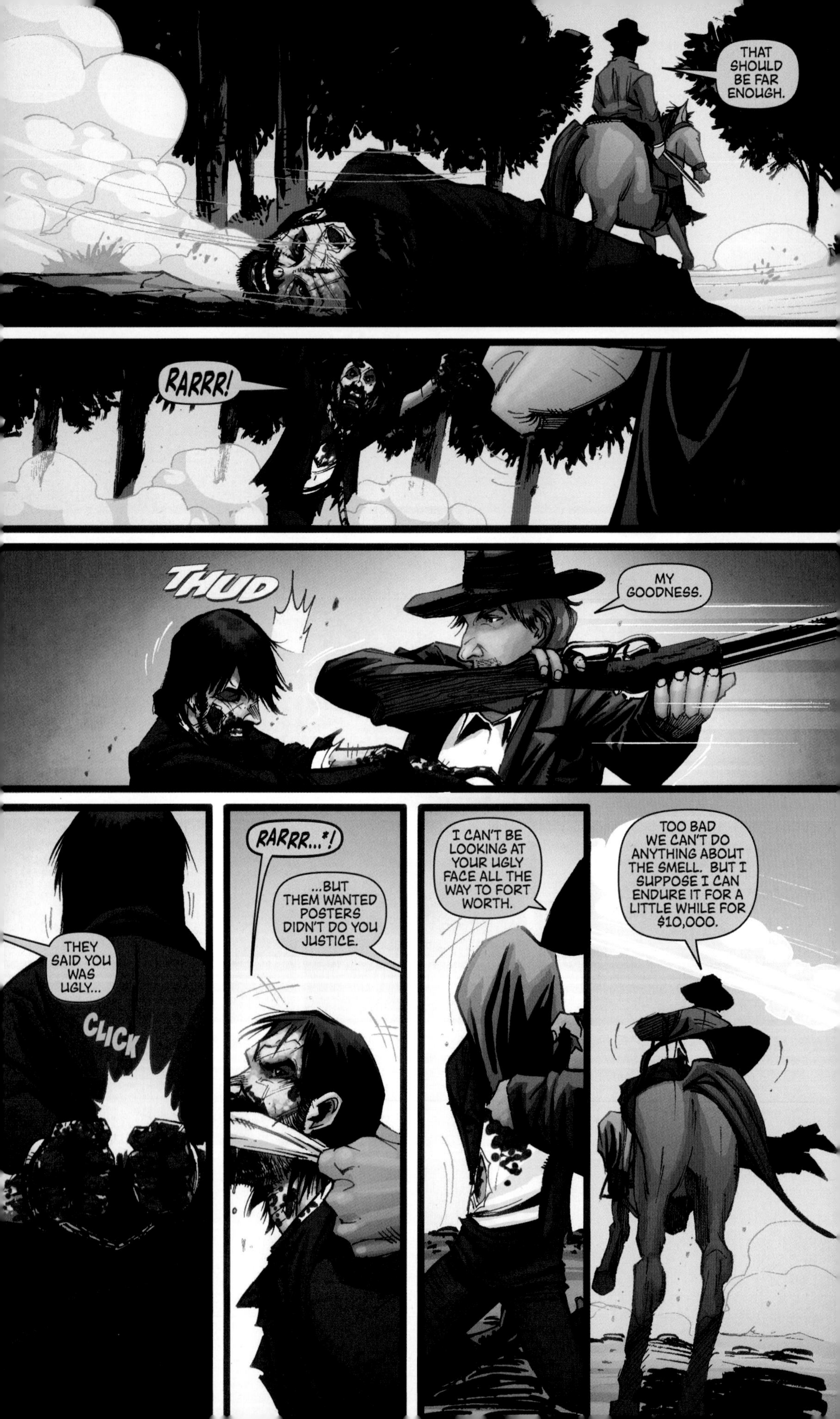
THAT SHOULD BE FAR ENOUGH.
RARRR!
THUD
MY GOODNESS.
THEY SAID YOU WAS UGLY...
CLICK
RARRR...*!
...BUT THEM WANTED POSTERS DIDN'T DO YOU JUSTICE.
I CAN'T BE LOOKING AT YOUR UGLY FACE ALL THE WAY TO FORT WORTH.
TOO BAD WE CAN'T DO ANYTHING ABOUT THE SMELL. BUT I SUPPOSE I CAN ENDURE IT FOR A LITTLE WHILE FOR $10,000.

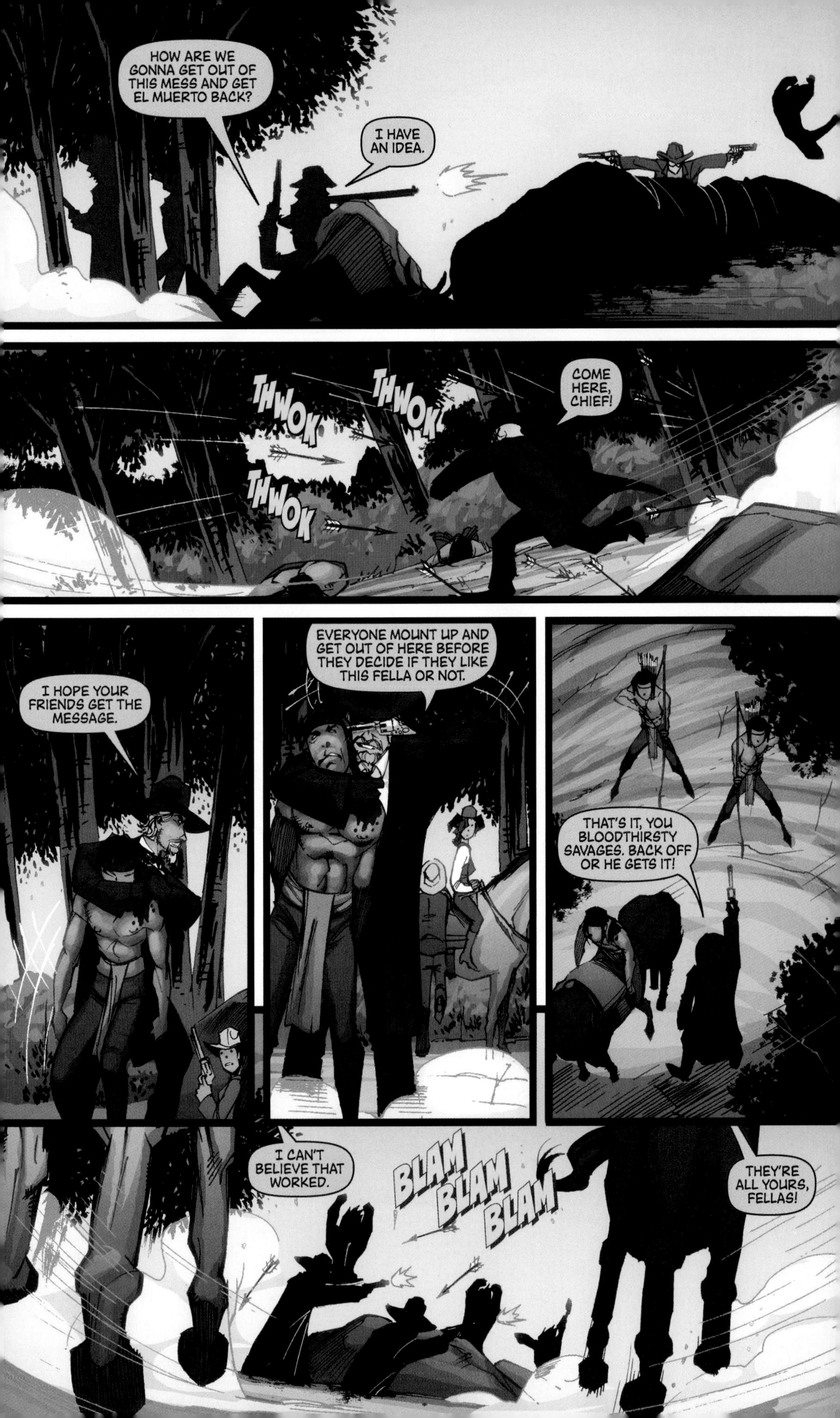
HOW ARE WE GONNA GET OUT OF THIS MESS AND GET EL MUERTO BACK?
I HAVE AN IDEA.
THWOK
THWOK
THWOK
COME HERE, CHIEF!
I HOPE YOUR FRIENDS GET THE MESSAGE.
EVERYONE MOUNT UP AND GET OUT OF HERE BEFORE THEY DECIDE IF THEY LIKE THIS FELLA OR NOT.
THAT'S IT, YOU BLOODTHIRSTY SAVAGES. BACK OFF OR HE GETS IT!
I CAN'T BELIEVE THAT WORKED.
BLAM
BLAM
BLAM
THEY'RE ALL YOURS, FELLAS!

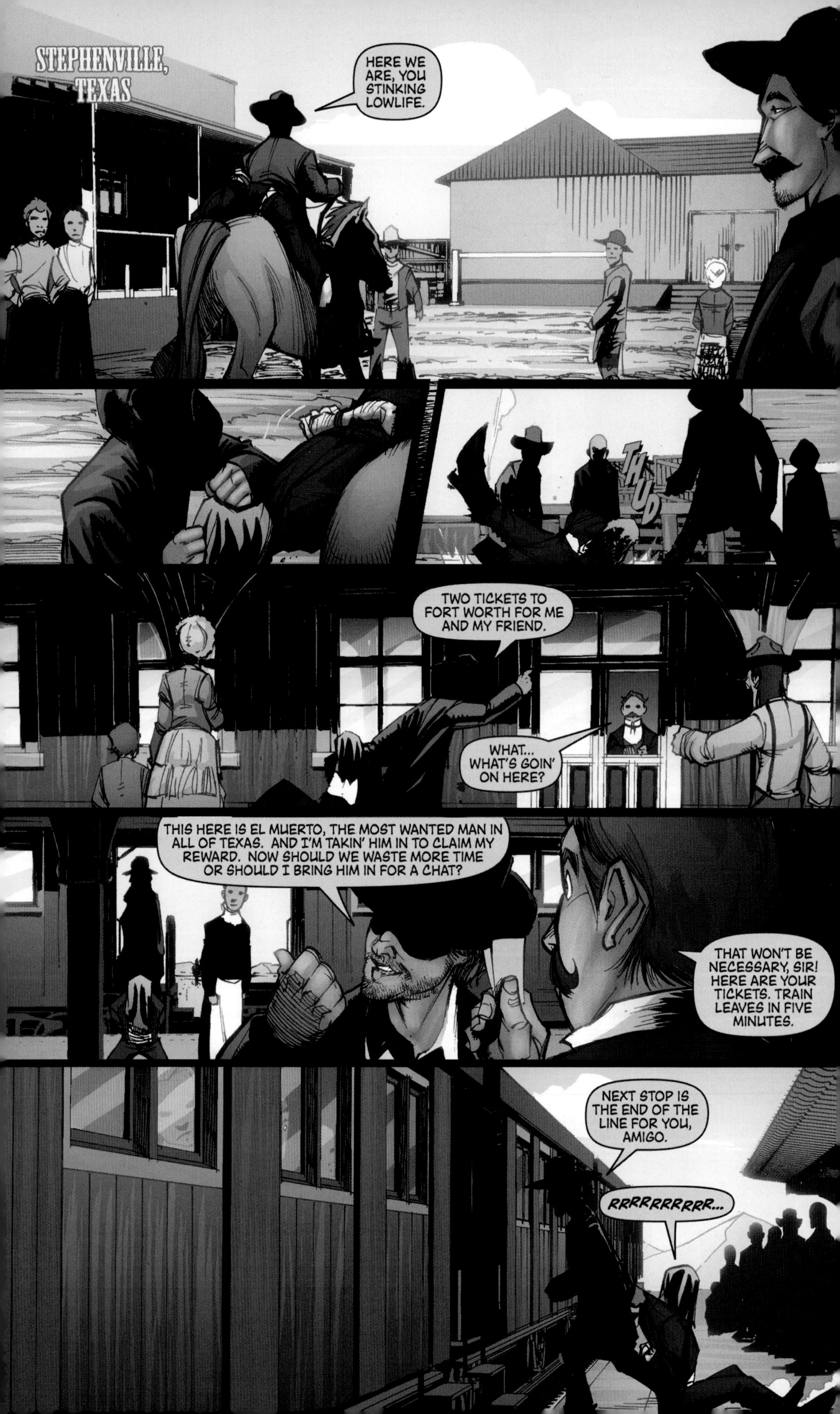

STEPHENVILLE, TEXAS
HERE WE ARE, YOU STINKING LOWLIFE.
THUD
TWO TICKETS TO FORT WORTH FOR ME AND MY FRIEND.
WHAT... WHAT'S GOIN' ON HERE?
THIS HERE IS EL MUERTO, THE MOST WANTED MAN IN ALL OF TEXAS. AND I'M TAKIN' HIM IN TO CLAIM MY REWARD. NOW SHOULD WE WASTE MORE TIME OR SHOULD I BRING HIM IN FOR A CHAT?
THAT WON'T BE NECESSARY, SIR! HERE ARE YOUR TICKETS. TRAIN LEAVES IN FIVE MINUTES.
NEXT STOP IS THE END OF THE LINE FOR YOU, AMIGO.
RRRRRRRRR...

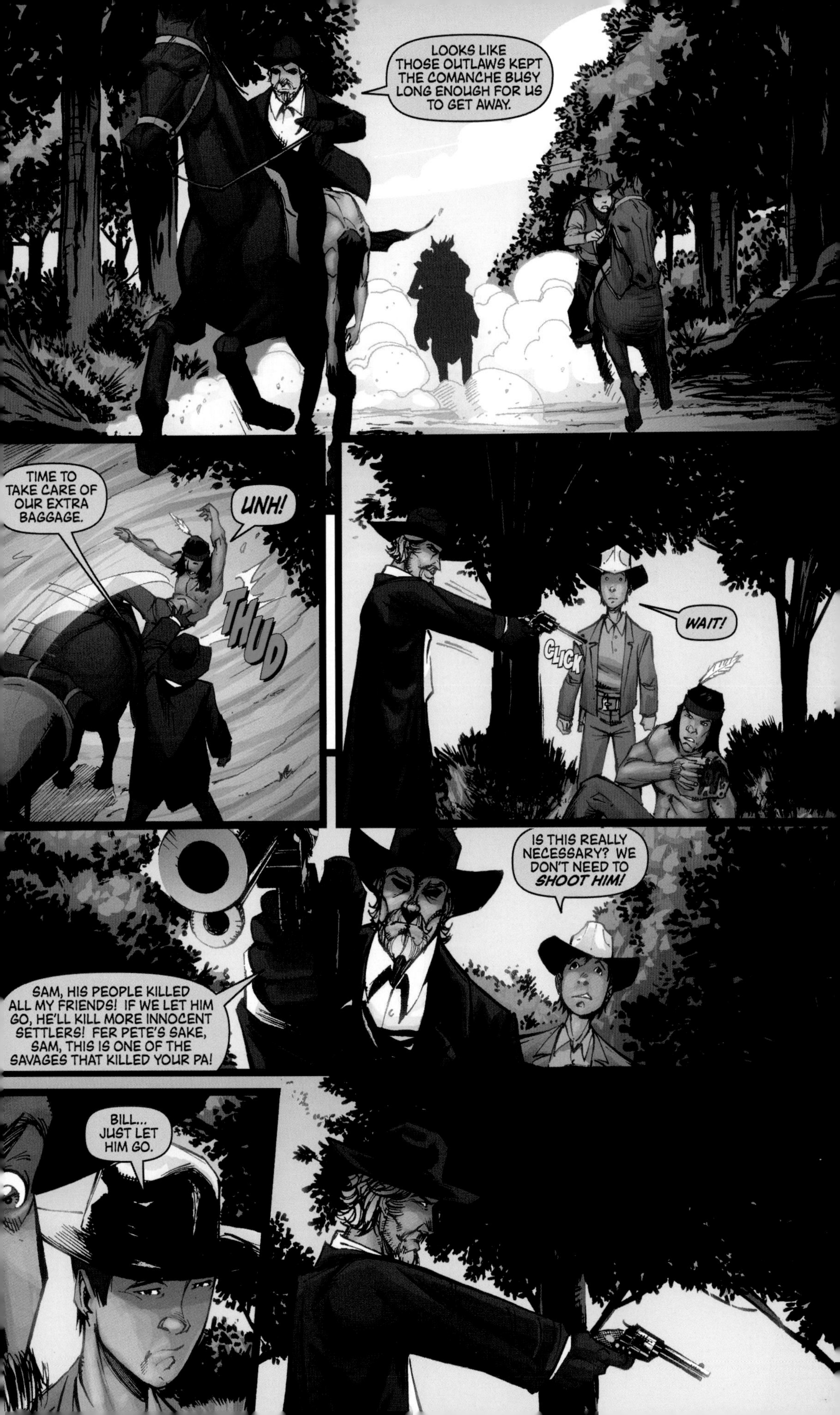
LOOKS LIKE THOSE OUTLAWS KEPT THE COMANCHE BUSY LONG ENOUGH FOR US TO GET AWAY.
TIME TO TAKE CARE OF OUR EXTRA BAGGAGE.
UNH!
THUD
WAIT!
CLICK
IS THIS REALLY NECESSARY? WE DON'T NEED TO SHOOT HIM!
SAM, HIS PEOPLE KILLED ALL MY FRIENDS! IF WE LET HIM GO, HE'LL KILL MORE INNOCENT SETTLERS! FER PETE'S SAKE, SAM, THIS IS ONE OF THE SAVAGES THAT KILLED YOUR PA!
BILL... JUST LET HIM GO.

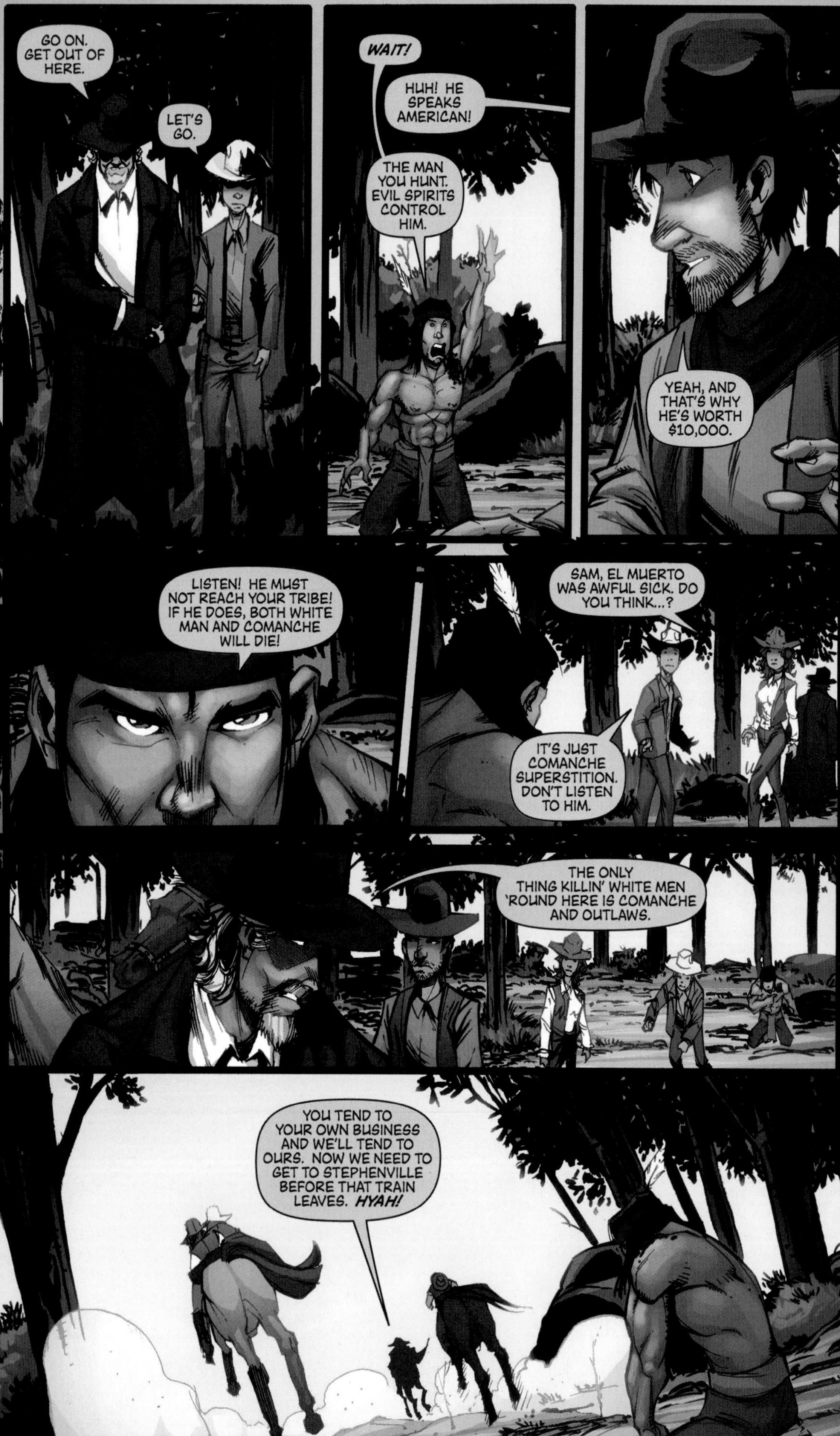
GO ON. GET OUT OF HERE.
LET'S GO.
WAIT!
HUH! HE SPEAKS AMERICAN!
THE MAN YOU HUNT. EVIL SPIRITS CONTROL HIM.
YEAH, AND THAT'S WHY HE'S WORTH $10,000.
LISTEN! HE MUST NOT REACH YOUR TRIBE! IF HE DOES, BOTH WHITE MAN AND COMANCHE WILL DIE!
SAM, EL MUERTO WAS AWFUL SICK. DO YOU THINK...?
IT'S JUST COMANCHE SUPERSTITION. DON'T LISTEN TO HIM.
THE ONLY THING KILLIN' WHITE MEN 'ROUND HERE IS COMANCHE AND OUTLAWS.
YOU TEND TO YOUR OWN BUSINESS AND WE'LL TEND TO OURS. NOW WE NEED TO GET TO STEPHENVILLE BEFORE THAT TRAIN LEAVES. HYAH!

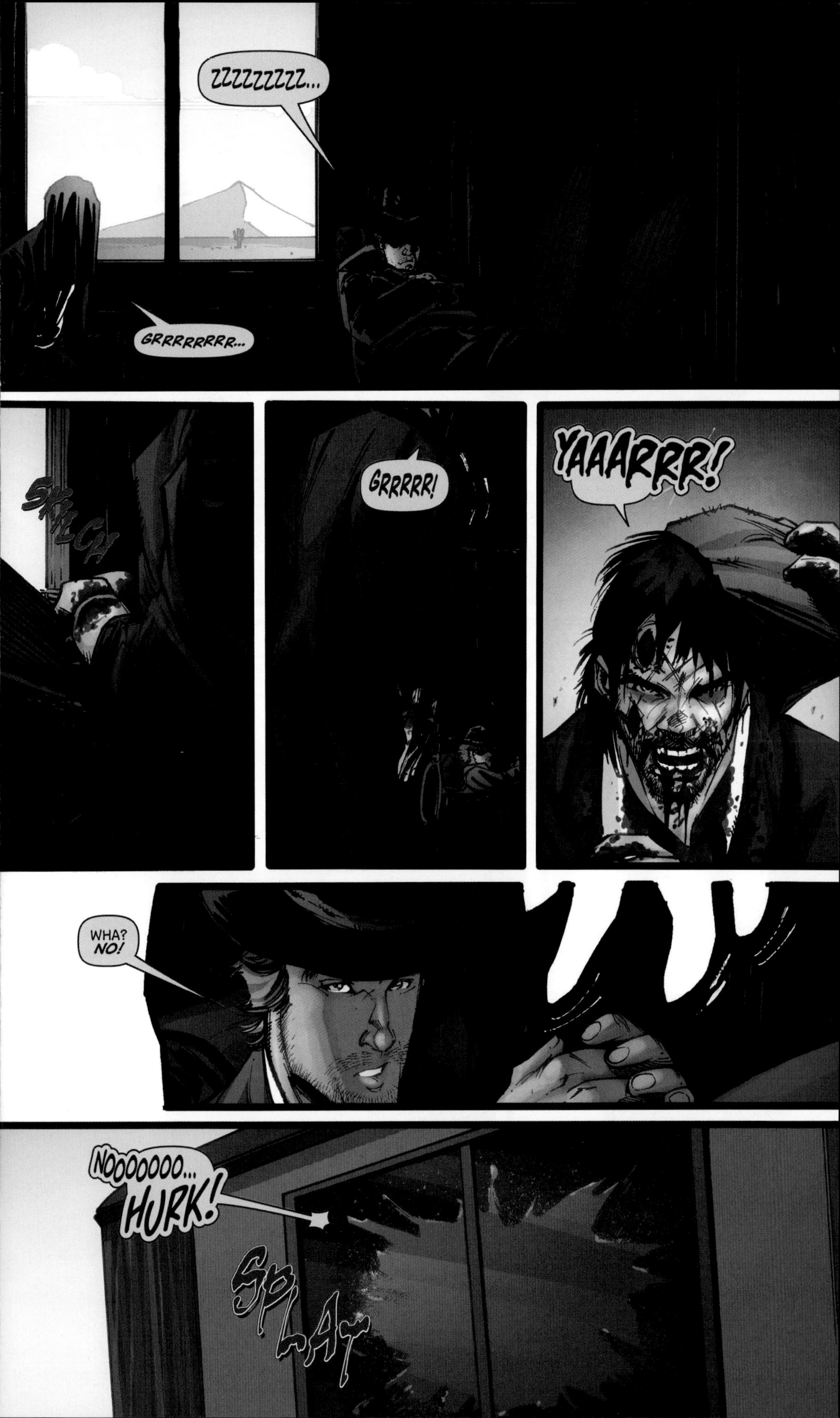
ZZZZZZZZZ...
GRRRRRRRR...
SKLCH
GRRRRR!
YAAARRR!
WHA? NO!
NOOOOOOO... HURK!
SPLAT

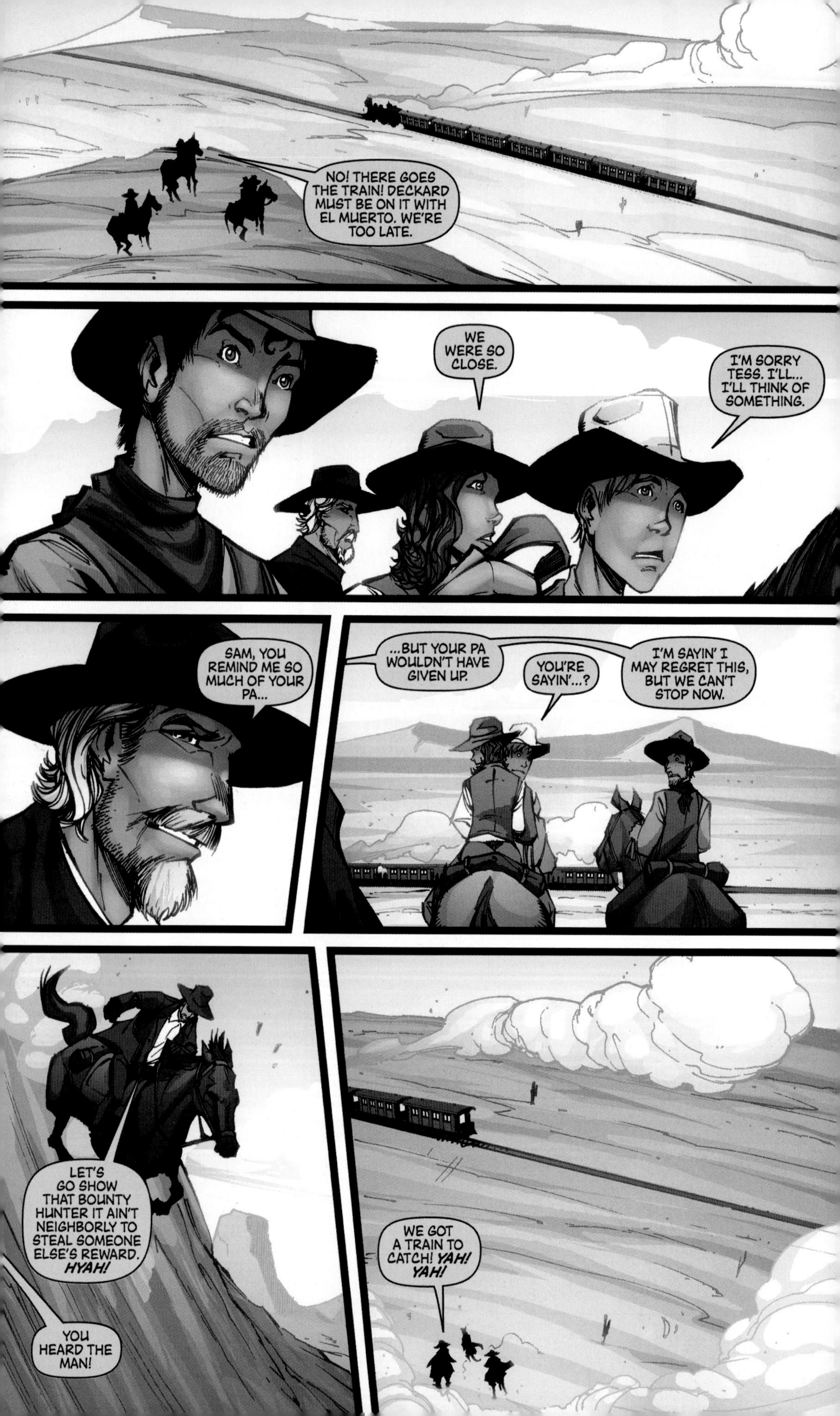

NO! THERE GOES THE TRAIN! DECKARD MUST BE ON IT WITH EL MUERTO. WE'RE TOO LATE.
WE WERE SO CLOSE.
I'M SORRY TESS. I'LL... I'LL THINK OF SOMETHING.
SAM, YOU REMIND ME SO MUCH OF YOUR PA...
...BUT YOUR PA WOULDN'T HAVE GIVEN UP.
YOU'RE SAYIN'...?
I'M SAYIN' I MAY REGRET THIS, BUT WE CAN'T STOP NOW.
LET'S GO SHOW THAT BOUNTY HUNTER IT AIN'T NEIGHBORLY TO STEAL SOMEONE ELSE'S REWARD. *HYAH!*
YOU HEARD THE MAN!
WE GOT A TRAIN TO CATCH! *YAH! YAH!*

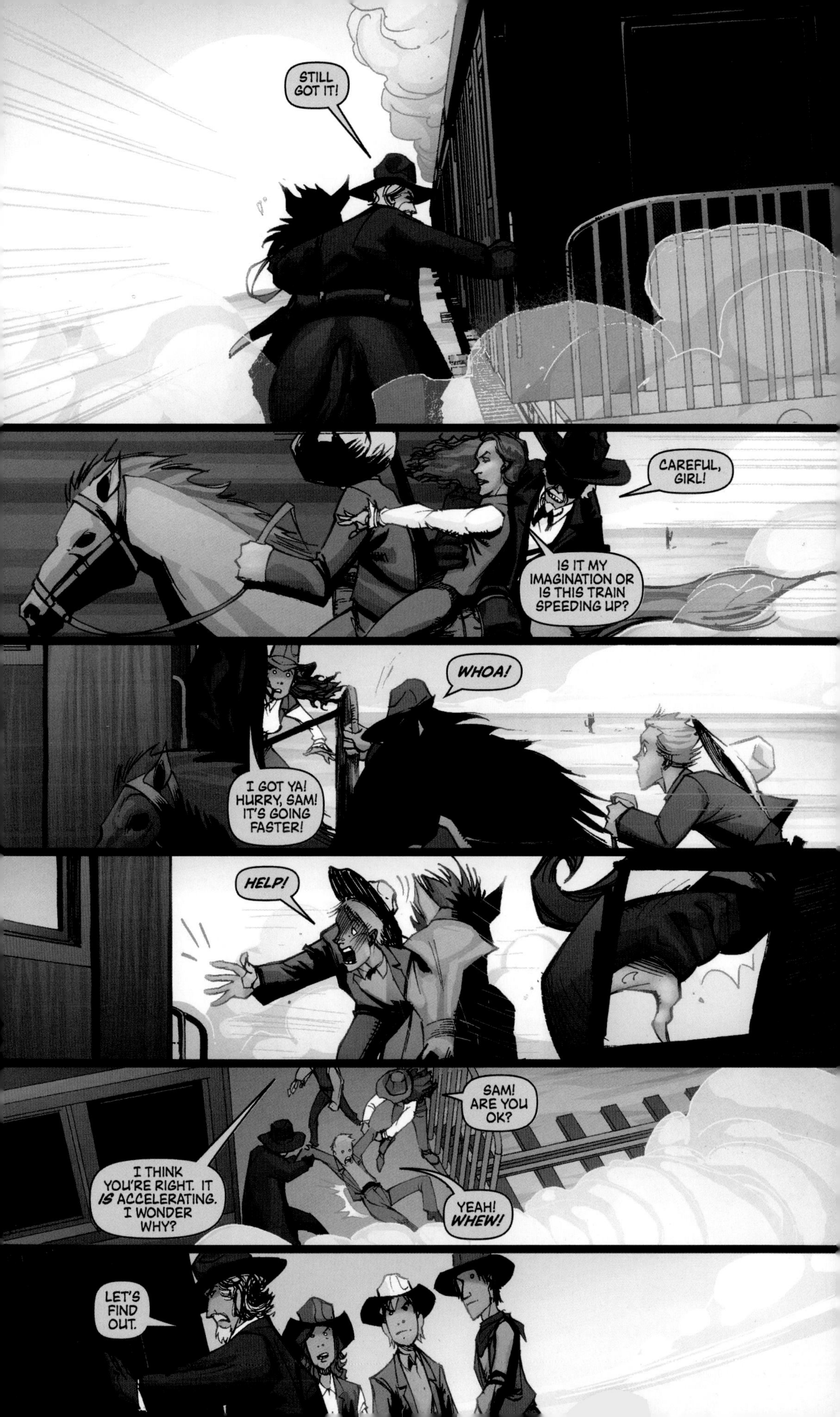
STILL GOT IT!
CAREFUL, GIRL!
IS IT MY IMAGINATION OR IS THIS TRAIN SPEEDING UP?
WHOA!
I GOT YA! HURRY, SAM! IT'S GOING FASTER!
HELP!
SAM! ARE YOU OK?
I THINK YOU'RE RIGHT. IT *IS* ACCELERATING. I WONDER WHY?
YEAH! *WHEW!*
LET'S FIND OUT.

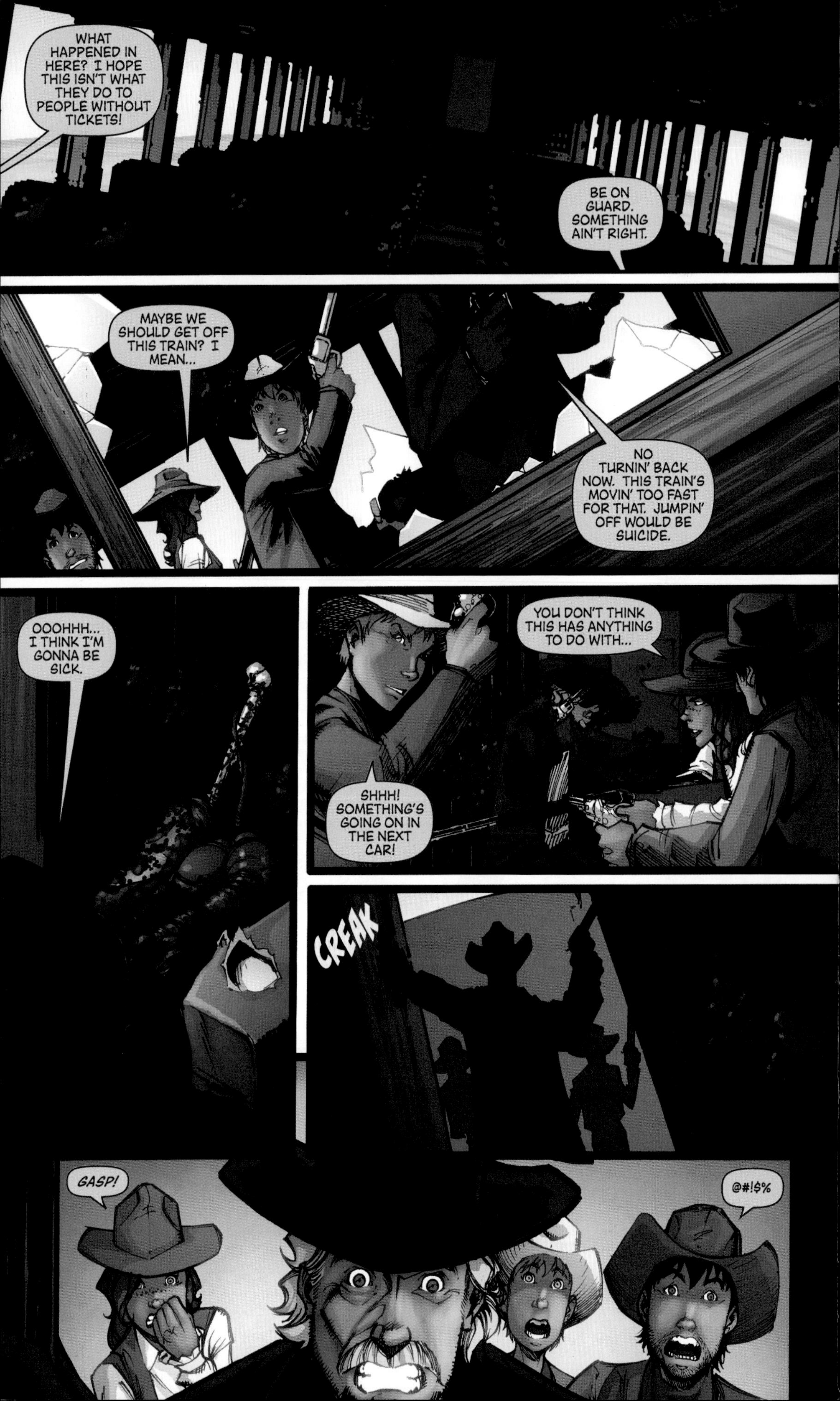
WHAT HAPPENED IN HERE? I HOPE THIS ISN'T WHAT THEY DO TO PEOPLE WITHOUT TICKETS!
BE ON GUARD. SOMETHING AIN'T RIGHT.
MAYBE WE SHOULD GET OFF THIS TRAIN? I MEAN...
NO TURNIN' BACK NOW. THIS TRAIN'S MOVIN' TOO FAST FOR THAT. JUMPIN' OFF WOULD BE SUICIDE.
OOOHHH... I THINK I'M GONNA BE SICK.
YOU DON'T THINK THIS HAS ANYTHING TO DO WITH...
SHHH! SOMETHING'S GOING ON IN THE NEXT CAR!
CREAK
GASP!
@#!$%

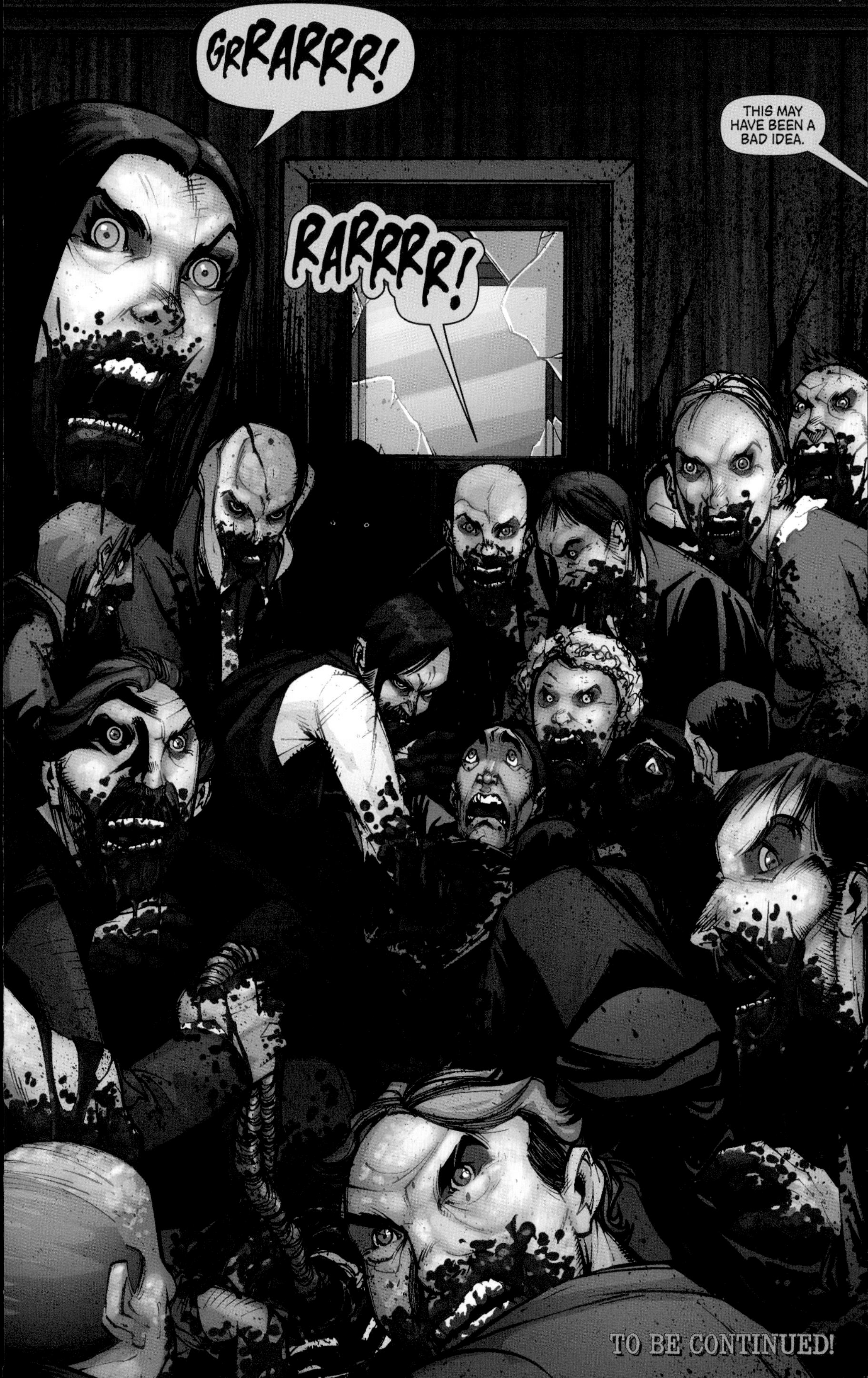
GrRARRR!
THIS MAY HAVE BEEN A BAD IDEA.
RARRRR!
TO BE CONTINUED!

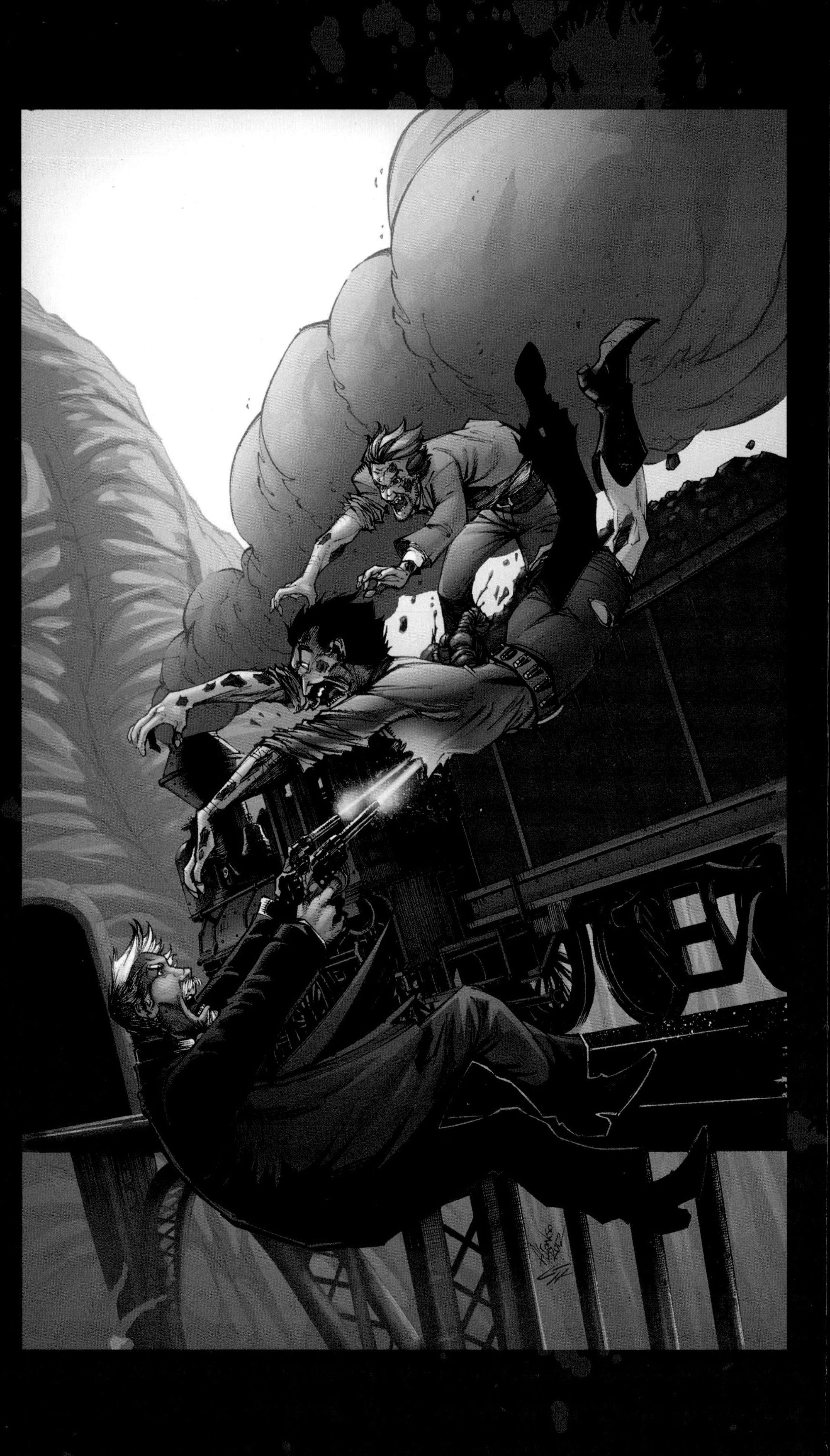

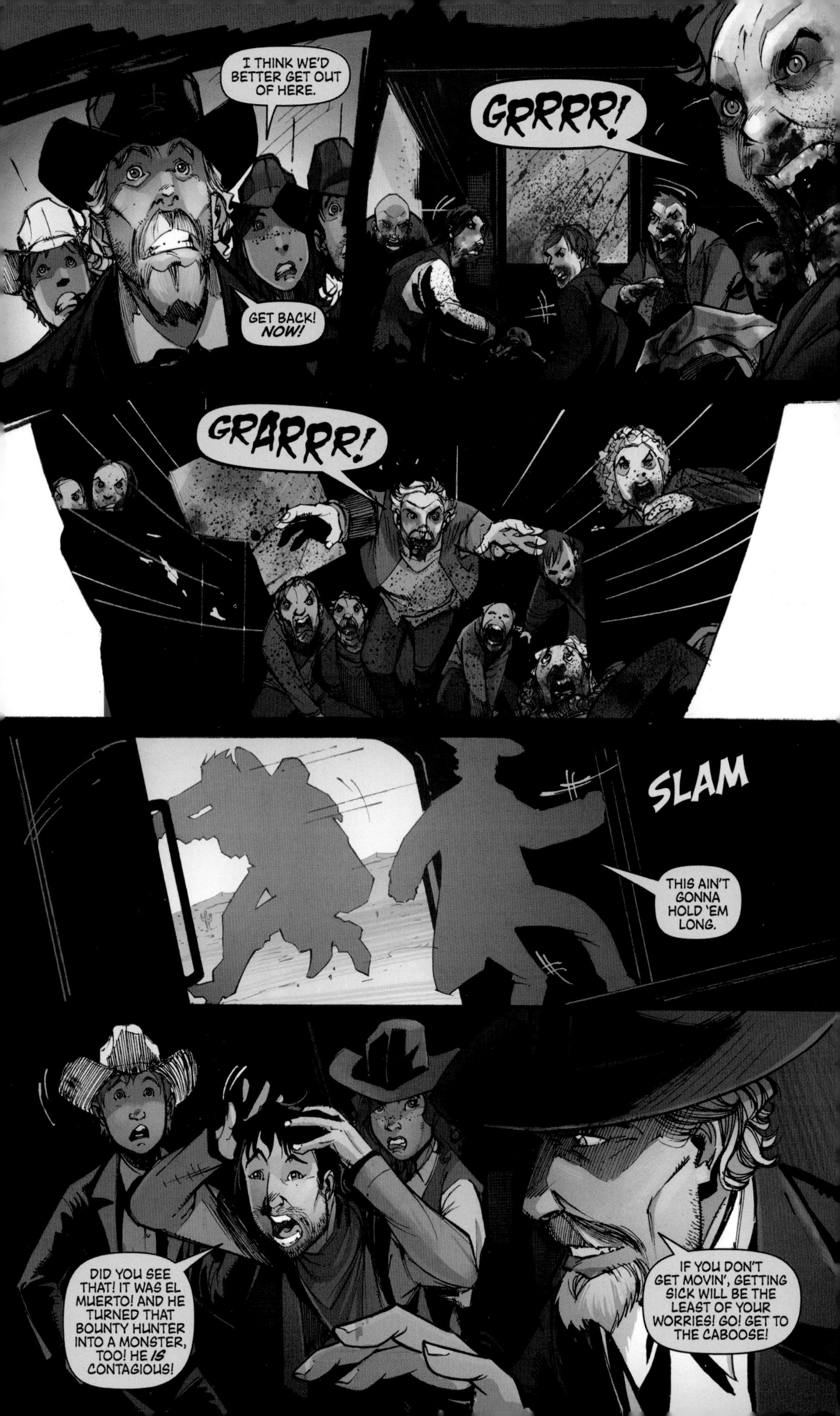
I THINK WE'D BETTER GET OUT OF HERE.
GET BACK! *NOW!*
GRRRR!
GRARRR!
SLAM
THIS AIN'T GONNA HOLD 'EM LONG.
DID YOU SEE THAT! IT WAS EL MUERTO! AND HE TURNED THAT BOUNTY HUNTER INTO A MONSTER, TOO! HE *IS* CONTAGIOUS!
IF YOU DON'T GET MOVIN', GETTING SICK WILL BE THE LEAST OF YOUR WORRIES! GO! GET TO THE CABOOSE!

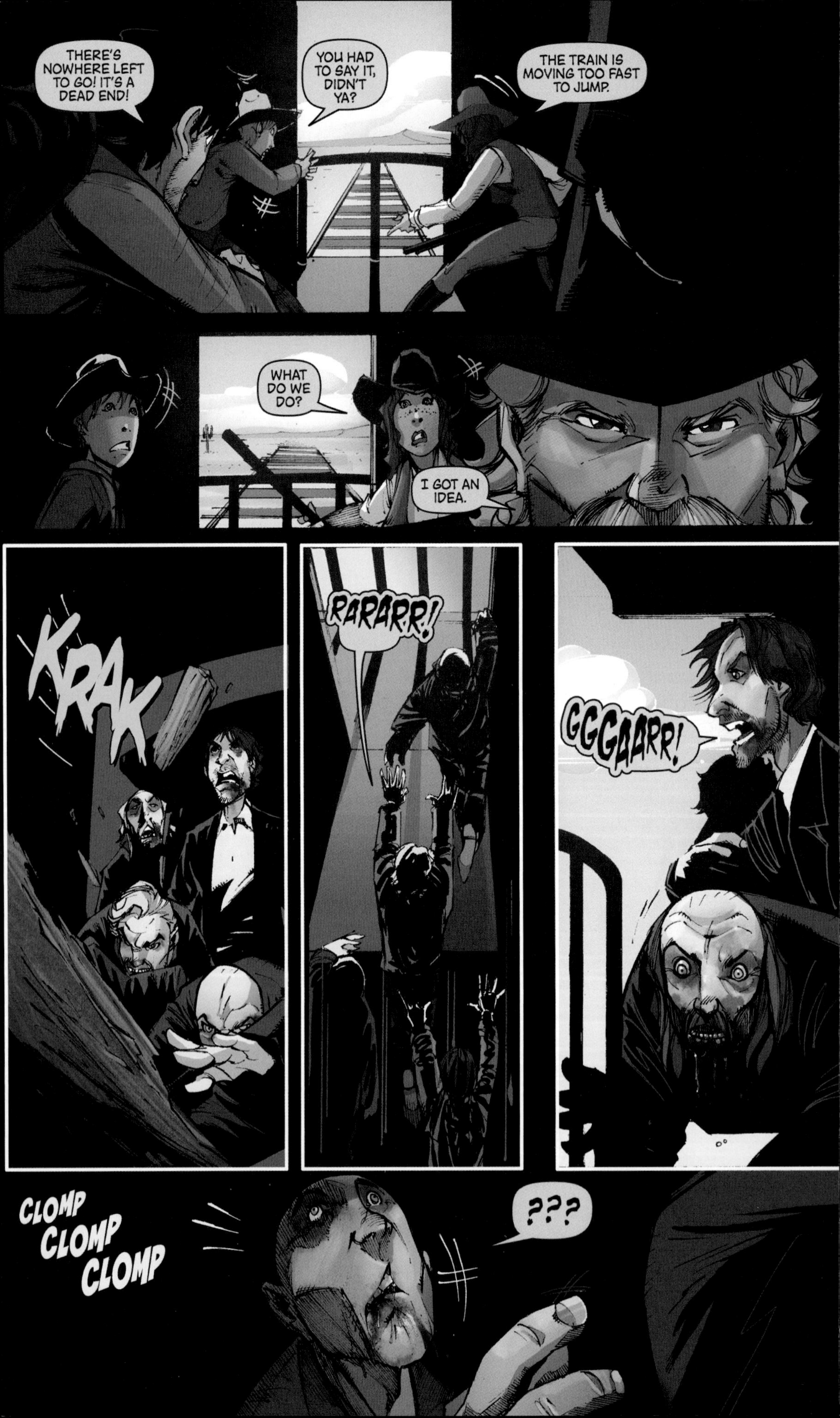
THERE'S NOWHERE LEFT TO GO! IT'S A DEAD END!
YOU HAD TO SAY IT, DIDN'T YA?
THE TRAIN IS MOVING TOO FAST TO JUMP.
WHAT DO WE DO?
I GOT AN IDEA.
KRAK
RARARR!
GGGAARR!
CLOMP CLOMP CLOMP
???

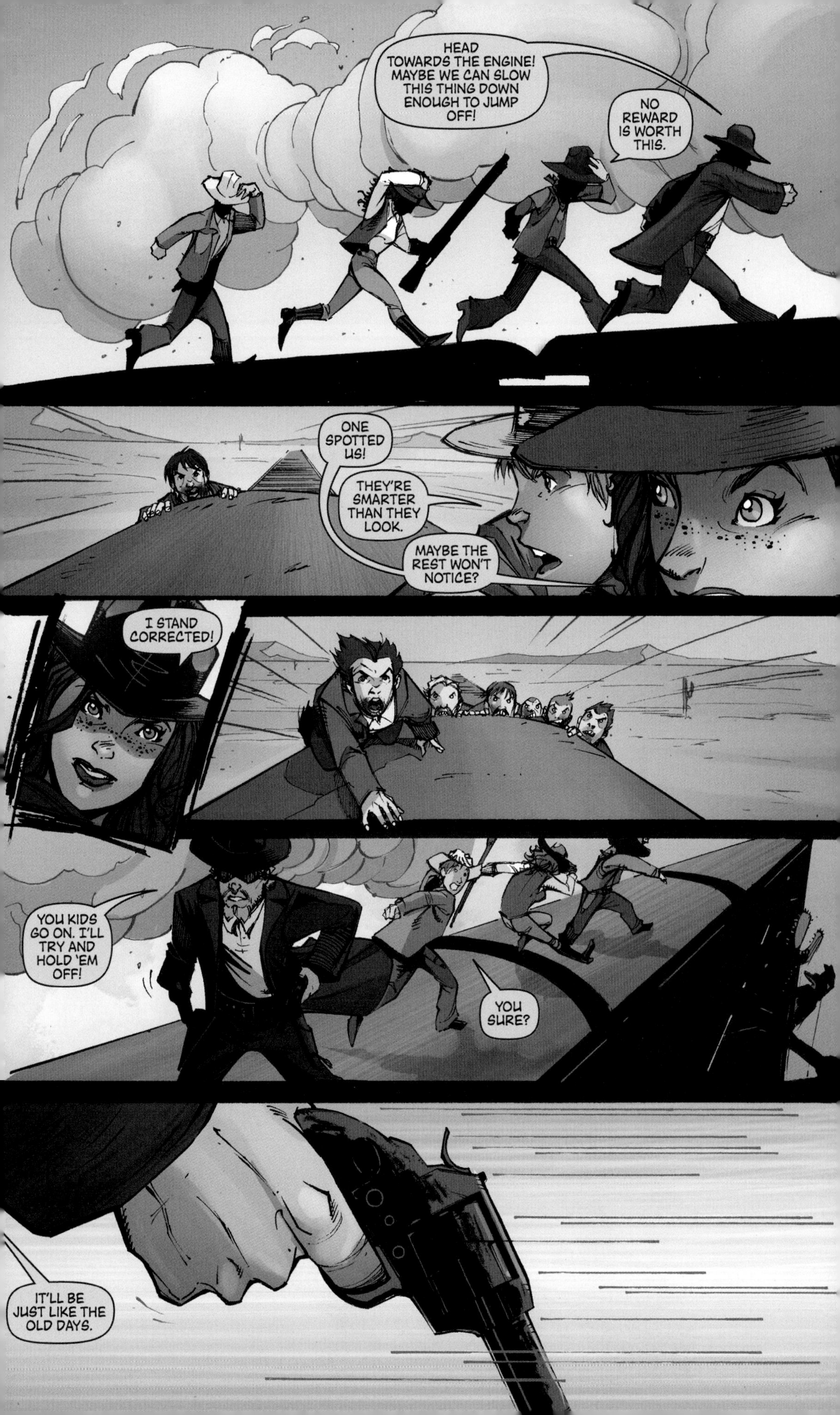
HEAD TOWARDS THE ENGINE! MAYBE WE CAN SLOW THIS THING DOWN ENOUGH TO JUMP OFF!
NO REWARD IS WORTH THIS.
ONE SPOTTED US!
THEY'RE SMARTER THAN THEY LOOK.
MAYBE THE REST WON'T NOTICE?
I STAND CORRECTED!
YOU KIDS GO ON. I'LL TRY AND HOLD 'EM OFF!
YOU SURE?
IT'LL BE JUST LIKE THE OLD DAYS.

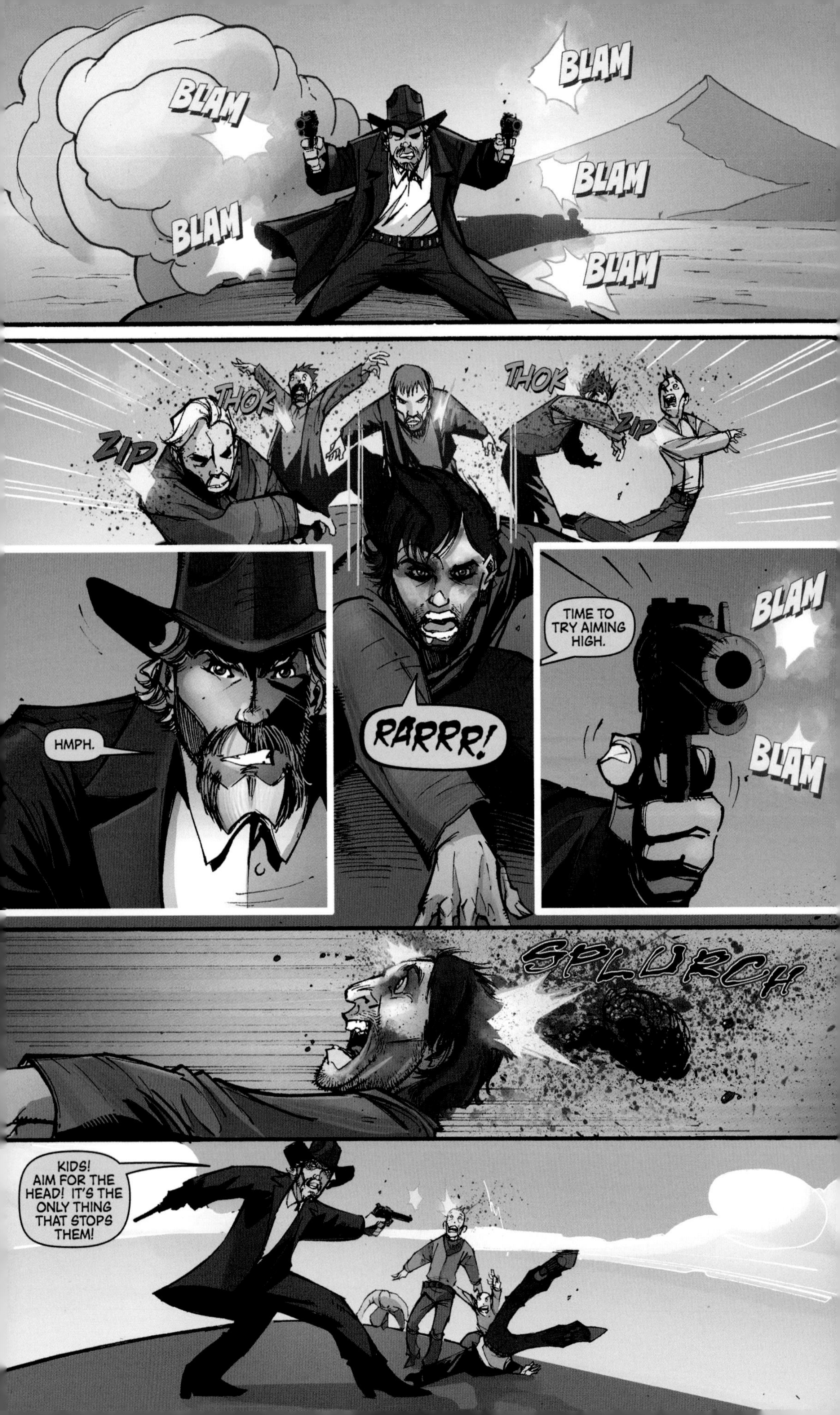
BLAM
BLAM
BLAM
BLAM
BLAM
ZIP
THOK
THOK
ZIP
HMPH.
RARRR!
TIME TO TRY AIMING HIGH.
BLAM
BLAM
SPLURCH
KIDS! AIM FOR THE HEAD! IT'S THE ONLY THING THAT STOPS THEM!

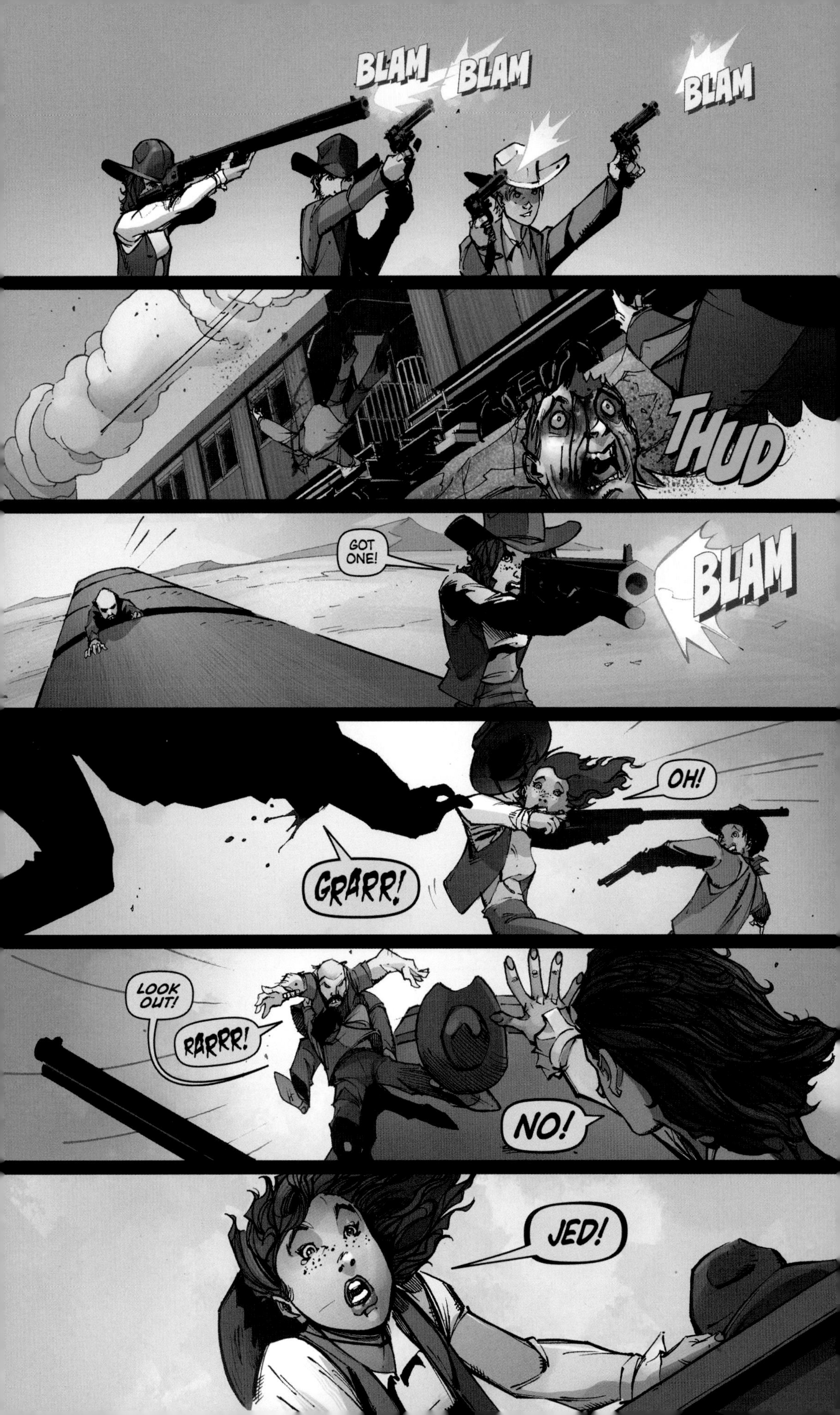
BLAM
BLAM
BLAM
THUD
GOT ONE!
BLAM
OH!
GRARR!
LOOK OUT!
RARRR!
NO!
JED!

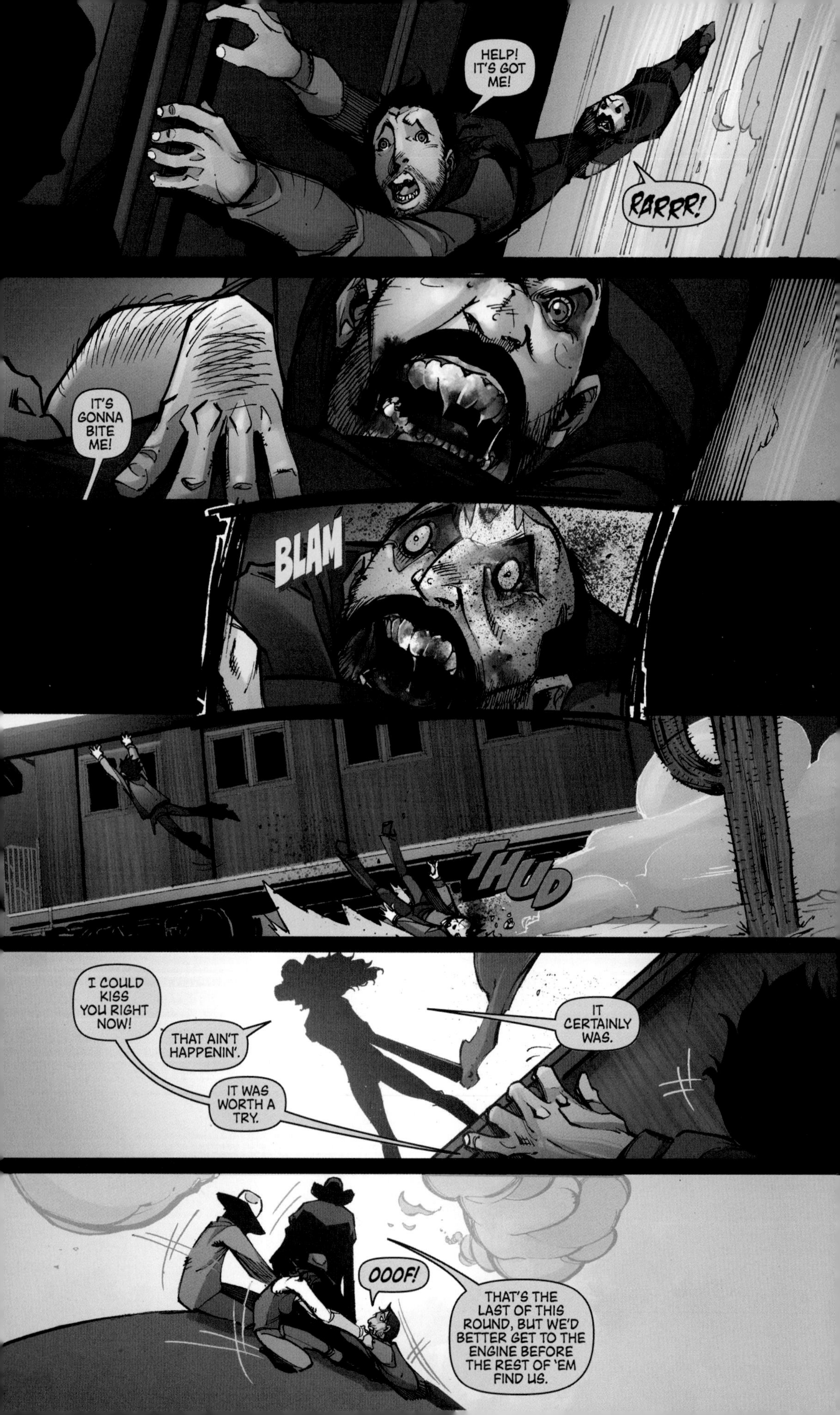
HELP! IT'S GOT ME!
RARRR!
IT'S GONNA BITE ME!
BLAM
THUD
I COULD KISS YOU RIGHT NOW!
THAT AIN'T HAPPENIN'.
IT WAS WORTH A TRY.
IT CERTAINLY WAS.
OOOF!
THAT'S THE LAST OF THIS ROUND, BUT WE'D BETTER GET TO THE ENGINE BEFORE THE REST OF 'EM FIND US.

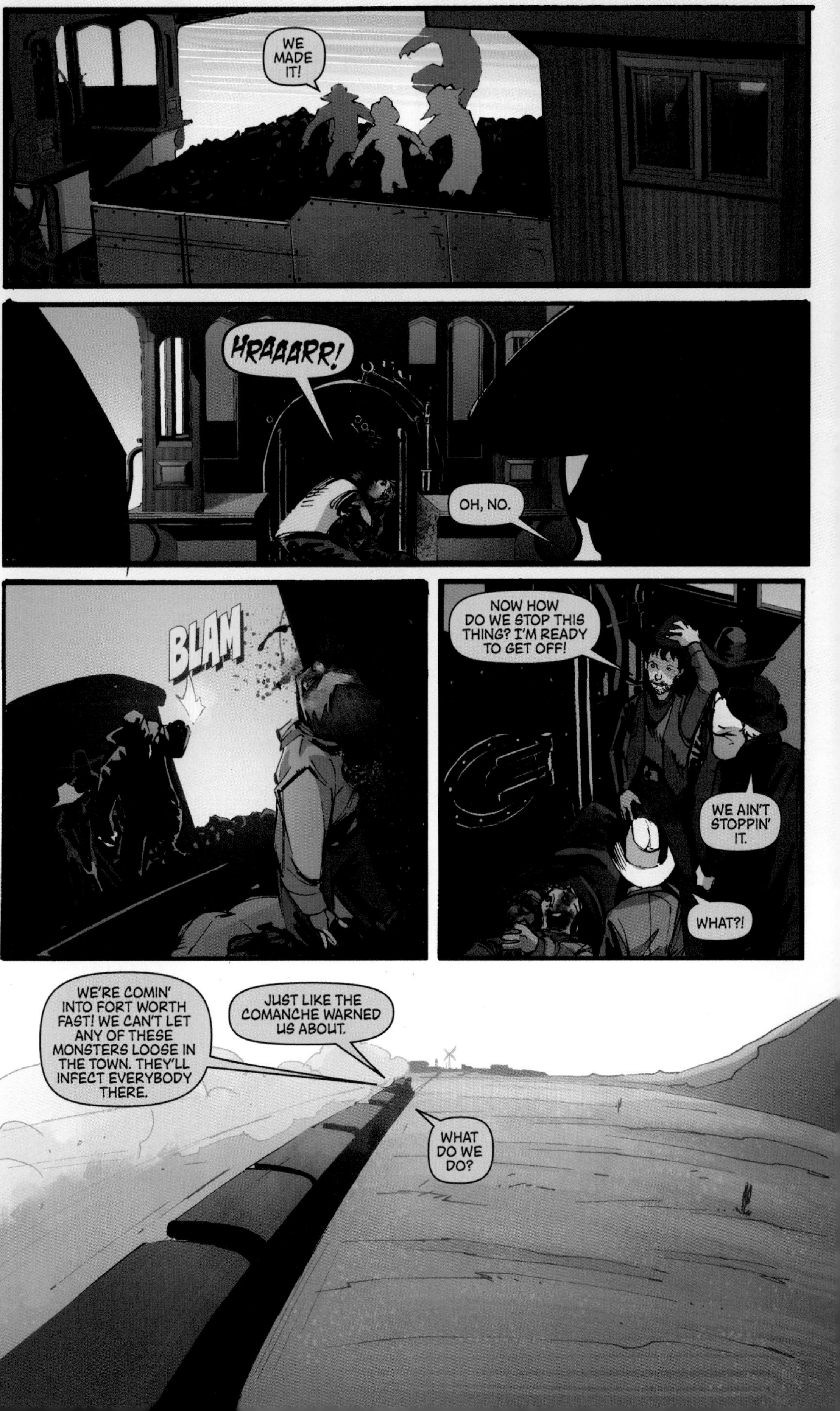
WE MADE IT!
HRAAARR!
OH, NO.
BLAM
NOW HOW DO WE STOP THIS THING? I'M READY TO GET OFF!
WE AIN'T STOPPIN' IT.
WHAT?!
WE'RE COMIN' INTO FORT WORTH FAST! WE CAN'T LET ANY OF THESE MONSTERS LOOSE IN THE TOWN. THEY'LL INFECT EVERYBODY THERE.
JUST LIKE THE COMANCHE WARNED US ABOUT.
WHAT DO WE DO?

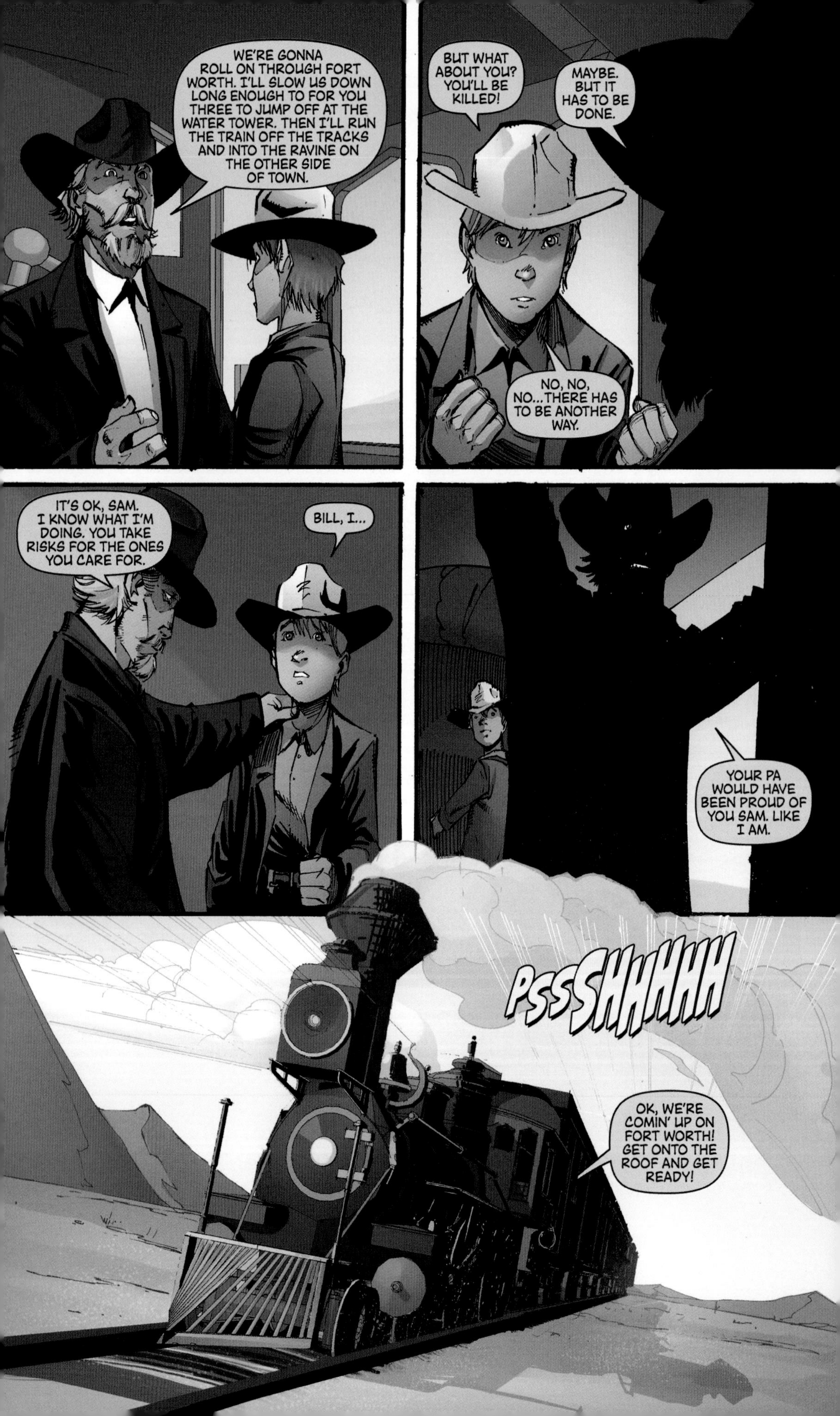
WE'RE GONNA ROLL ON THROUGH FORT WORTH. I'LL SLOW US DOWN LONG ENOUGH TO FOR YOU THREE TO JUMP OFF AT THE WATER TOWER. THEN I'LL RUN THE TRAIN OFF THE TRACKS AND INTO THE RAVINE ON THE OTHER SIDE OF TOWN.
BUT WHAT ABOUT YOU? YOU'LL BE KILLED!
MAYBE. BUT IT HAS TO BE DONE.
NO, NO, NO...THERE HAS TO BE ANOTHER WAY.
IT'S OK, SAM. I KNOW WHAT I'M DOING. YOU TAKE RISKS FOR THE ONES YOU CARE FOR.
BILL, I...
YOUR PA WOULD HAVE BEEN PROUD OF YOU SAM. LIKE I AM.
PSSSHHHHH
OK, WE'RE COMIN' UP ON FORT WORTH! GET ONTO THE ROOF AND GET READY!

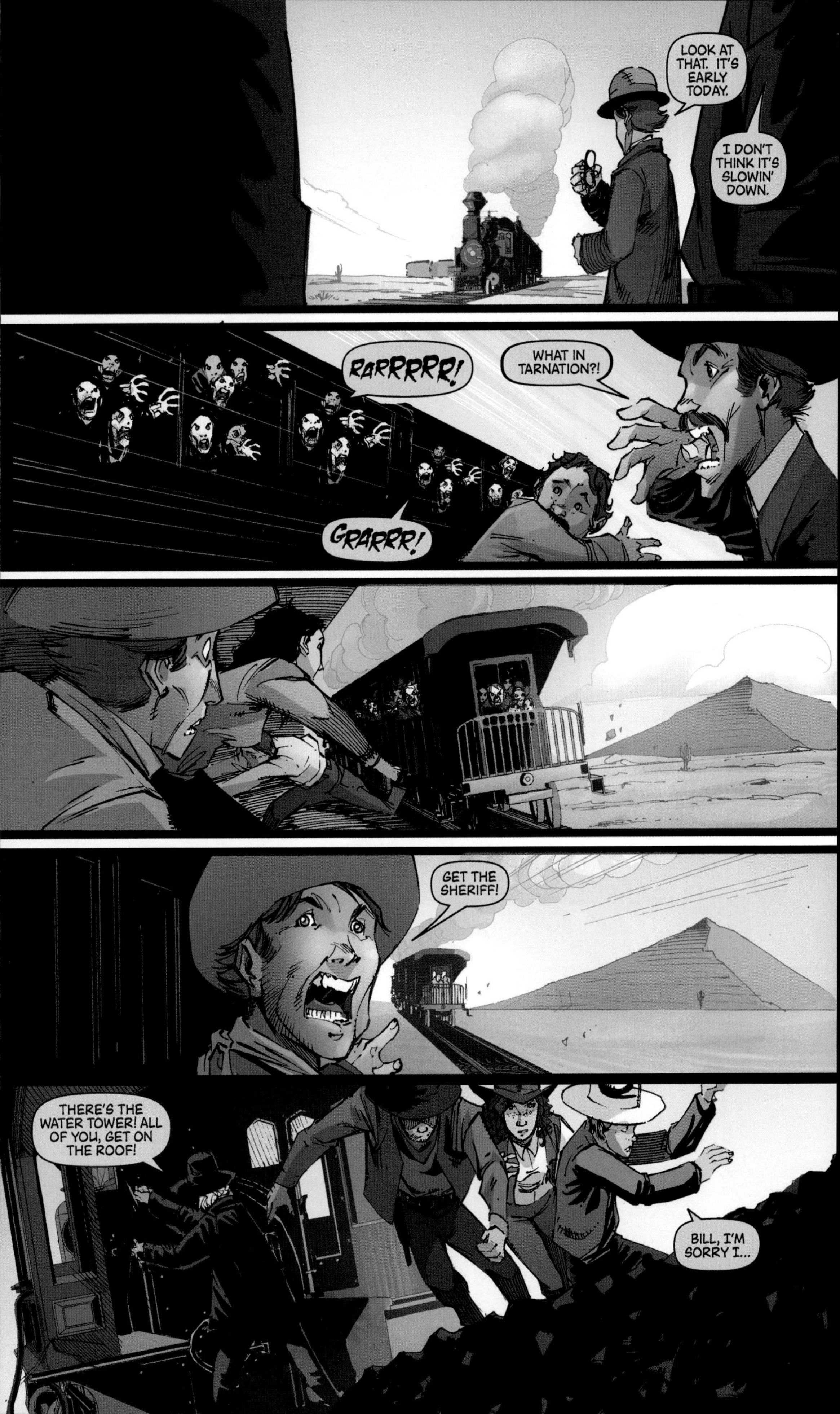
LOOK AT THAT. IT'S EARLY TODAY.
I DON'T THINK IT'S SLOWIN' DOWN.
RaRRRRR!
WHAT IN TARNATION?!
GRARRR!
GET THE SHERIFF!
THERE'S THE WATER TOWER! ALL OF YOU, GET ON THE ROOF!
BILL, I'M SORRY I...

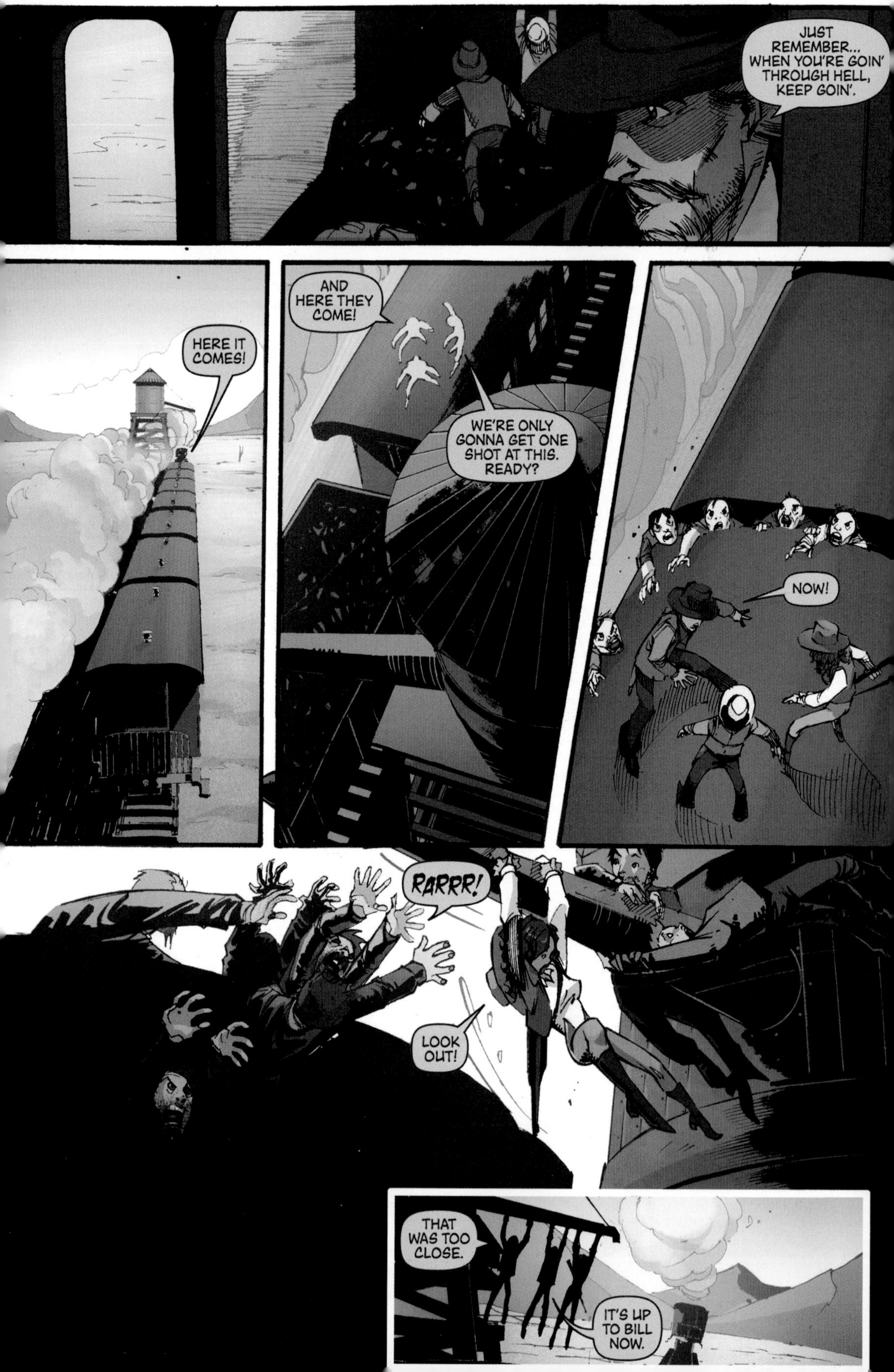
JUST REMEMBER... WHEN YOU'RE GOIN' THROUGH HELL, KEEP GOIN'.
HERE IT COMES!
AND HERE THEY COME!
WE'RE ONLY GONNA GET ONE SHOT AT THIS. READY?
NOW!
RARRR!
LOOK OUT!
THAT WAS TOO CLOSE.
IT'S UP TO BILL NOW.

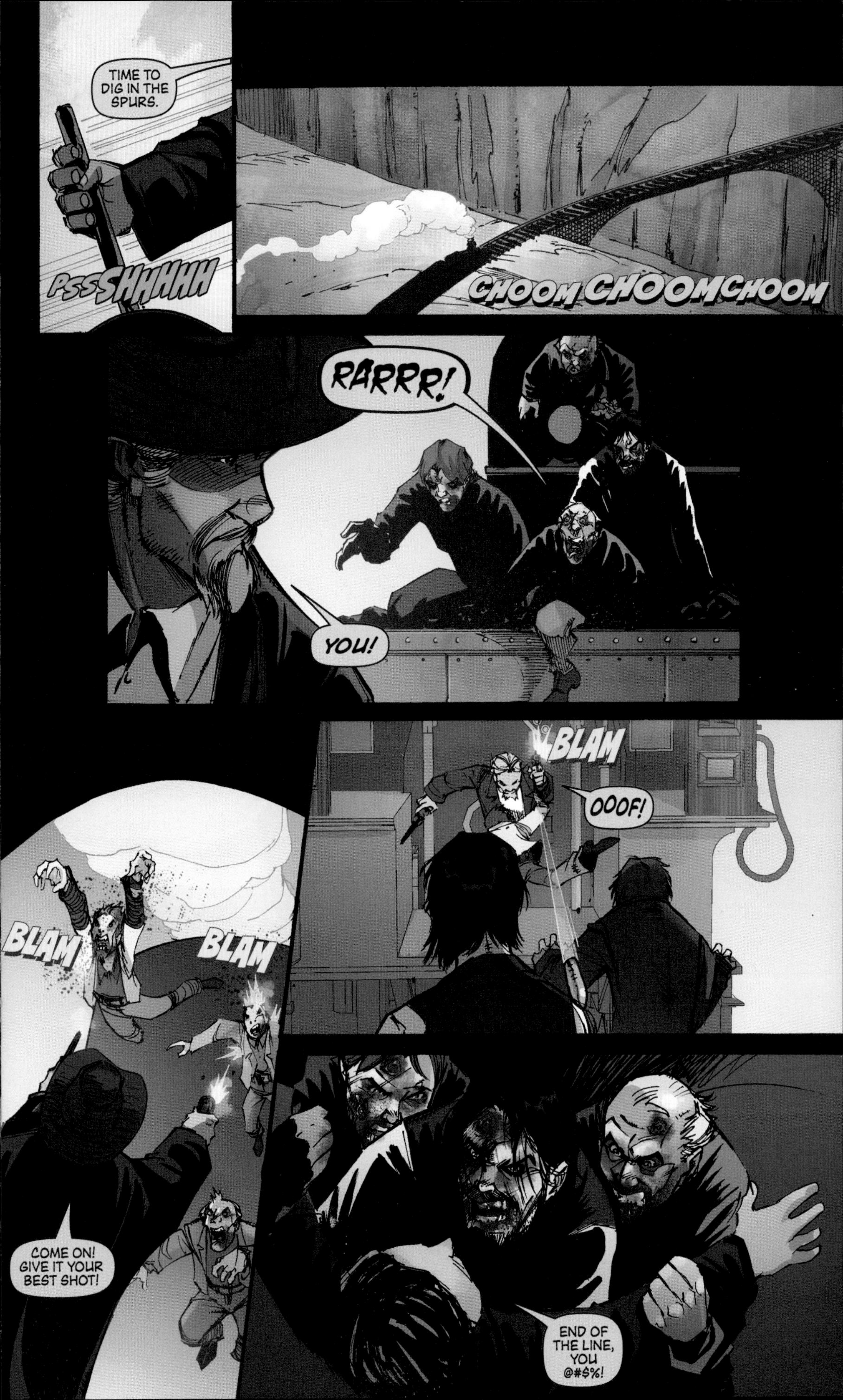
TIME TO DIG IN THE SPURS.
PSSSHHHHH
CHOOM CHOOMCHOOM
RARRR!
YOU!
BLAM
OOOF!
BLAM
BLAM
COME ON! GIVE IT YOUR BEST SHOT!
END OF THE LINE, YOU @#$%!

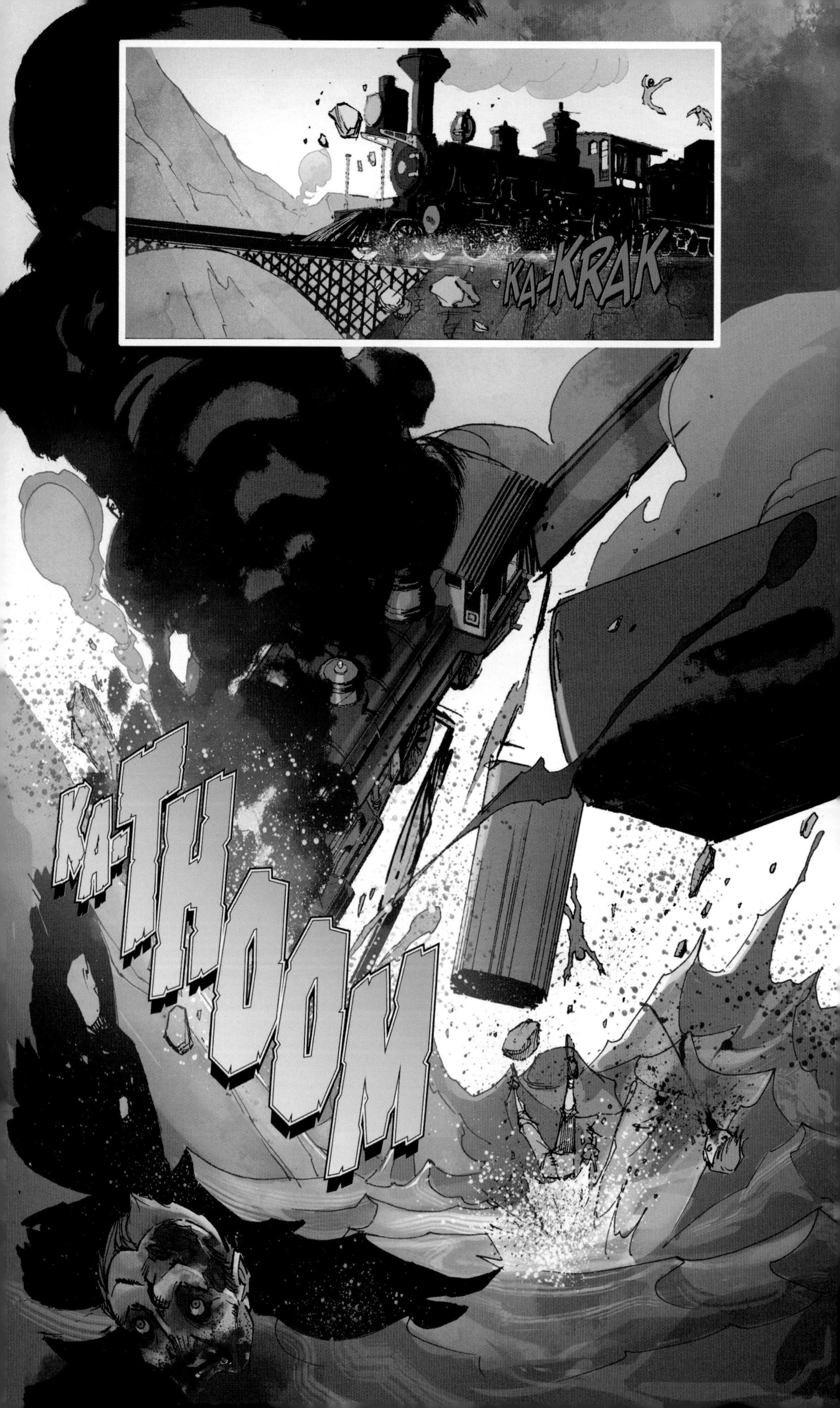
KA-KRAK
KA-THOOM

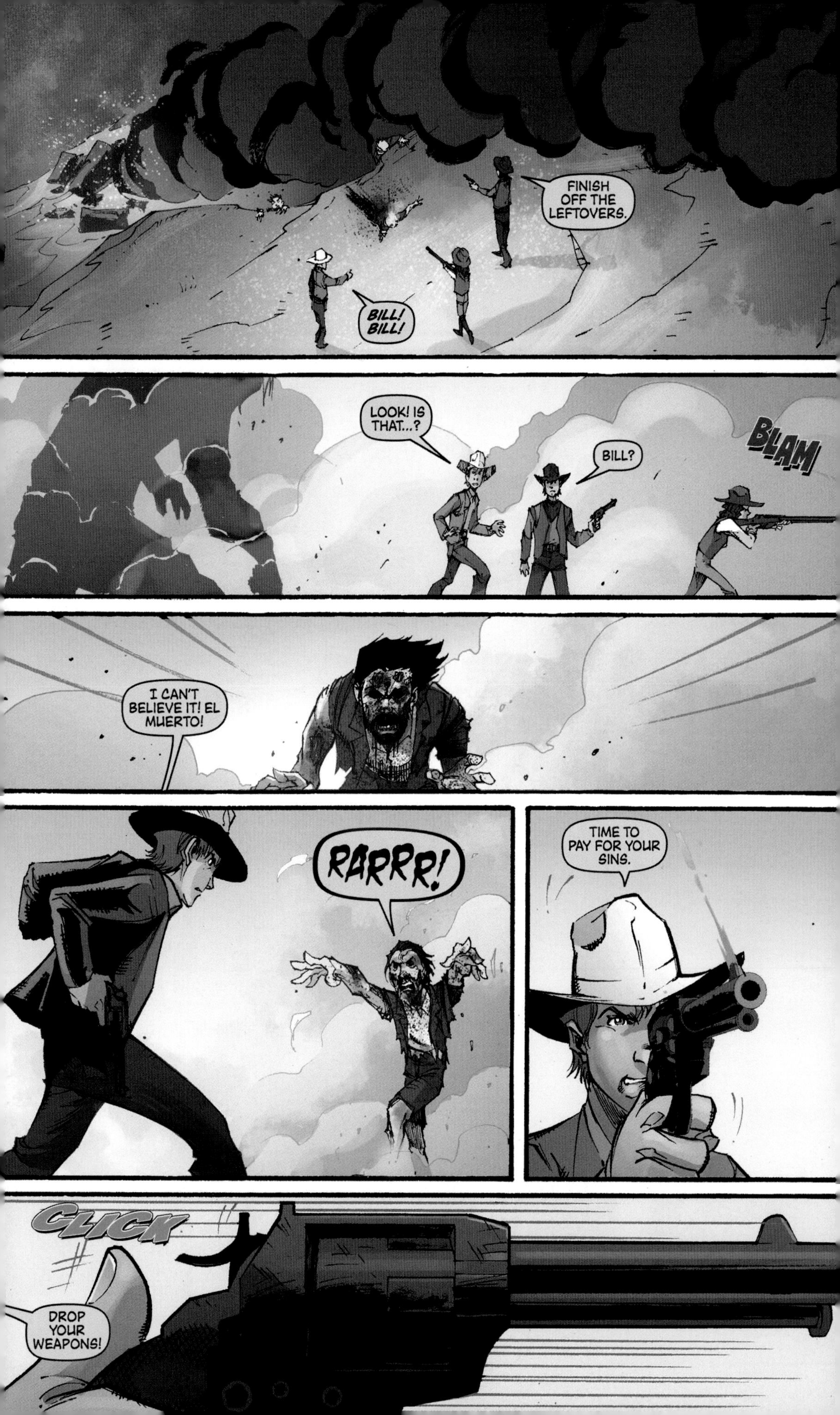
FINISH OFF THE LEFTOVERS.
BILL! BILL!
LOOK! IS THAT...?
BILL?
BLAM
I CAN'T BELIEVE IT! EL MUERTO!
RARRR!
TIME TO PAY FOR YOUR SINS.
CLICK
DROP YOUR WEAPONS!

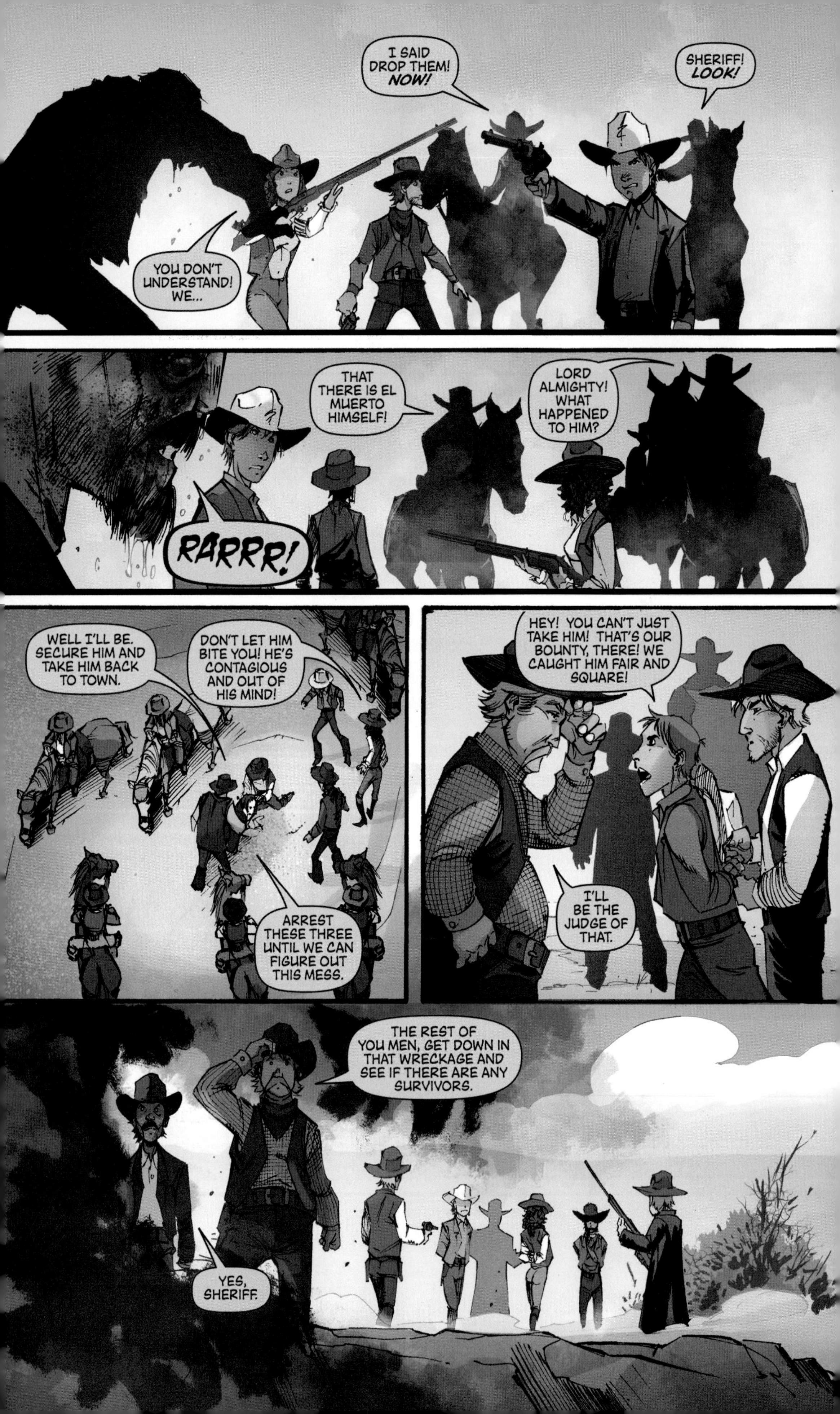
I SAID DROP THEM! NOW!
SHERIFF! LOOK!
YOU DON'T UNDERSTAND! WE...
THAT THERE IS EL MUERTO HIMSELF!
LORD ALMIGHTY! WHAT HAPPENED TO HIM?
RARRR!
WELL I'LL BE. SECURE HIM AND TAKE HIM BACK TO TOWN.
DON'T LET HIM BITE YOU! HE'S CONTAGIOUS AND OUT OF HIS MIND!
ARREST THESE THREE UNTIL WE CAN FIGURE OUT THIS MESS.
HEY! YOU CAN'T JUST TAKE HIM! THAT'S OUR BOUNTY, THERE! WE CAUGHT HIM FAIR AND SQUARE!
I'LL BE THE JUDGE OF THAT.
THE REST OF YOU MEN, GET DOWN IN THAT WRECKAGE AND SEE IF THERE ARE ANY SURVIVORS.
YES, SHERIFF.

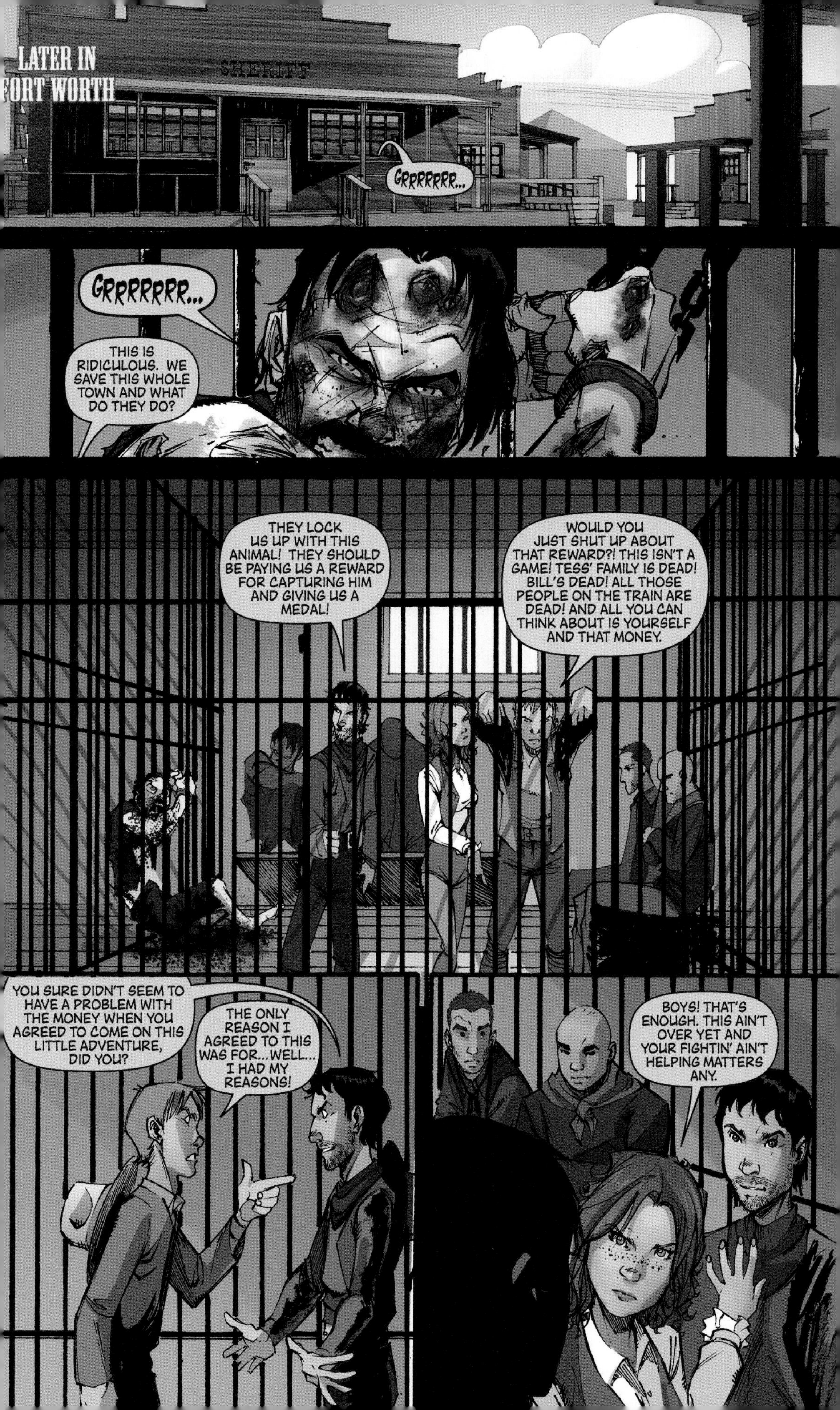
LATER IN FORT WORTH
SHERIFF
GRRRRRRR...
GRRRRRRR...
THIS IS RIDICULOUS. WE SAVE THIS WHOLE TOWN AND WHAT DO THEY DO?
THEY LOCK US UP WITH THIS ANIMAL! THEY SHOULD BE PAYING US A REWARD FOR CAPTURING HIM AND GIVING US A MEDAL!
WOULD YOU JUST SHUT UP ABOUT THAT REWARD?! THIS ISN'T A GAME! TESS' FAMILY IS DEAD! BILL'S DEAD! ALL THOSE PEOPLE ON THE TRAIN ARE DEAD! AND ALL YOU CAN THINK ABOUT IS YOURSELF AND THAT MONEY.
YOU SURE DIDN'T SEEM TO HAVE A PROBLEM WITH THE MONEY WHEN YOU AGREED TO COME ON THIS LITTLE ADVENTURE, DID YOU?
THE ONLY REASON I AGREED TO THIS WAS FOR...WELL... I HAD MY REASONS!
BOYS! THAT'S ENOUGH. THIS AIN'T OVER YET AND YOUR FIGHTIN' AIN'T HELPING MATTERS ANY.

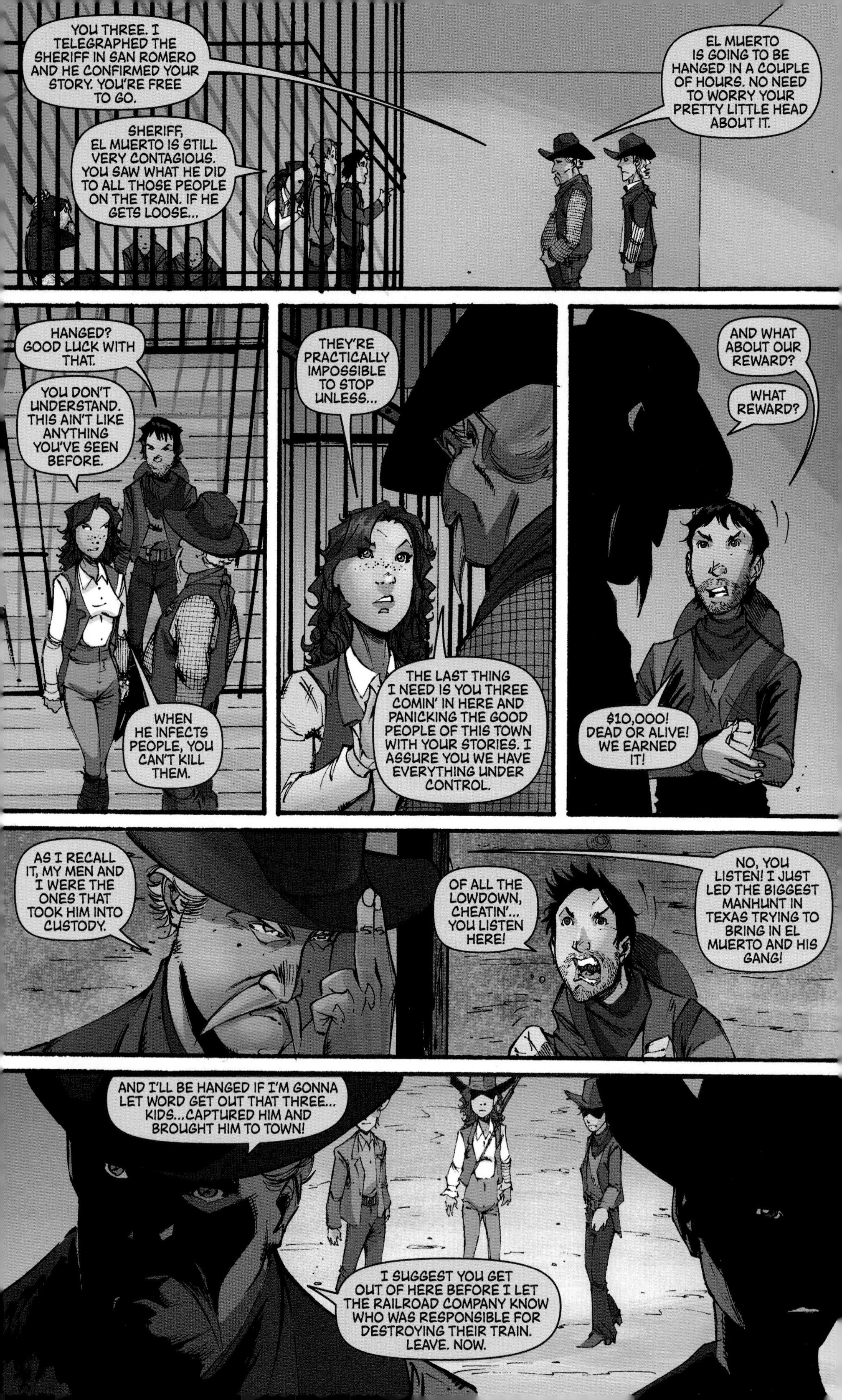
YOU THREE. I TELEGRAPHED THE SHERIFF IN SAN ROMERO AND HE CONFIRMED YOUR STORY. YOU'RE FREE TO GO.
SHERIFF, EL MUERTO IS STILL VERY CONTAGIOUS. YOU SAW WHAT HE DID TO ALL THOSE PEOPLE ON THE TRAIN. IF HE GETS LOOSE...
EL MUERTO IS GOING TO BE HANGED IN A COUPLE OF HOURS. NO NEED TO WORRY YOUR PRETTY LITTLE HEAD ABOUT IT.
HANGED? GOOD LUCK WITH THAT.
YOU DON'T UNDERSTAND. THIS AIN'T LIKE ANYTHING YOU'VE SEEN BEFORE.
WHEN HE INFECTS PEOPLE, YOU CAN'T KILL THEM.
THEY'RE PRACTICALLY IMPOSSIBLE TO STOP UNLESS...
THE LAST THING I NEED IS YOU THREE COMIN' IN HERE AND PANICKING THE GOOD PEOPLE OF THIS TOWN WITH YOUR STORIES. I ASSURE YOU WE HAVE EVERYTHING UNDER CONTROL.
AND WHAT ABOUT OUR REWARD?
WHAT REWARD?
$10,000! DEAD OR ALIVE! WE EARNED IT!
AS I RECALL IT, MY MEN AND I WERE THE ONES THAT TOOK HIM INTO CUSTODY.
OF ALL THE LOWDOWN, CHEATIN'... YOU LISTEN HERE!
NO, YOU LISTEN! I JUST LED THE BIGGEST MANHUNT IN TEXAS TRYING TO BRING IN EL MUERTO AND HIS GANG!
AND I'LL BE HANGED IF I'M GONNA LET WORD GET OUT THAT THREE... KIDS...CAPTURED HIM AND BROUGHT HIM TO TOWN!
I SUGGEST YOU GET OUT OF HERE BEFORE I LET THE RAILROAD COMPANY KNOW WHO WAS RESPONSIBLE FOR DESTROYING THEIR TRAIN. LEAVE. NOW.

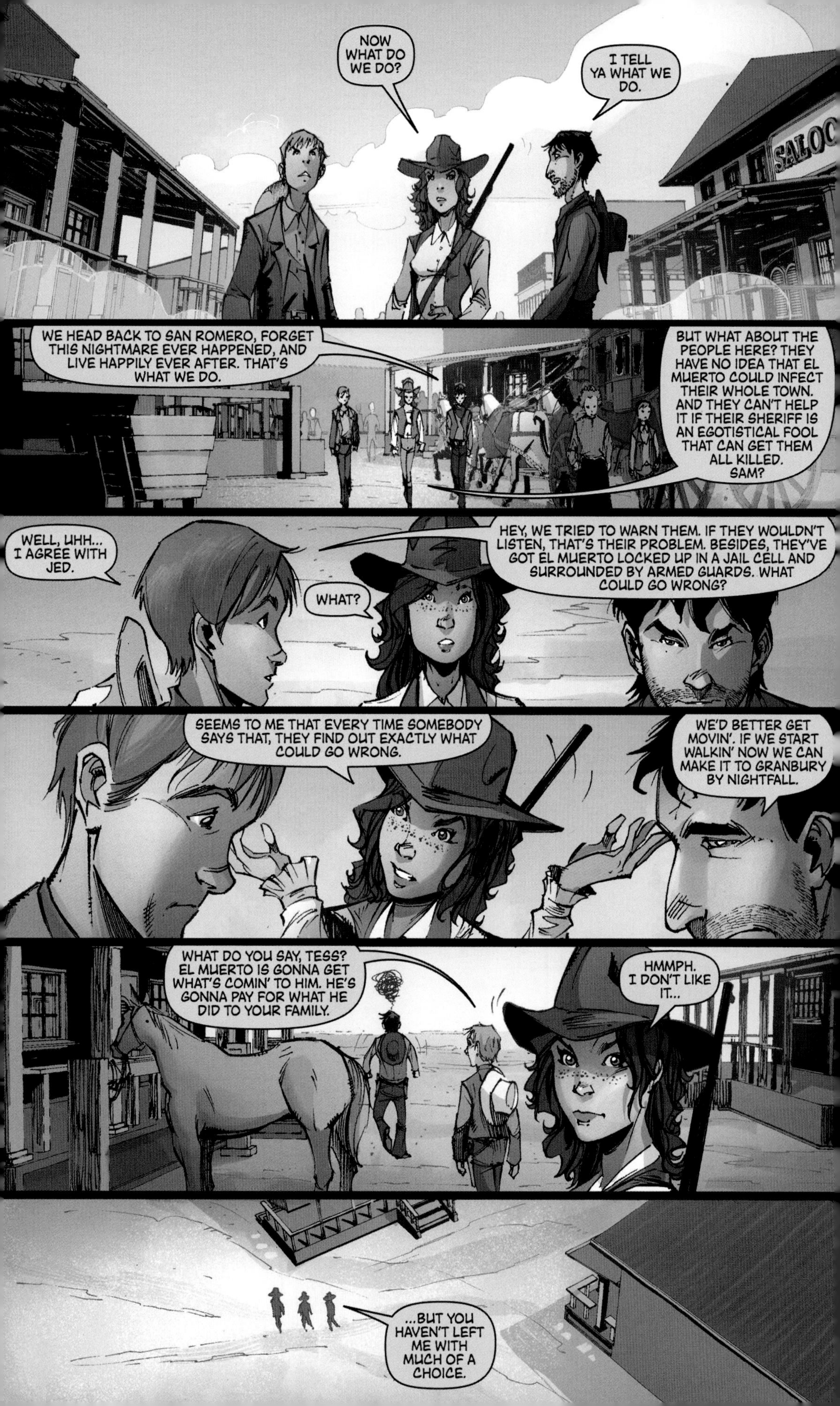
NOW WHAT DO WE DO?
I TELL YA WHAT WE DO.
SALOO
WE HEAD BACK TO SAN ROMERO, FORGET THIS NIGHTMARE EVER HAPPENED, AND LIVE HAPPILY EVER AFTER. THAT'S WHAT WE DO.
BUT WHAT ABOUT THE PEOPLE HERE? THEY HAVE NO IDEA THAT EL MUERTO COULD INFECT THEIR WHOLE TOWN. AND THEY CAN'T HELP IT IF THEIR SHERIFF IS AN EGOTISTICAL FOOL THAT CAN GET THEM ALL KILLED. SAM?
WELL, UHH... I AGREE WITH JED.
WHAT?
HEY, WE TRIED TO WARN THEM. IF THEY WOULDN'T LISTEN, THAT'S THEIR PROBLEM. BESIDES, THEY'VE GOT EL MUERTO LOCKED UP IN A JAIL CELL AND SURROUNDED BY ARMED GUARDS. WHAT COULD GO WRONG?
SEEMS TO ME THAT EVERY TIME SOMEBODY SAYS THAT, THEY FIND OUT EXACTLY WHAT COULD GO WRONG.
WE'D BETTER GET MOVIN'. IF WE START WALKIN' NOW WE CAN MAKE IT TO GRANBURY BY NIGHTFALL.
WHAT DO YOU SAY, TESS? EL MUERTO IS GONNA GET WHAT'S COMIN' TO HIM. HE'S GONNA PAY FOR WHAT HE DID TO YOUR FAMILY.
HMMPH. I DON'T LIKE IT...
...BUT YOU HAVEN'T LEFT ME WITH MUCH OF A CHOICE.

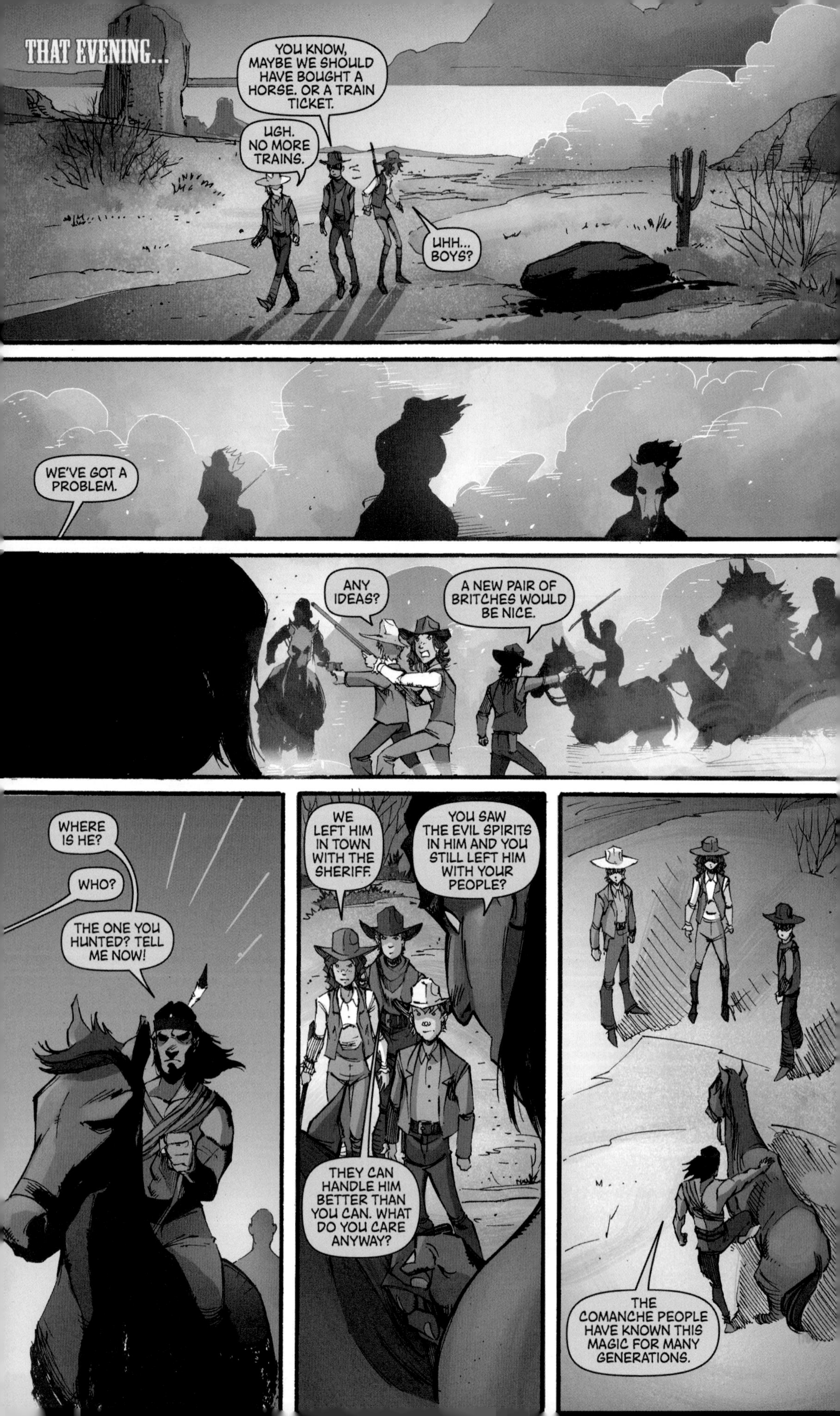
THAT EVENING...
YOU KNOW, MAYBE WE SHOULD HAVE BOUGHT A HORSE. OR A TRAIN TICKET.
UGH. NO MORE TRAINS.
UHH... BOYS?
WE'VE GOT A PROBLEM.
ANY IDEAS?
A NEW PAIR OF BRITCHES WOULD BE NICE.
WHERE IS HE?
WHO?
THE ONE YOU HUNTED? TELL ME NOW!
WE LEFT HIM IN TOWN WITH THE SHERIFF.
YOU SAW THE EVIL SPIRITS IN HIM AND YOU STILL LEFT HIM WITH YOUR PEOPLE?
THEY CAN HANDLE HIM BETTER THAN YOU CAN. WHAT DO YOU CARE ANYWAY?
THE COMANCHE PEOPLE HAVE KNOWN THIS MAGIC FOR MANY GENERATIONS.

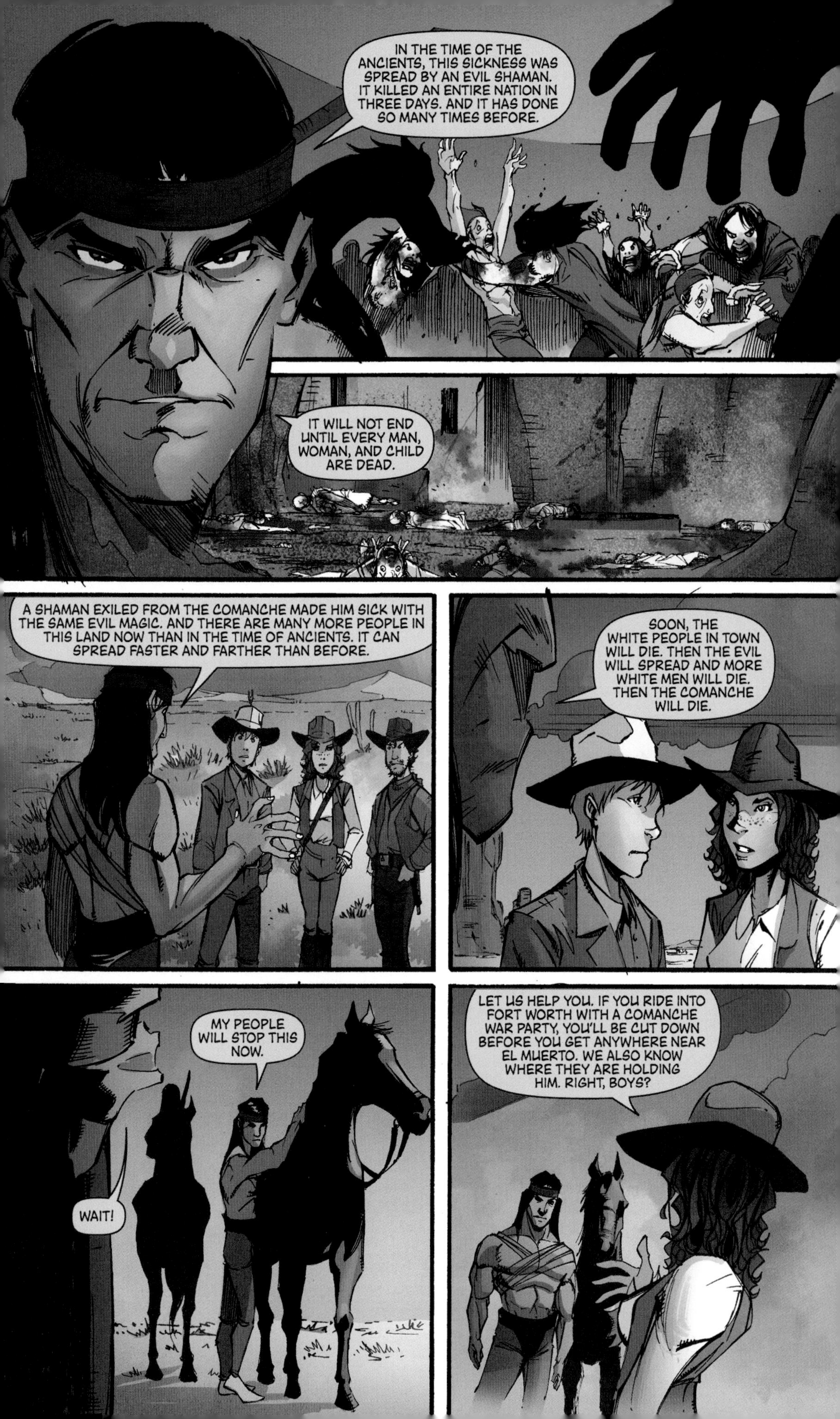
IN THE TIME OF THE ANCIENTS, THIS SICKNESS WAS SPREAD BY AN EVIL SHAMAN. IT KILLED AN ENTIRE NATION IN THREE DAYS. AND IT HAS DONE SO MANY TIMES BEFORE.
IT WILL NOT END UNTIL EVERY MAN, WOMAN, AND CHILD ARE DEAD.
A SHAMAN EXILED FROM THE COMANCHE MADE HIM SICK WITH THE SAME EVIL MAGIC. AND THERE ARE MANY MORE PEOPLE IN THIS LAND NOW THAN IN THE TIME OF ANCIENTS. IT CAN SPREAD FASTER AND FARTHER THAN BEFORE.
SOON, THE WHITE PEOPLE IN TOWN WILL DIE. THEN THE EVIL WILL SPREAD AND MORE WHITE MEN WILL DIE. THEN THE COMANCHE WILL DIE.
MY PEOPLE WILL STOP THIS NOW.
WAIT!
LET US HELP YOU. IF YOU RIDE INTO FORT WORTH WITH A COMANCHE WAR PARTY, YOU'LL BE CUT DOWN BEFORE YOU GET ANYWHERE NEAR EL MUERTO. WE ALSO KNOW WHERE THEY ARE HOLDING HIM. RIGHT, BOYS?

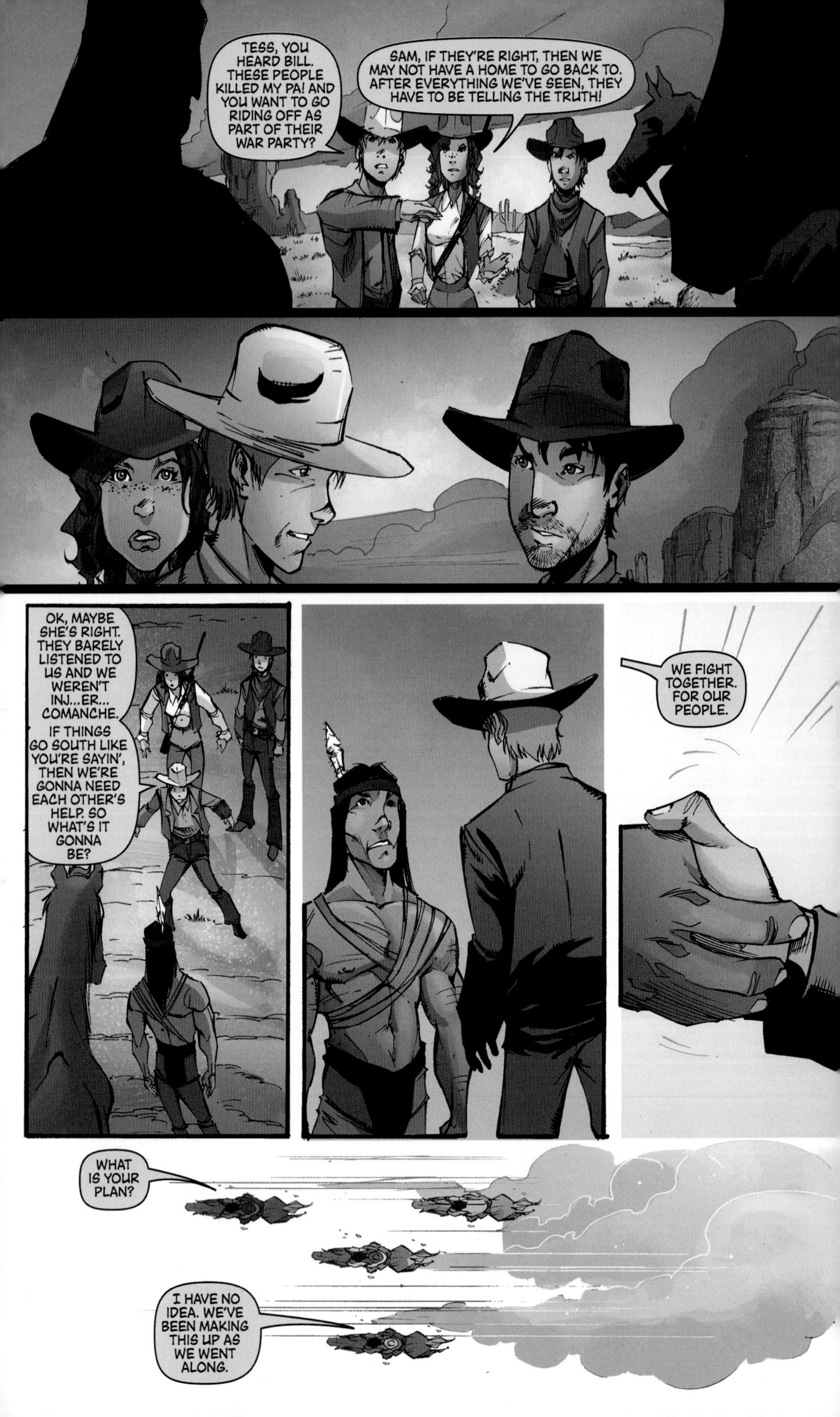
TESS, YOU HEARD BILL. THESE PEOPLE KILLED MY PA! AND YOU WANT TO GO RIDING OFF AS PART OF THEIR WAR PARTY?
SAM, IF THEY'RE RIGHT, THEN WE MAY NOT HAVE A HOME TO GO BACK TO. AFTER EVERYTHING WE'VE SEEN, THEY HAVE TO BE TELLING THE TRUTH!
OK, MAYBE SHE'S RIGHT. THEY BARELY LISTENED TO US AND WE WEREN'T INJ...ER... COMANCHE.
IF THINGS GO SOUTH LIKE YOU'RE SAYIN', THEN WE'RE GONNA NEED EACH OTHER'S HELP. SO WHAT'S IT GONNA BE?
WE FIGHT TOGETHER. FOR OUR PEOPLE.
WHAT IS YOUR PLAN?
I HAVE NO IDEA. WE'VE BEEN MAKING THIS UP AS WE WENT ALONG.

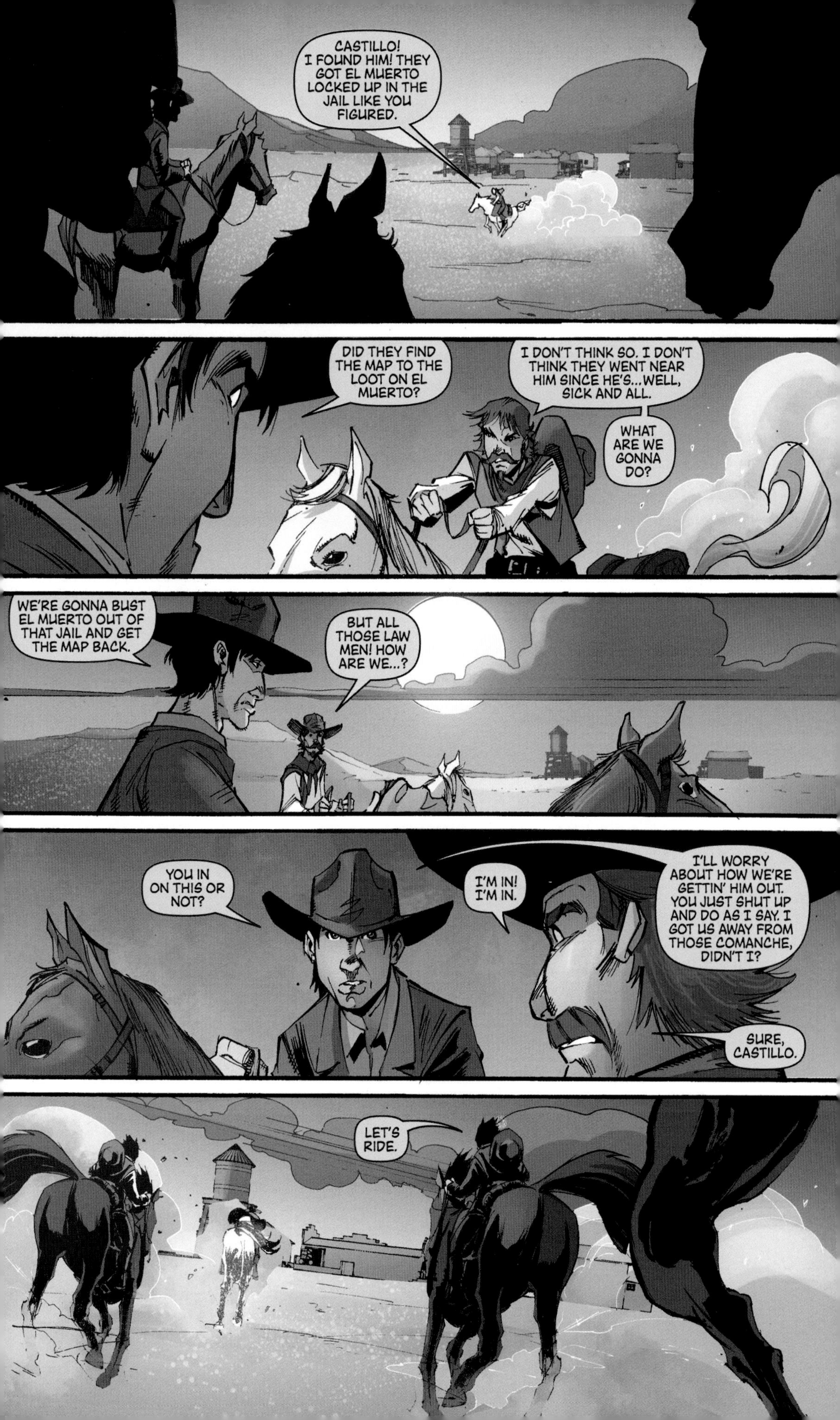
CASTILLO! I FOUND HIM! THEY GOT EL MUERTO LOCKED UP IN THE JAIL LIKE YOU FIGURED.
DID THEY FIND THE MAP TO THE LOOT ON EL MUERTO?
I DON'T THINK SO. I DON'T THINK THEY WENT NEAR HIM SINCE HE'S...WELL, SICK AND ALL.
WHAT ARE WE GONNA DO?
WE'RE GONNA BUST EL MUERTO OUT OF THAT JAIL AND GET THE MAP BACK.
BUT ALL THOSE LAW MEN! HOW ARE WE...?
YOU IN ON THIS OR NOT?
I'M IN! I'M IN.
I'LL WORRY ABOUT HOW WE'RE GETTIN' HIM OUT. YOU JUST SHUT UP AND DO AS I SAY. I GOT US AWAY FROM THOSE COMANCHE, DIDN'T I?
SURE, CASTILLO.
LET'S RIDE.

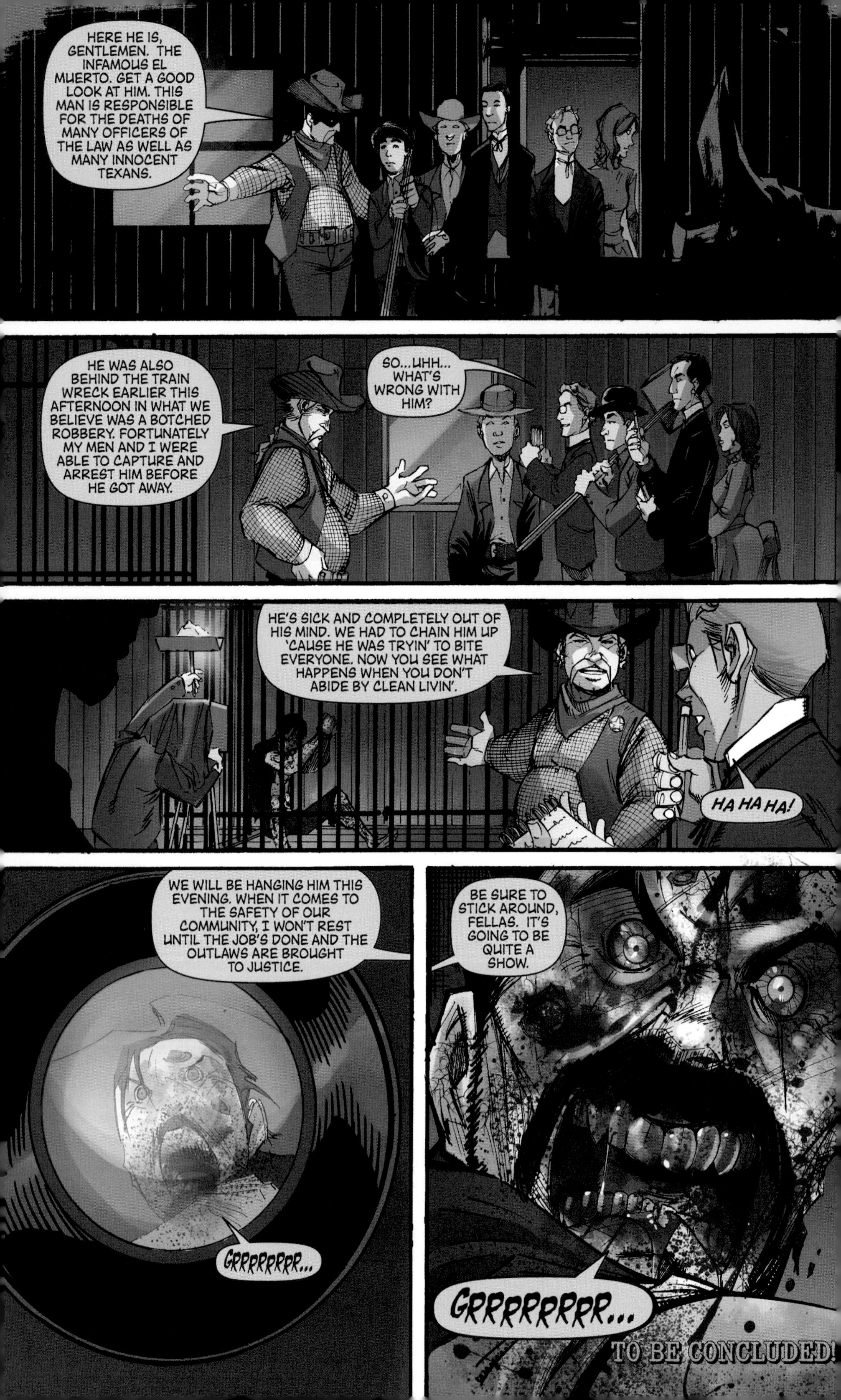
HERE HE IS, GENTLEMEN. THE INFAMOUS EL MUERTO. GET A GOOD LOOK AT HIM. THIS MAN IS RESPONSIBLE FOR THE DEATHS OF MANY OFFICERS OF THE LAW AS WELL AS MANY INNOCENT TEXANS.
HE WAS ALSO BEHIND THE TRAIN WRECK EARLIER THIS AFTERNOON IN WHAT WE BELIEVE WAS A BOTCHED ROBBERY. FORTUNATELY MY MEN AND I WERE ABLE TO CAPTURE AND ARREST HIM BEFORE HE GOT AWAY.
SO...UHH... WHAT'S WRONG WITH HIM?
HE'S SICK AND COMPLETELY OUT OF HIS MIND. WE HAD TO CHAIN HIM UP 'CAUSE HE WAS TRYIN' TO BITE EVERYONE. NOW YOU SEE WHAT HAPPENS WHEN YOU DON'T ABIDE BY CLEAN LIVIN'.
HA HA HA!
WE WILL BE HANGING HIM THIS EVENING. WHEN IT COMES TO THE SAFETY OF OUR COMMUNITY, I WON'T REST UNTIL THE JOB'S DONE AND THE OUTLAWS ARE BROUGHT TO JUSTICE.
GRRRRRRR...
BE SURE TO STICK AROUND, FELLAS. IT'S GOING TO BE QUITE A SHOW.
GRRRRRRRR...
TO BE CONCLUDED!

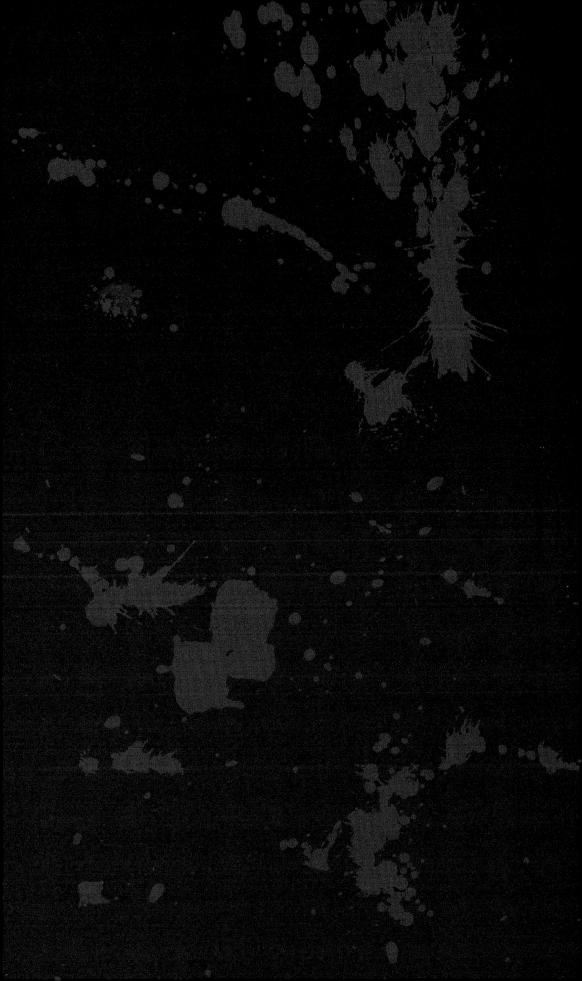

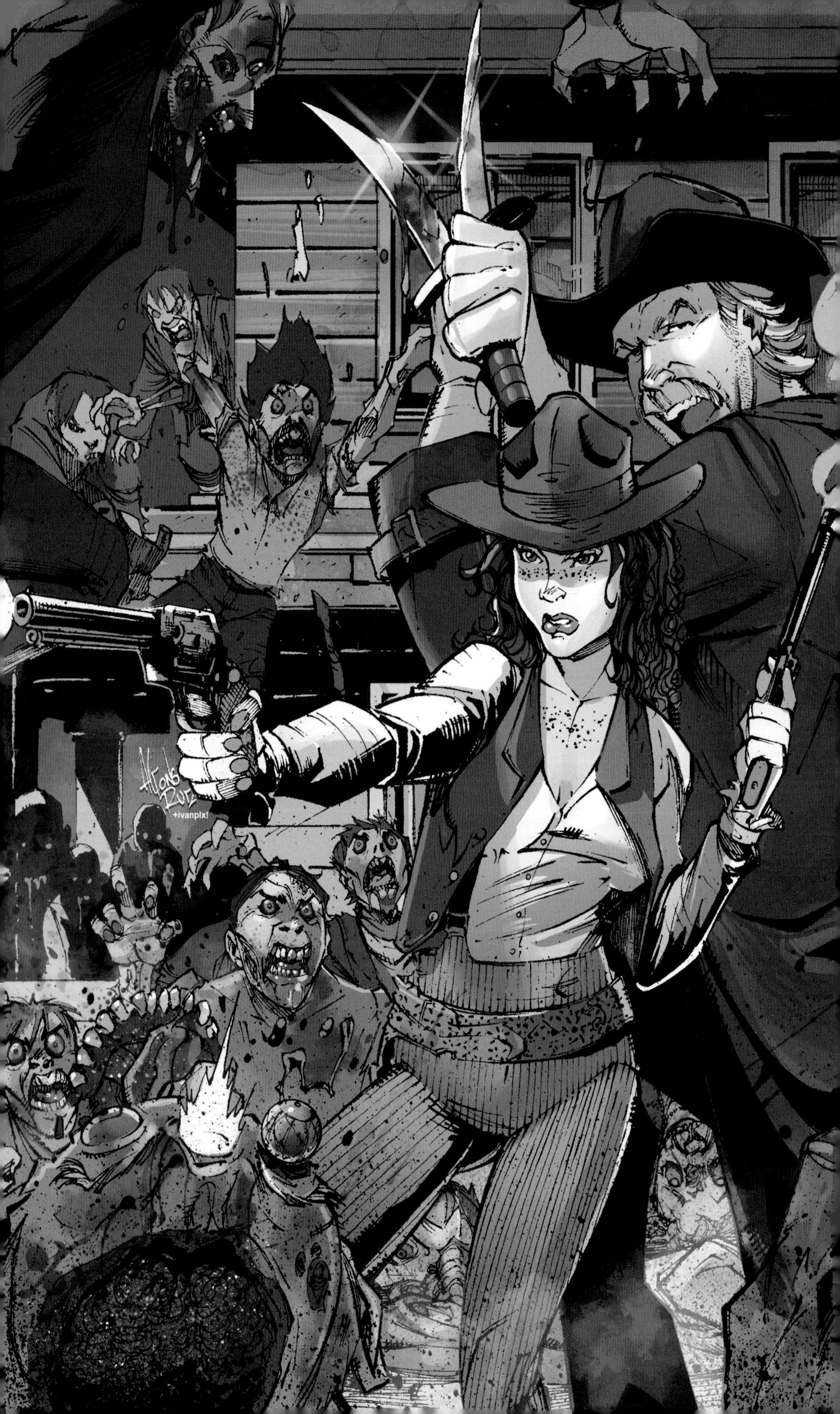
+ivanplx!

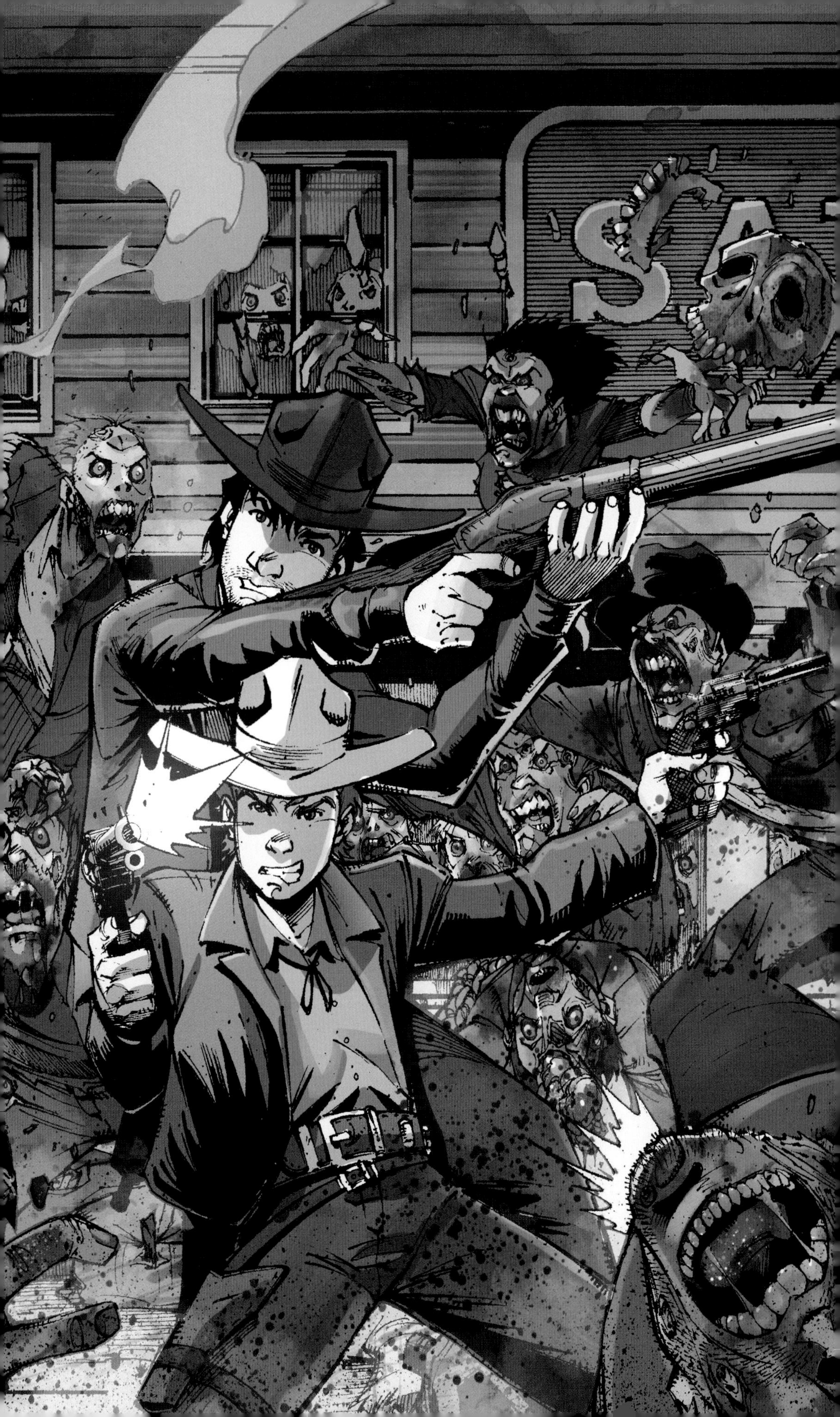

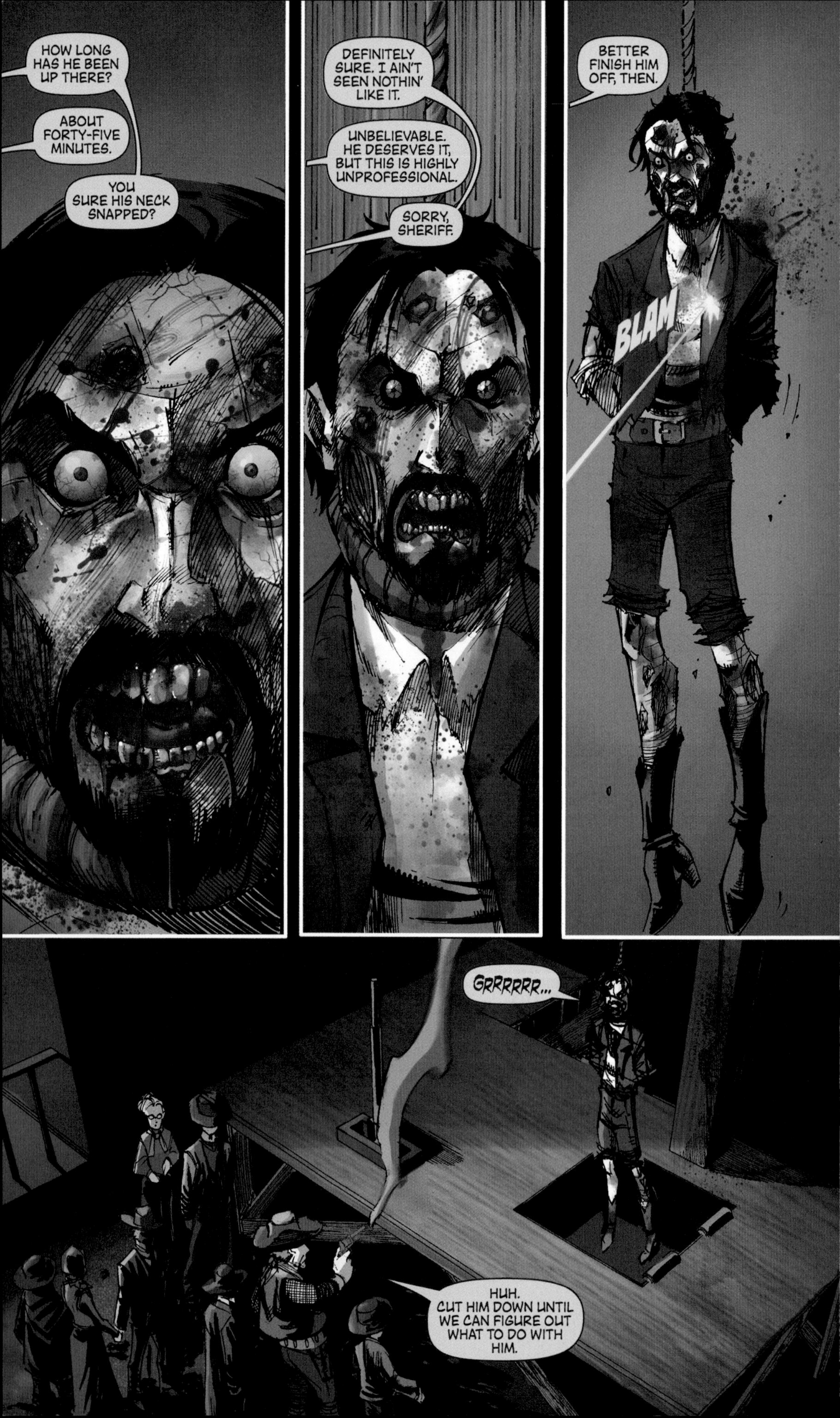
HOW LONG HAS HE BEEN UP THERE?
ABOUT FORTY-FIVE MINUTES.
YOU SURE HIS NECK SNAPPED?
DEFINITELY SURE. I AIN'T SEEN NOTHIN' LIKE IT.
UNBELIEVABLE. HE DESERVES IT, BUT THIS IS HIGHLY UNPROFESSIONAL.
SORRY, SHERIFF.
BETTER FINISH HIM OFF, THEN.
BLAM
GRRRRRR...
HUH. CUT HIM DOWN UNTIL WE CAN FIGURE OUT WHAT TO DO WITH HIM.

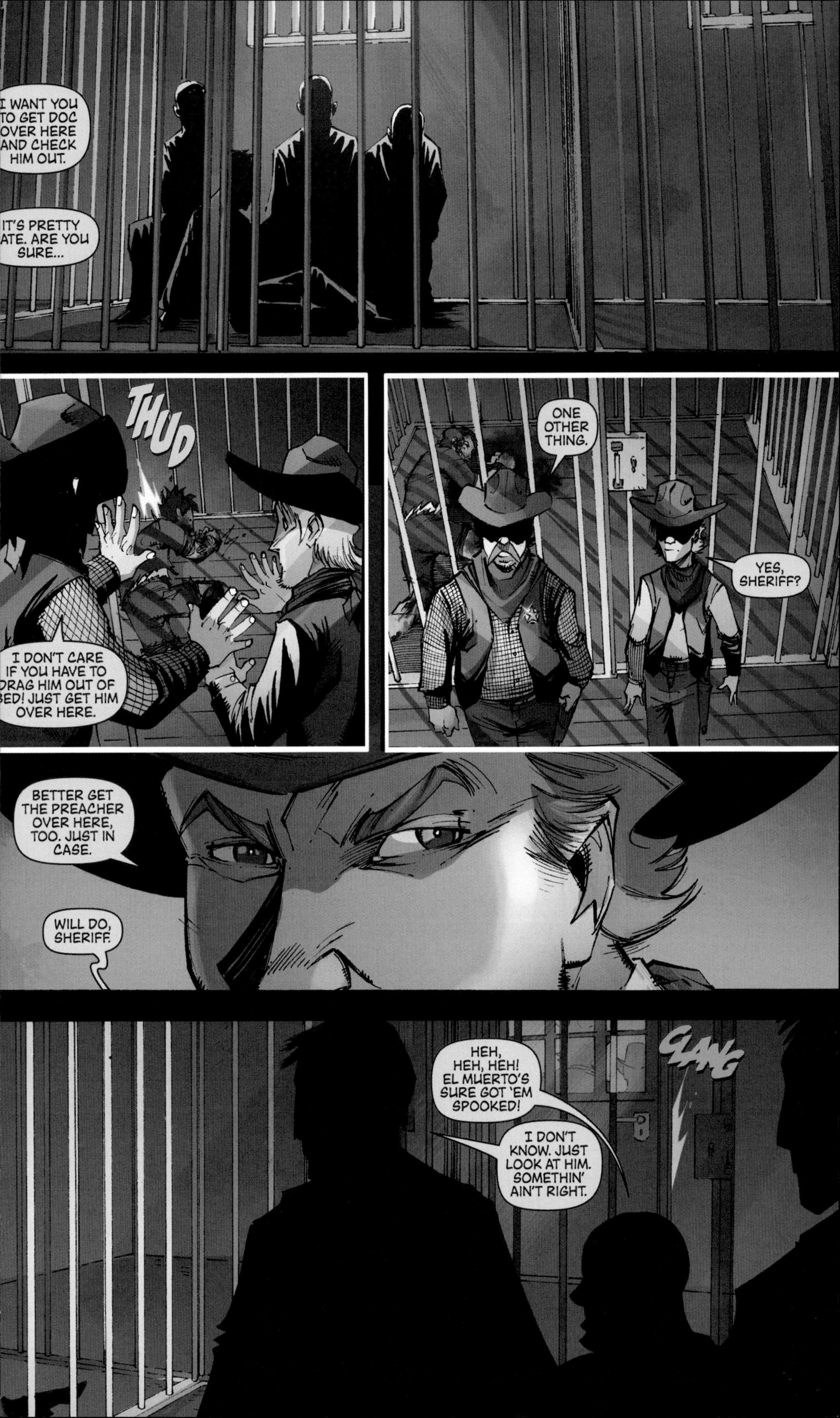
I WANT YOU TO GET DOC OVER HERE AND CHECK HIM OUT.
IT'S PRETTY LATE. ARE YOU SURE...
THUD
I DON'T CARE IF YOU HAVE TO DRAG HIM OUT OF BED! JUST GET HIM OVER HERE.
ONE OTHER THING.
YES, SHERIFF?
BETTER GET THE PREACHER OVER HERE, TOO. JUST IN CASE.
WILL DO, SHERIFF.
CLANG
HEH, HEH, HEH! EL MUERTO'S SURE GOT 'EM SPOOKED!
I DON'T KNOW. JUST LOOK AT HIM. SOMETHIN' AIN'T RIGHT.

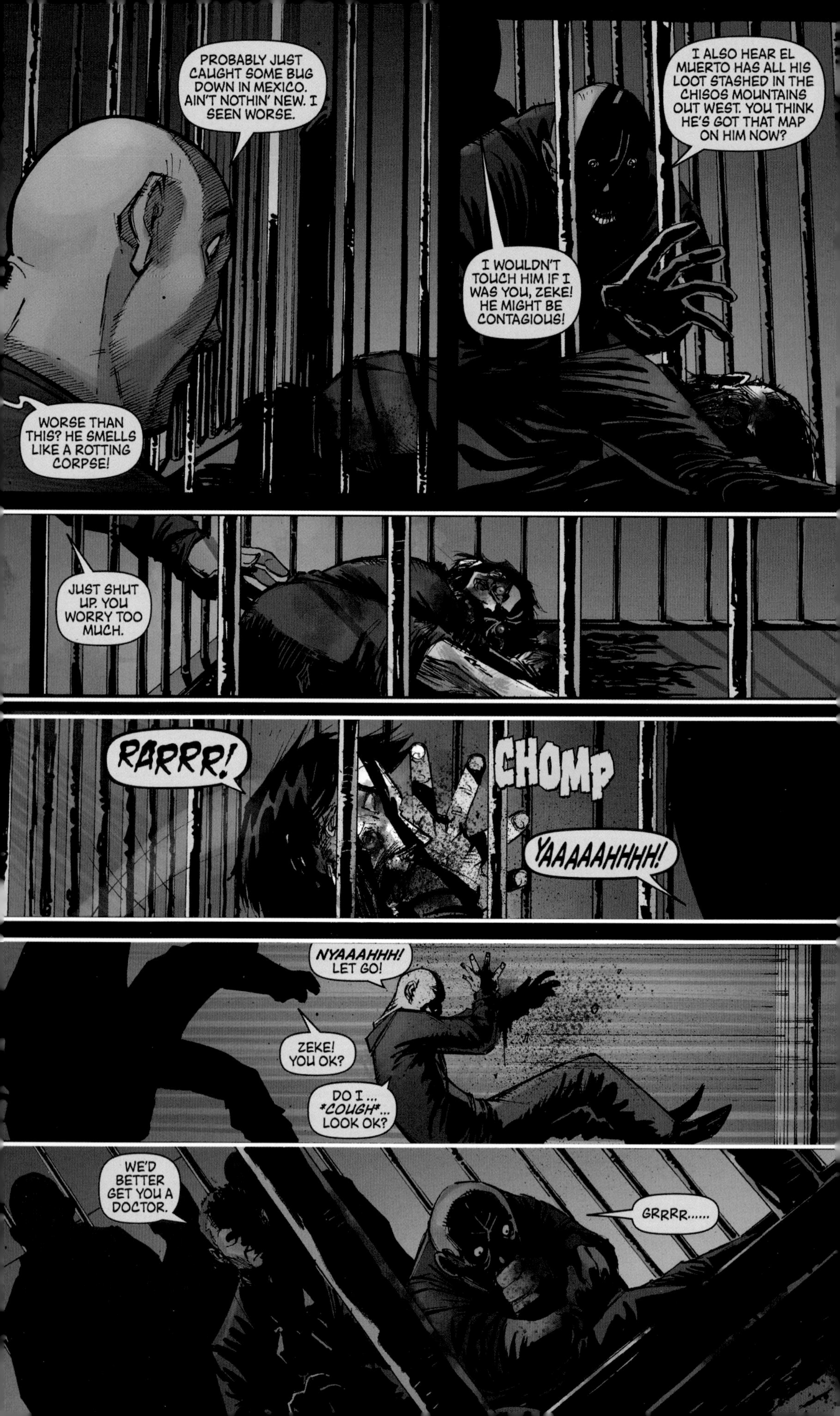
PROBABLY JUST CAUGHT SOME BUG DOWN IN MEXICO. AIN'T NOTHIN' NEW. I SEEN WORSE.
WORSE THAN THIS? HE SMELLS LIKE A ROTTING CORPSE!
I ALSO HEAR EL MUERTO HAS ALL HIS LOOT STASHED IN THE CHISOS MOUNTAINS OUT WEST. YOU THINK HE'S GOT THAT MAP ON HIM NOW?
I WOULDN'T TOUCH HIM IF I WAS YOU, ZEKE! HE MIGHT BE CONTAGIOUS!
JUST SHUT UP. YOU WORRY TOO MUCH.
RARRR!
CHOMP
YAAAAAHHHH!
NYAAAHHH! LET GO!
ZEKE! YOU OK?
DO I ... *COUGH*... LOOK OK?
WE'D BETTER GET YOU A DOCTOR.
GRRRR......

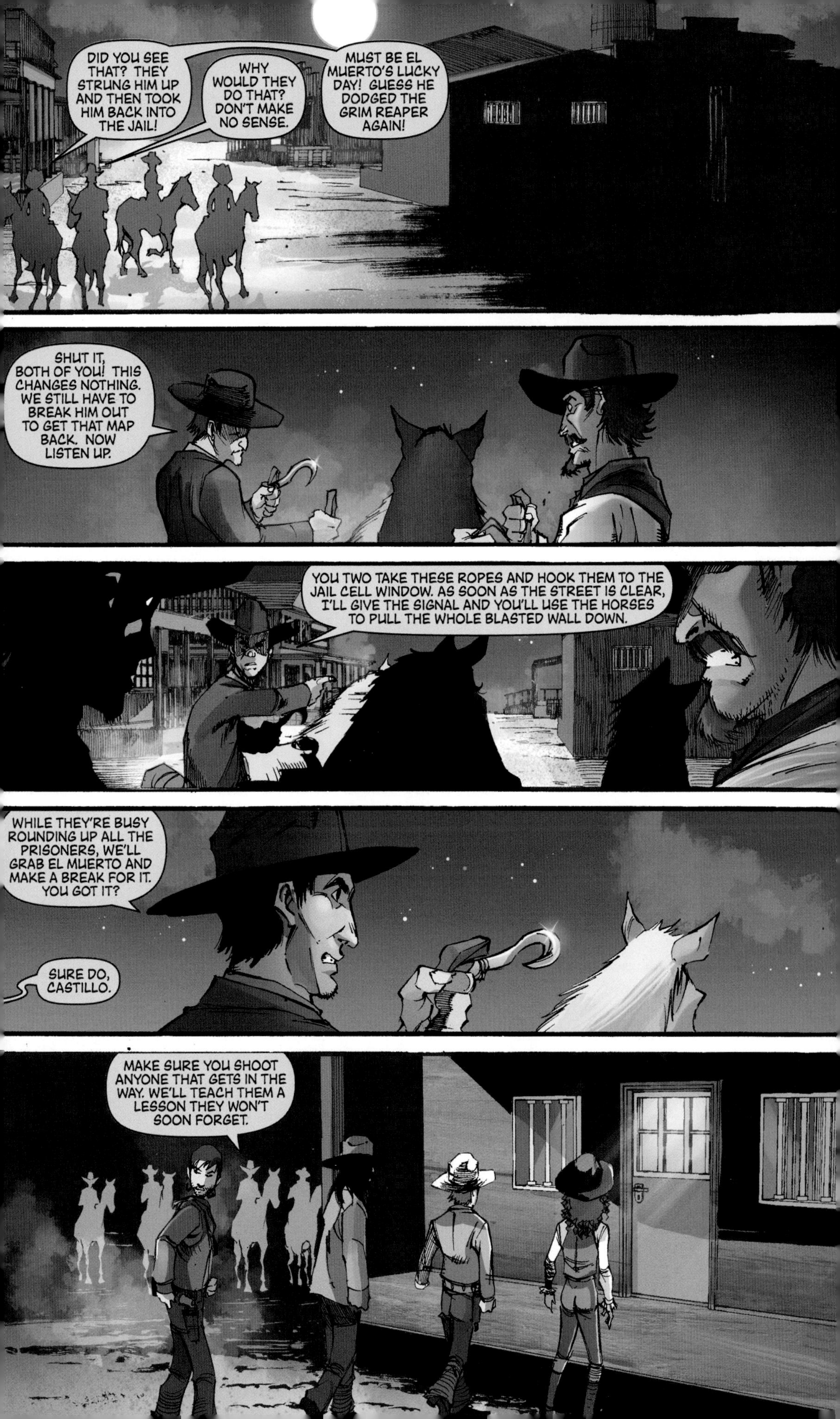
DID YOU SEE THAT? THEY STRUNG HIM UP AND THEN TOOK HIM BACK INTO THE JAIL!
WHY WOULD THEY DO THAT? DON'T MAKE NO SENSE.
MUST BE EL MUERTO'S LUCKY DAY! GUESS HE DODGED THE GRIM REAPER AGAIN!
SHUT IT, BOTH OF YOU! THIS CHANGES NOTHING. WE STILL HAVE TO BREAK HIM OUT TO GET THAT MAP BACK. NOW LISTEN UP.
YOU TWO TAKE THESE ROPES AND HOOK THEM TO THE JAIL CELL WINDOW. AS SOON AS THE STREET IS CLEAR, I'LL GIVE THE SIGNAL AND YOU'LL USE THE HORSES TO PULL THE WHOLE BLASTED WALL DOWN.
WHILE THEY'RE BUSY ROUNDING UP ALL THE PRISONERS, WE'LL GRAB EL MUERTO AND MAKE A BREAK FOR IT. YOU GOT IT?
SURE DO, CASTILLO.
MAKE SURE YOU SHOOT ANYONE THAT GETS IN THE WAY. WE'LL TEACH THEM A LESSON THEY WON'T SOON FORGET.

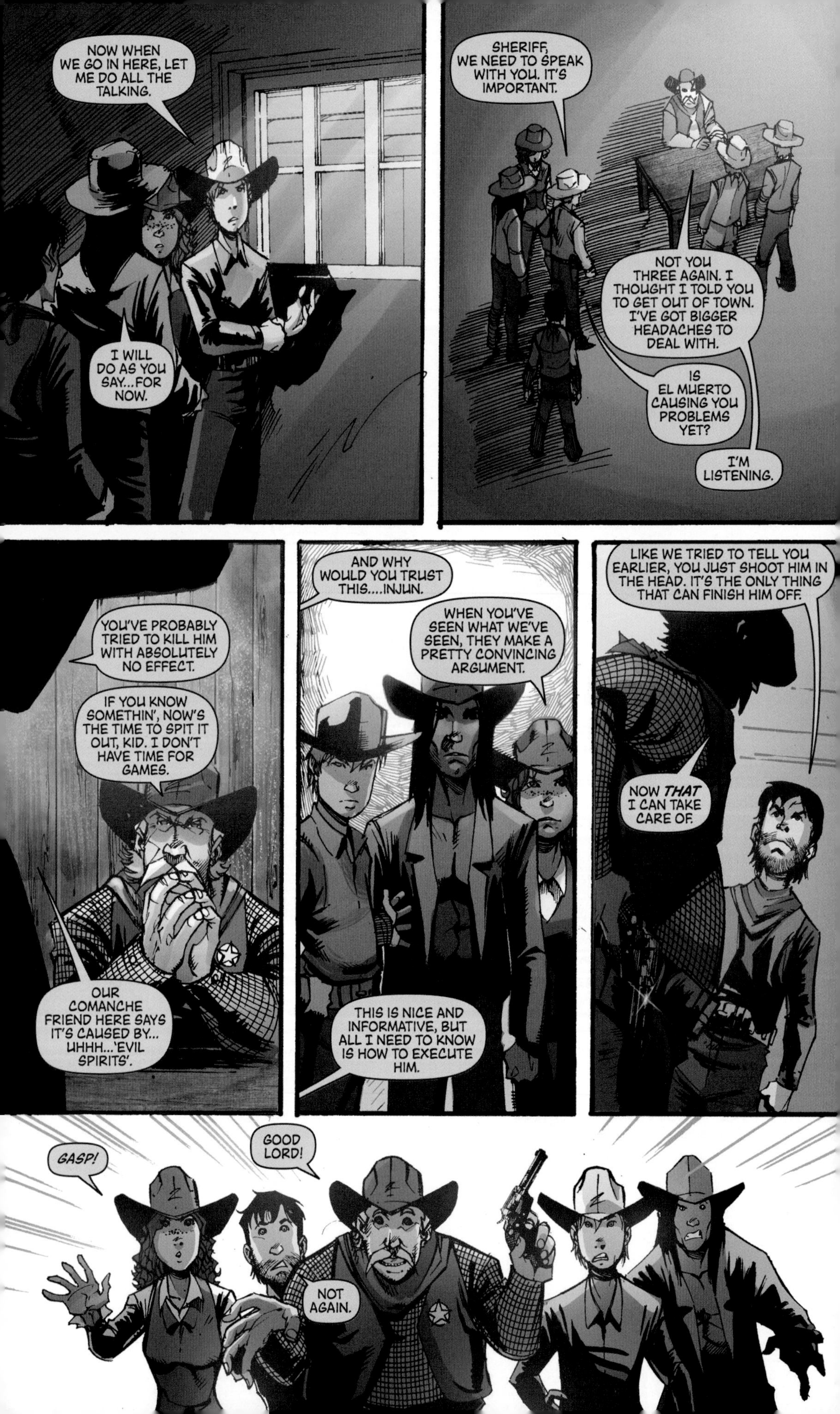
NOW WHEN WE GO IN HERE, LET ME DO ALL THE TALKING.
I WILL DO AS YOU SAY...FOR NOW.
SHERIFF, WE NEED TO SPEAK WITH YOU. IT'S IMPORTANT.
NOT YOU THREE AGAIN. I THOUGHT I TOLD YOU TO GET OUT OF TOWN. I'VE GOT BIGGER HEADACHES TO DEAL WITH.
IS EL MUERTO CAUSING YOU PROBLEMS YET?
I'M LISTENING.
YOU'VE PROBABLY TRIED TO KILL HIM WITH ABSOLUTELY NO EFFECT.
IF YOU KNOW SOMETHIN', NOW'S THE TIME TO SPIT IT OUT, KID. I DON'T HAVE TIME FOR GAMES.
OUR COMANCHE FRIEND HERE SAYS IT'S CAUSED BY... UHHH...'EVIL SPIRITS'.
AND WHY WOULD YOU TRUST THIS....INJUN.
WHEN YOU'VE SEEN WHAT WE'VE SEEN, THEY MAKE A PRETTY CONVINCING ARGUMENT.
THIS IS NICE AND INFORMATIVE, BUT ALL I NEED TO KNOW IS HOW TO EXECUTE HIM.
LIKE WE TRIED TO TELL YOU EARLIER, YOU JUST SHOOT HIM IN THE HEAD. IT'S THE ONLY THING THAT CAN FINISH HIM OFF.
NOW *THAT* I CAN TAKE CARE OF.
GASP!
GOOD LORD!
NOT AGAIN.

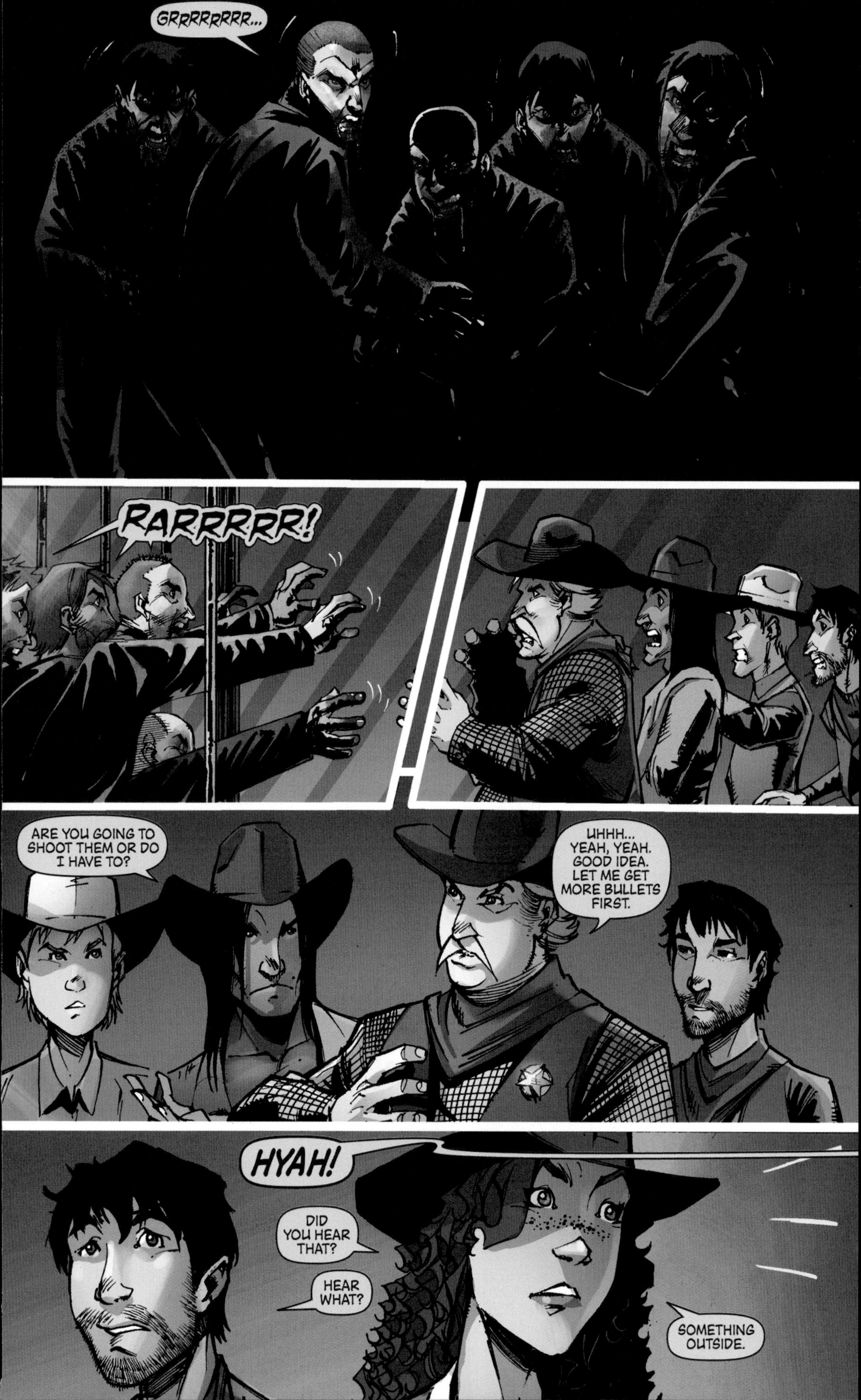
GRRRRRRRR...
RARRRRR!
ARE YOU GOING TO SHOOT THEM OR DO I HAVE TO?
UHHH... YEAH, YEAH. GOOD IDEA. LET ME GET MORE BULLETS FIRST.
HYAH!
DID YOU HEAR THAT?
HEAR WHAT?
SOMETHING OUTSIDE.

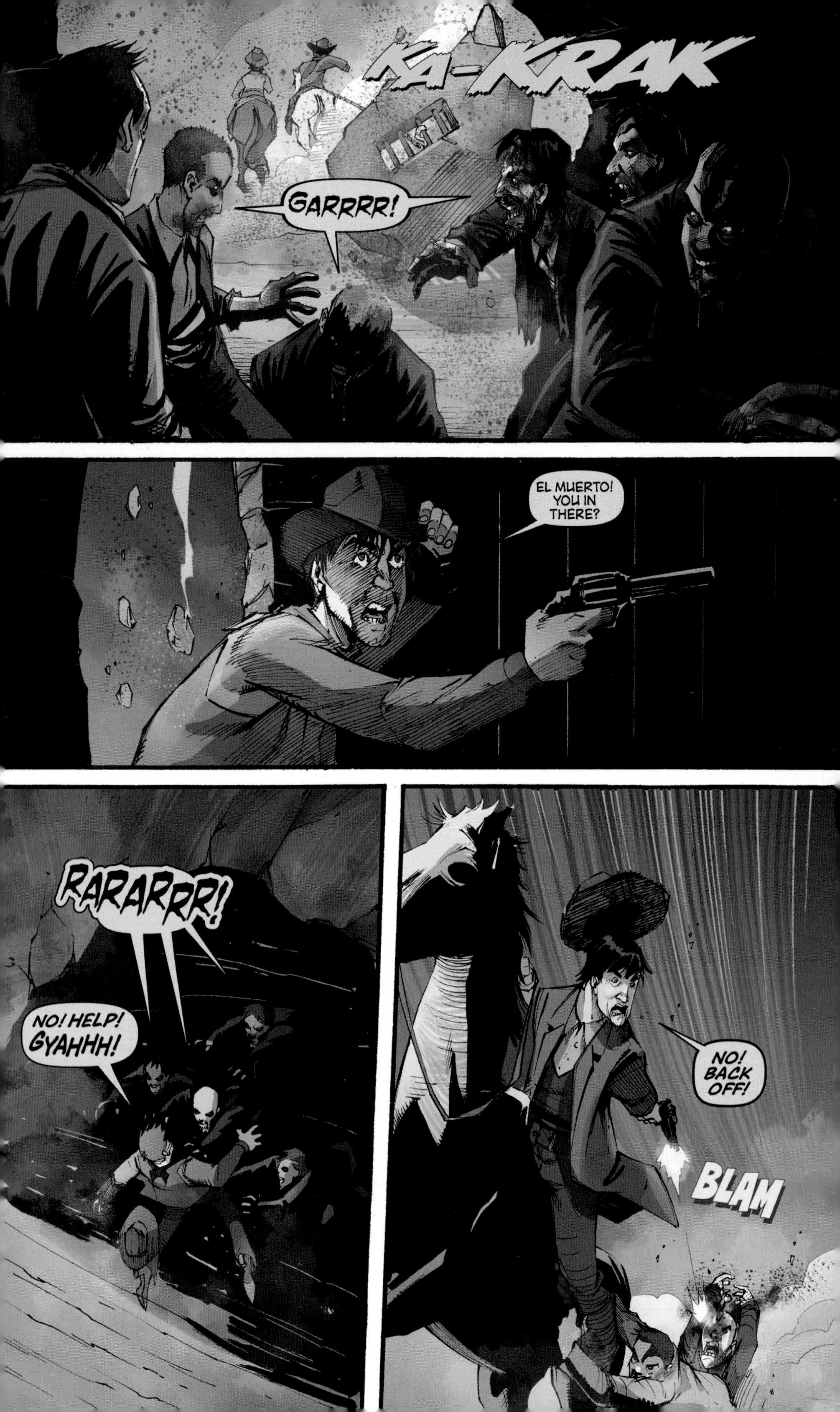
KA-KRAK
GARRRR!
EL MUERTO! YOU IN THERE?
RARARRR!
NO! HELP! GYAHHH!
NO! BACK OFF!
BLAM

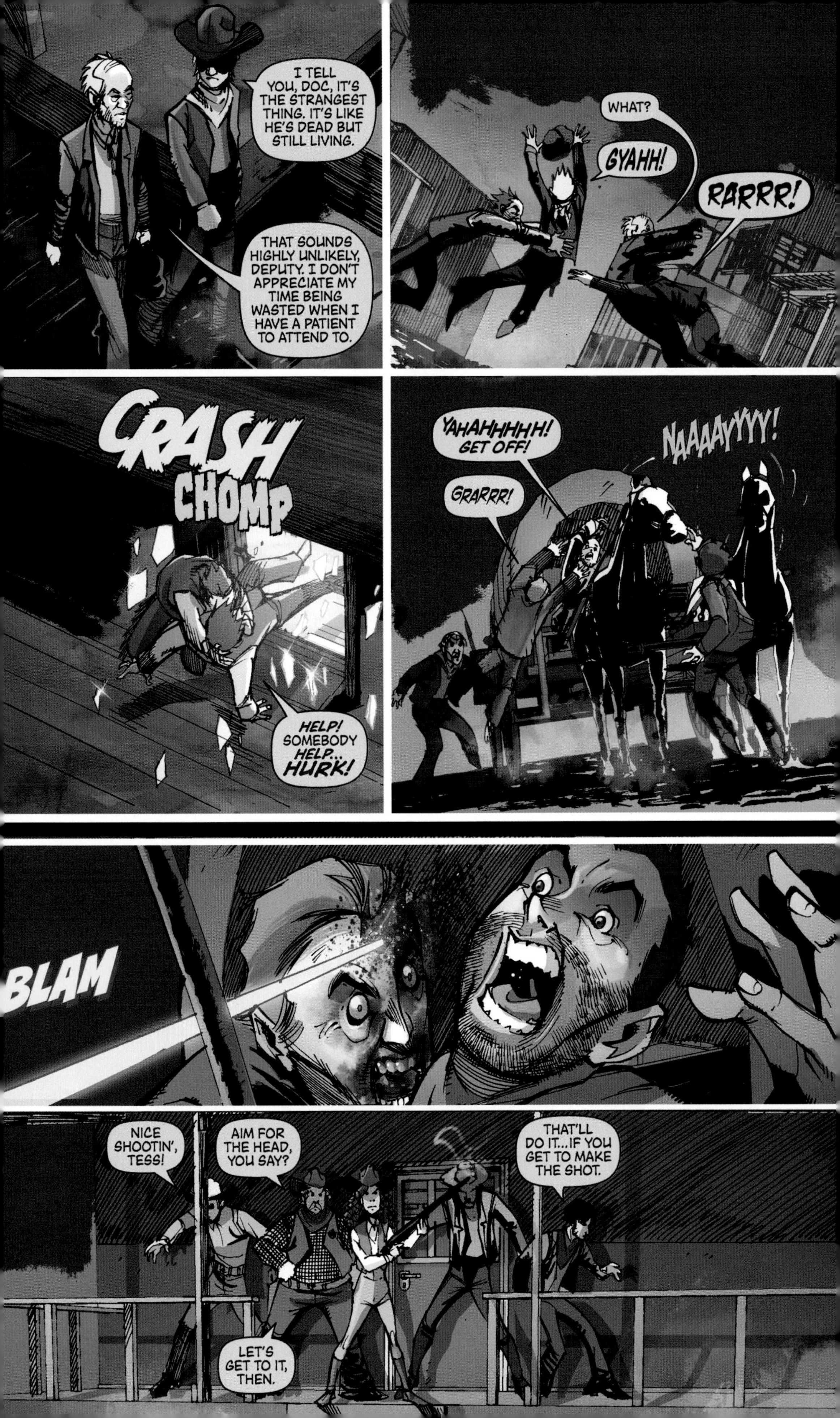
I TELL YOU, DOC, IT'S THE STRANGEST THING. IT'S LIKE HE'S DEAD BUT STILL LIVING.
THAT SOUNDS HIGHLY UNLIKELY, DEPUTY. I DON'T APPRECIATE MY TIME BEING WASTED WHEN I HAVE A PATIENT TO ATTEND TO.
WHAT?
GYAHH!
RARRR!
CRASH
CHOMP
HELP! SOMEBODY HELP... HURK!
YAHAHHHHH! GET OFF!
GRARRR!
NAAAAYYYY!
BLAM
NICE SHOOTIN', TESS!
AIM FOR THE HEAD, YOU SAY?
THAT'LL DO IT...IF YOU GET TO MAKE THE SHOT.
LET'S GET TO IT, THEN.

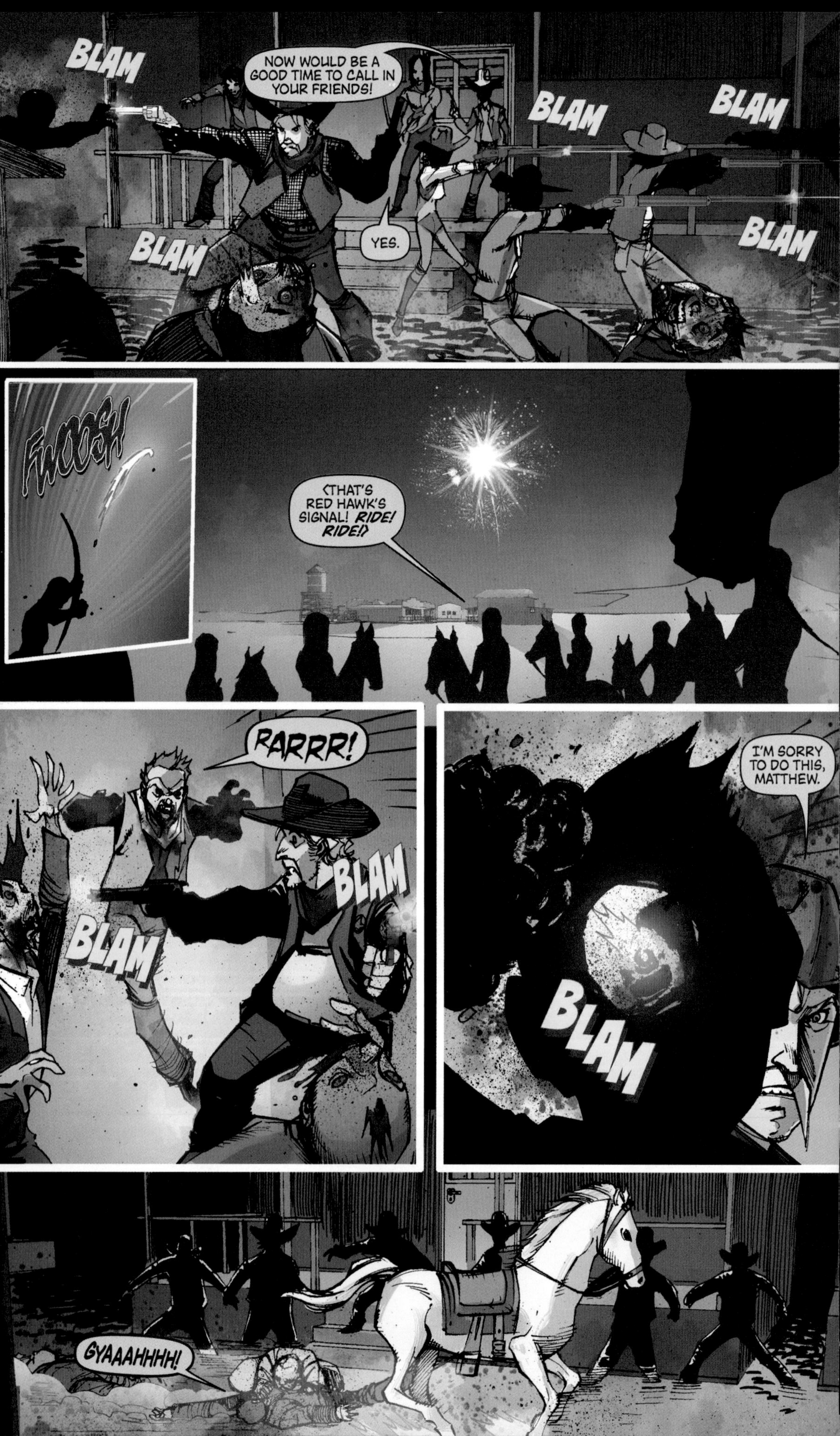
BLAM
NOW WOULD BE A GOOD TIME TO CALL IN YOUR FRIENDS!
BLAM
BLAM
YES.
BLAM
BLAM
FWOOSH
<THAT'S RED HAWK'S SIGNAL! RIDE! RIDE!>
RARRR!
BLAM
BLAM
I'M SORRY TO DO THIS, MATTHEW.
BLAM
GYAAAHHHH!

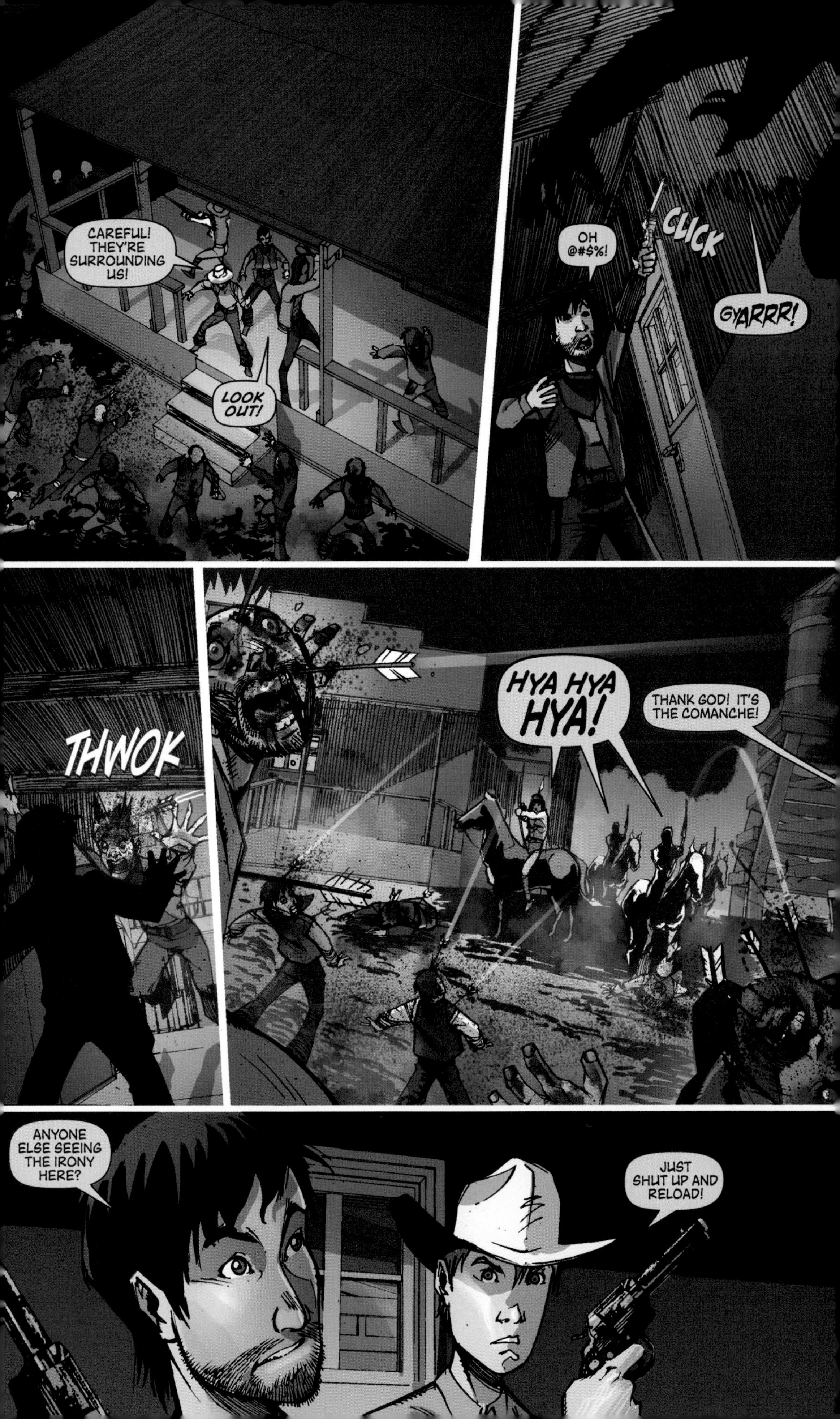
CAREFUL! THEY'RE SURROUNDING US!
LOOK OUT!
OH @#$%!
CLICK
GYARRR!
THWOK
HYA HYA HYA!
THANK GOD! IT'S THE COMANCHE!
ANYONE ELSE SEEING THE IRONY HERE?
JUST SHUT UP AND RELOAD!

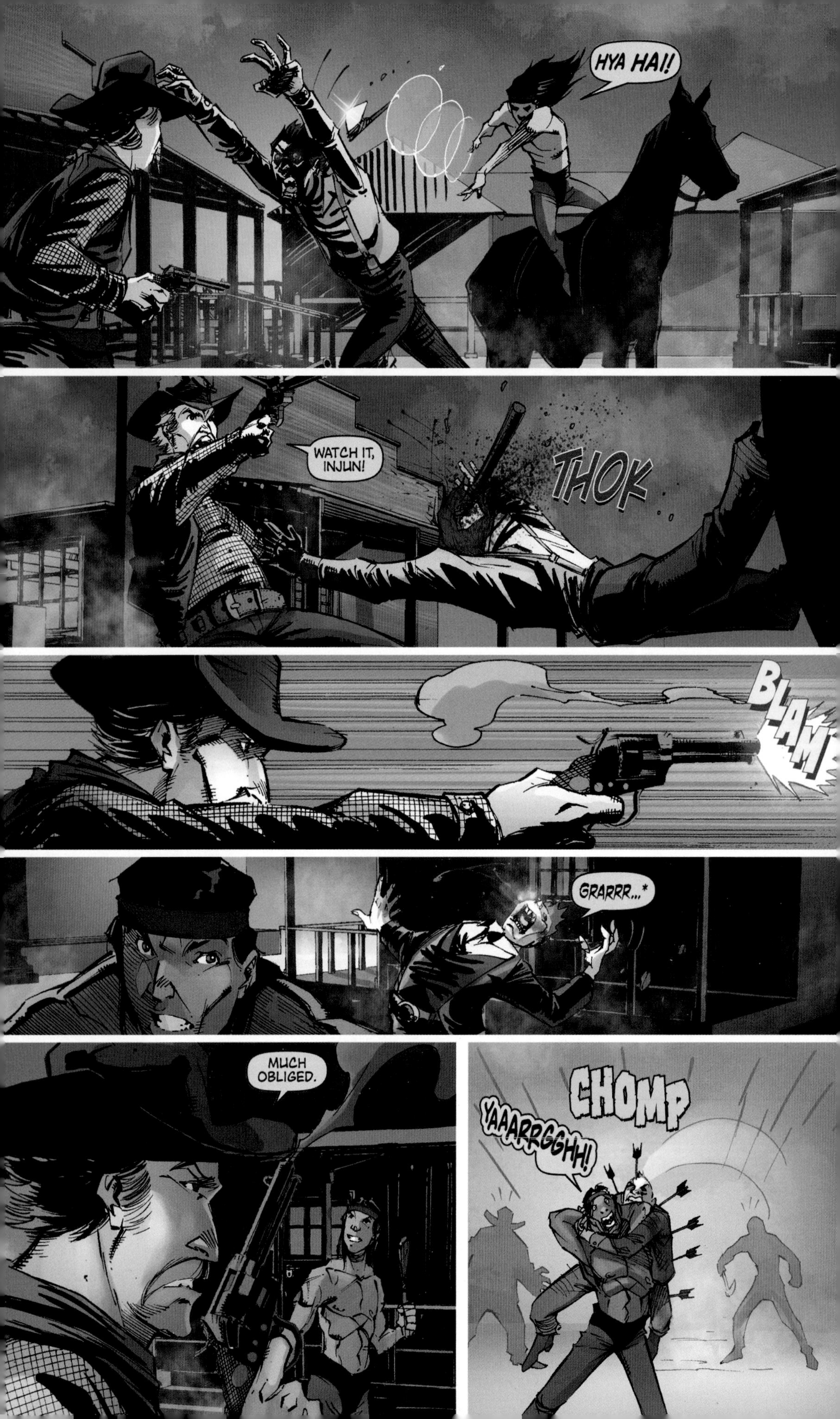
HYA HAI!
WATCH IT, INJUN!
THOK
BLAM
GRARRR...*
MUCH OBLIGED.
CHOMP
YAAARRGGHH!

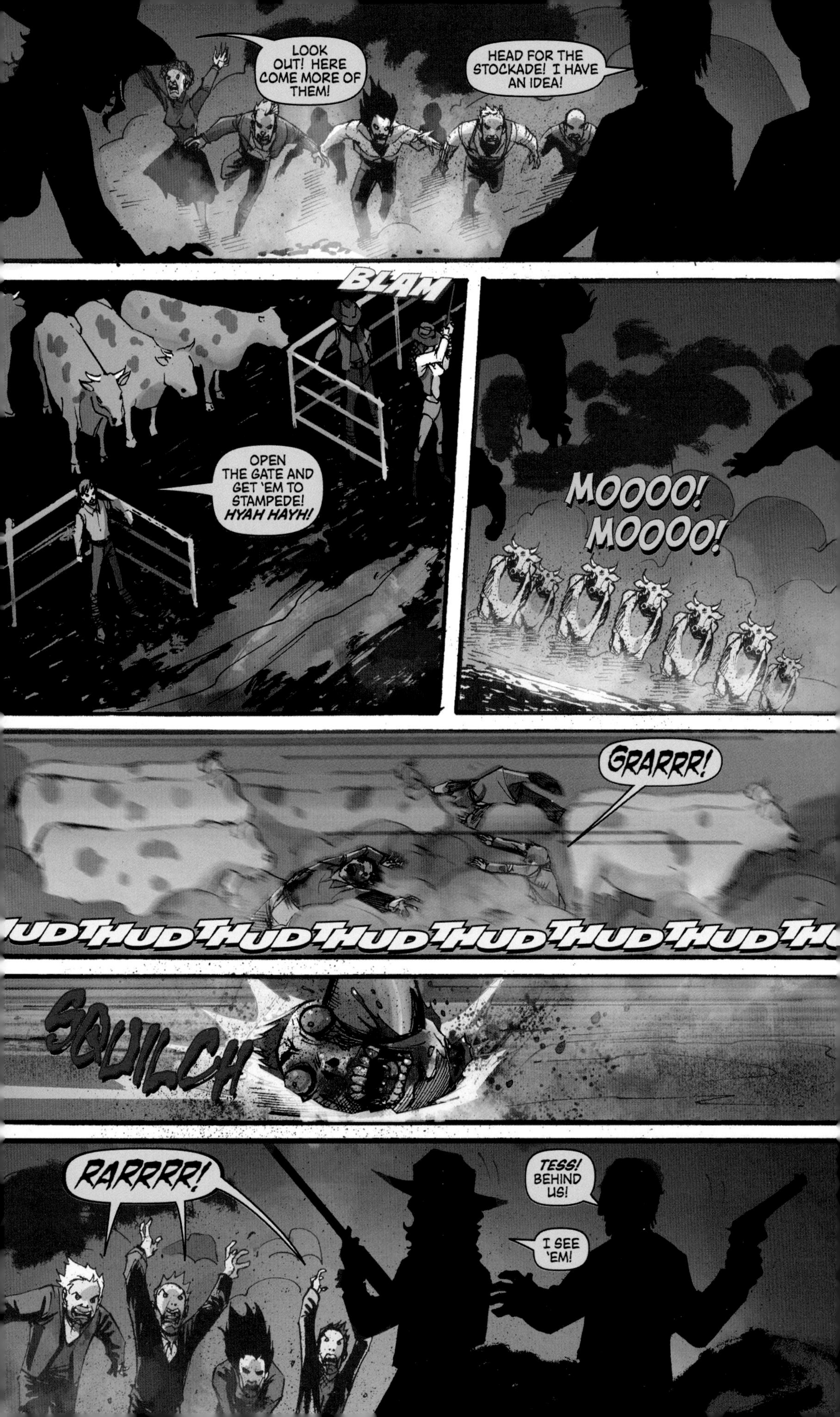

LOOK OUT! HERE COME MORE OF THEM!
HEAD FOR THE STOCKADE! I HAVE AN IDEA!
BLAM
OPEN THE GATE AND GET 'EM TO STAMPEDE! *HYAH HAYH!*
MOOOO! MOOOO!
GRARRR!
THUD THUD THUD THUD THUD THUD THUD THUD
SQUILCH
RARRRR!
TESS! BEHIND US!
I SEE 'EM!

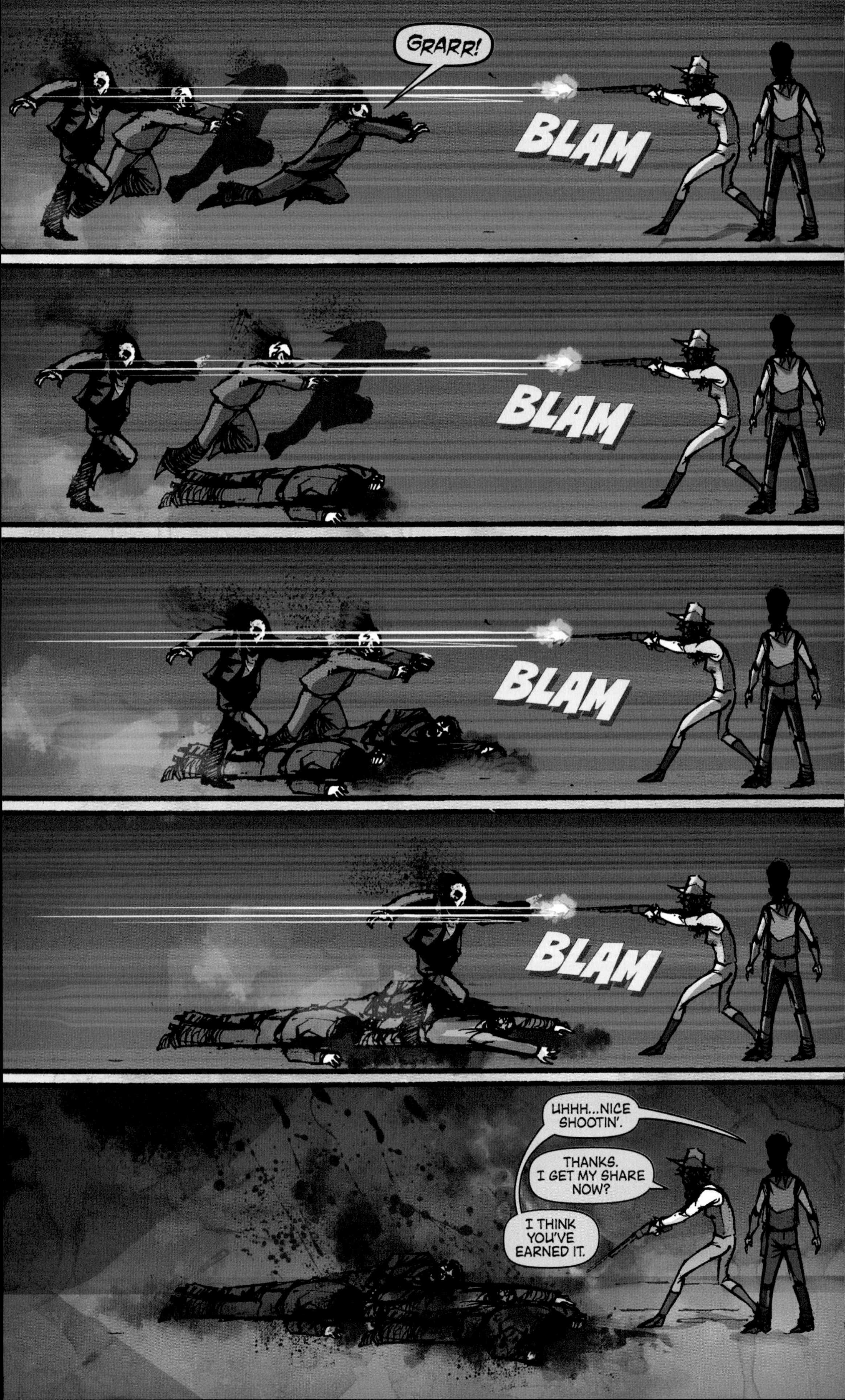
GRARR!
BLAM
BLAM
BLAM
BLAM
UHHH...NICE SHOOTIN'.
THANKS. I GET MY SHARE NOW?
I THINK YOU'VE EARNED IT.

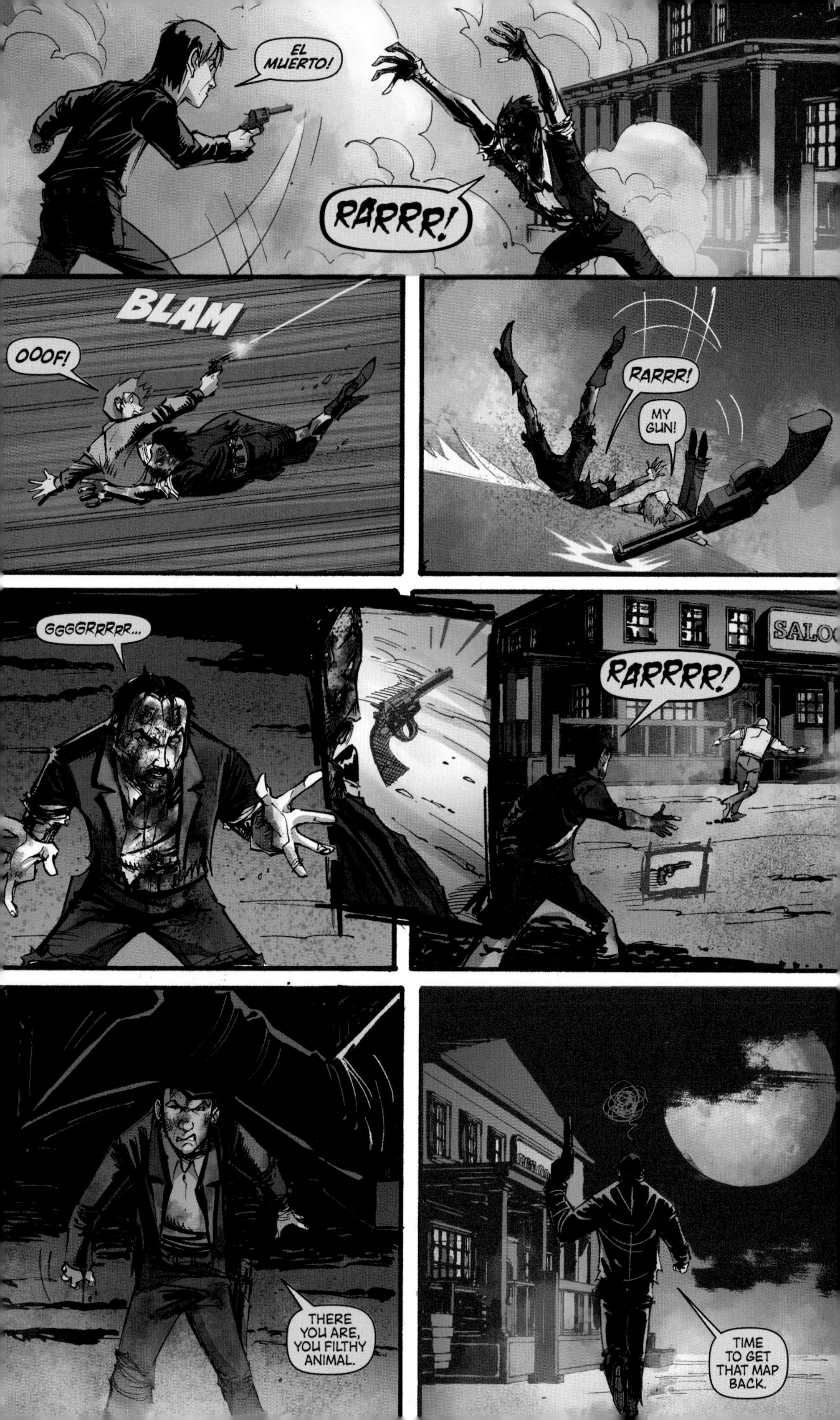
EL MUERTO!
RARRR!
BLAM
OOOF!
RARRR!
MY GUN!
GGGGRRRRR...
SALO
RARRRR!
THERE YOU ARE, YOU FILTHY ANIMAL.
TIME TO GET THAT MAP BACK.

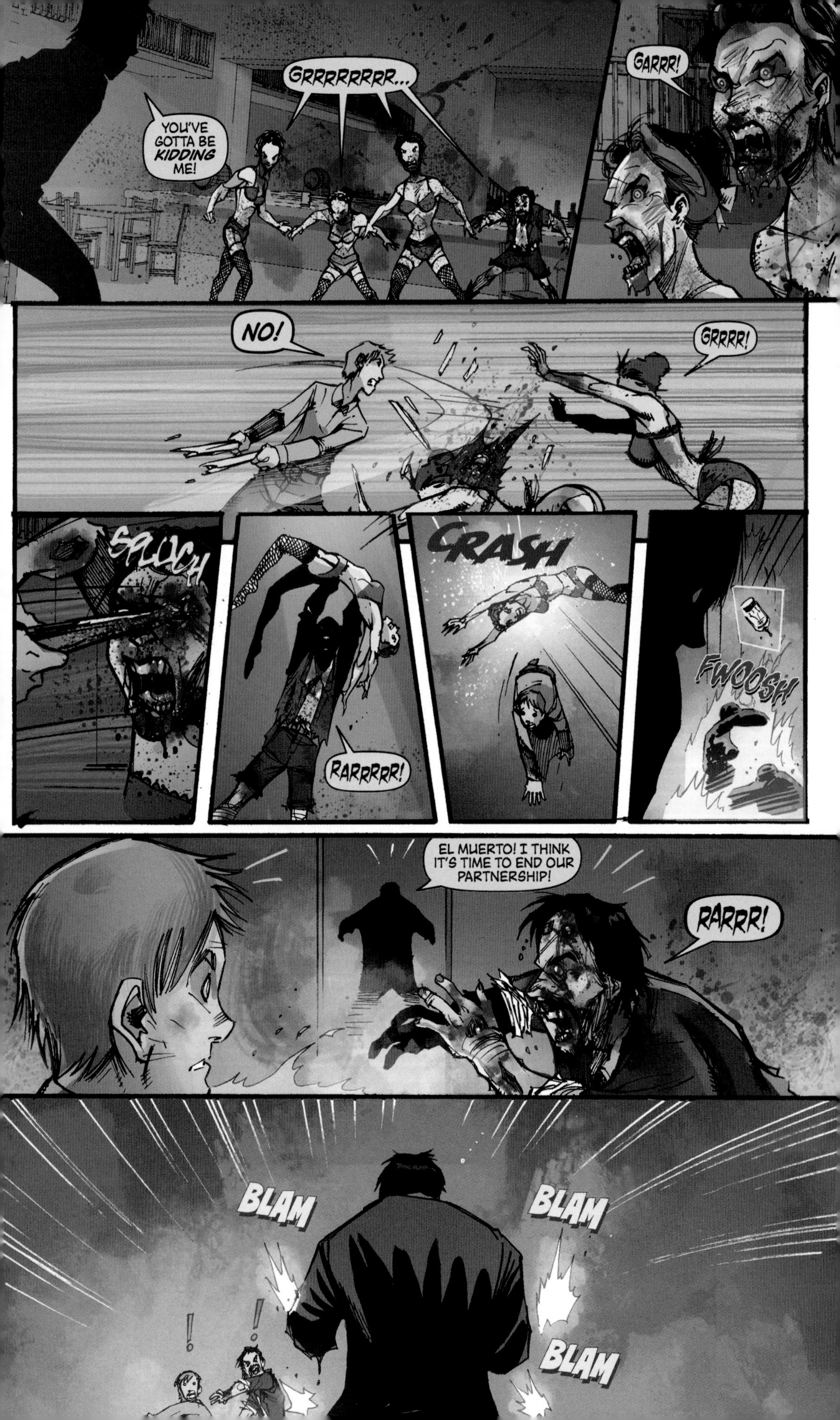
YOU'VE GOTTA BE KIDDING ME!
GRRRRRRRR...
GARRR!
NO!
GRRRR!
SPLOCH
RARRRRR!
CRASH
FWOOSH!
EL MUERTO! I THINK IT'S TIME TO END OUR PARTNERSHIP!
RARRR!
BLAM
BLAM
BLAM

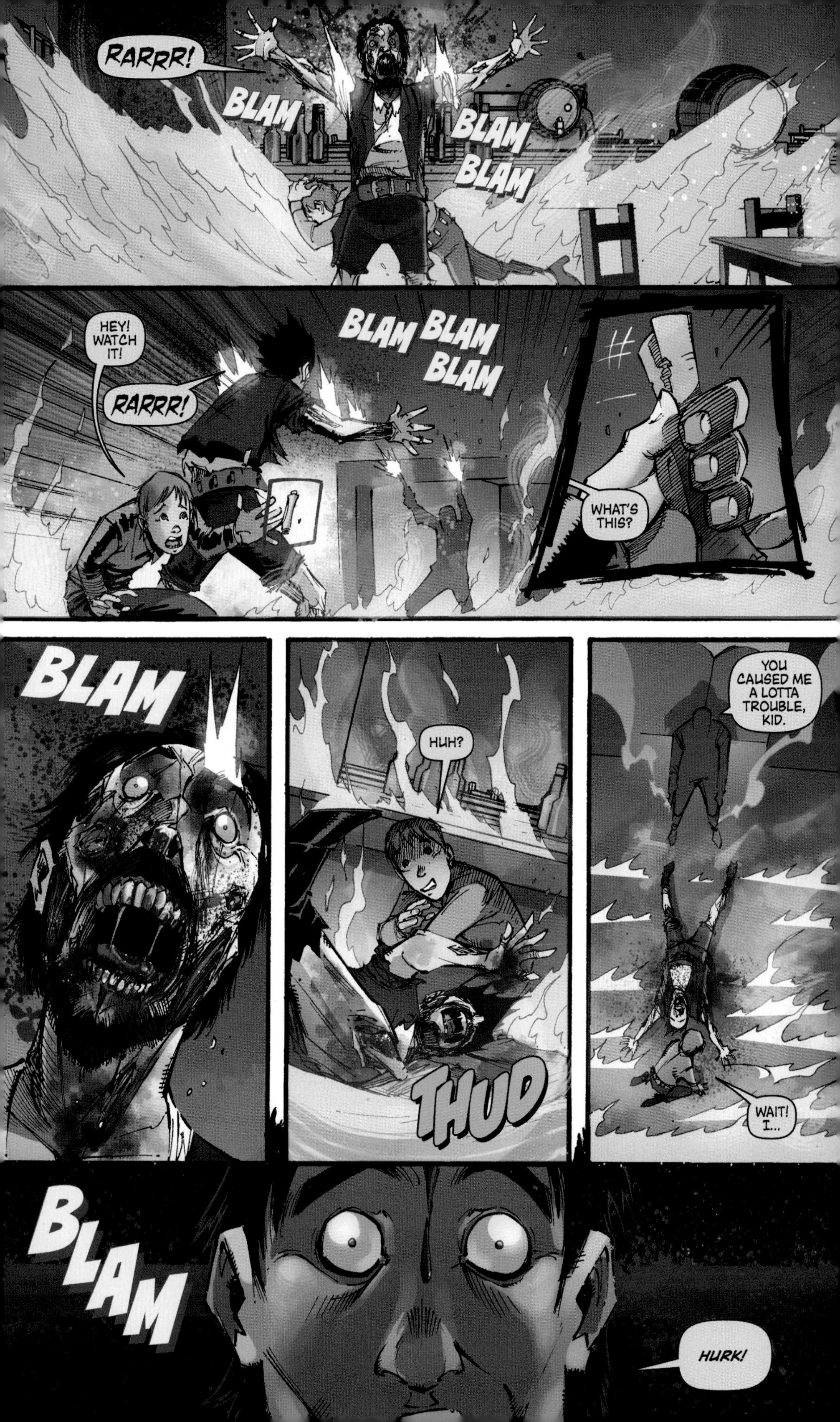
RARRR!
BLAM
BLAM
BLAM
HEY! WATCH IT!
RARRR!
BLAM BLAM
BLAM
WHAT'S THIS?
BLAM
HUH?
THUD
YOU CAUSED ME A LOTTA TROUBLE, KID.
WAIT! I...
BLAM
HURK!

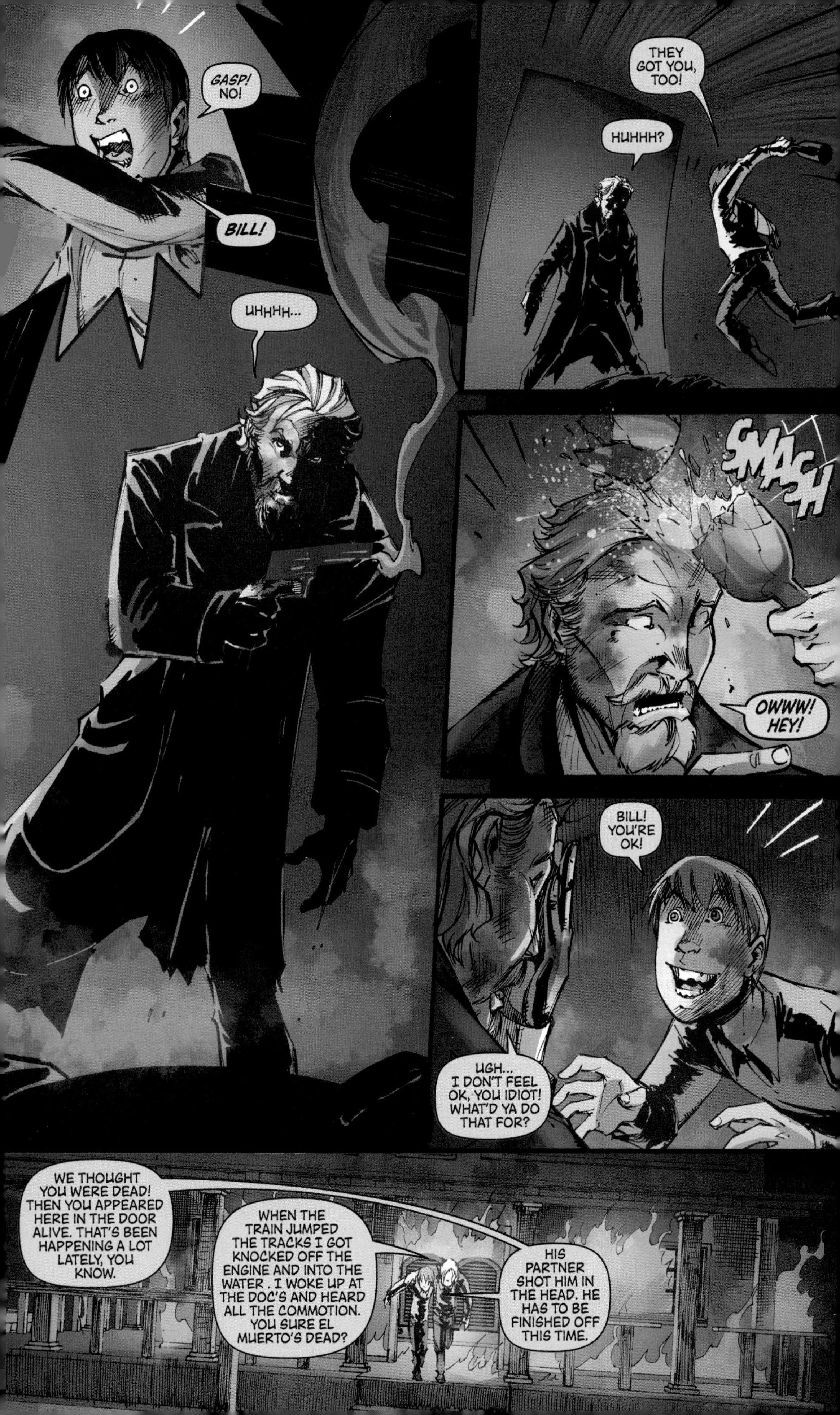
GASP! NO!
BILL!
UHHHH...
THEY GOT YOU, TOO!
HUHHH?
SMASH
OWWW! HEY!
BILL! YOU'RE OK!
UGH... I DON'T FEEL OK, YOU IDIOT! WHAT'D YA DO THAT FOR?
WE THOUGHT YOU WERE DEAD! THEN YOU APPEARED HERE IN THE DOOR ALIVE. THAT'S BEEN HAPPENING A LOT LATELY, YOU KNOW.
WHEN THE TRAIN JUMPED THE TRACKS I GOT KNOCKED OFF THE ENGINE AND INTO THE WATER . I WOKE UP AT THE DOC'S AND HEARD ALL THE COMMOTION. YOU SURE EL MUERTO'S DEAD?
HIS PARTNER SHOT HIM IN THE HEAD. HE HAS TO BE FINISHED OFF THIS TIME.

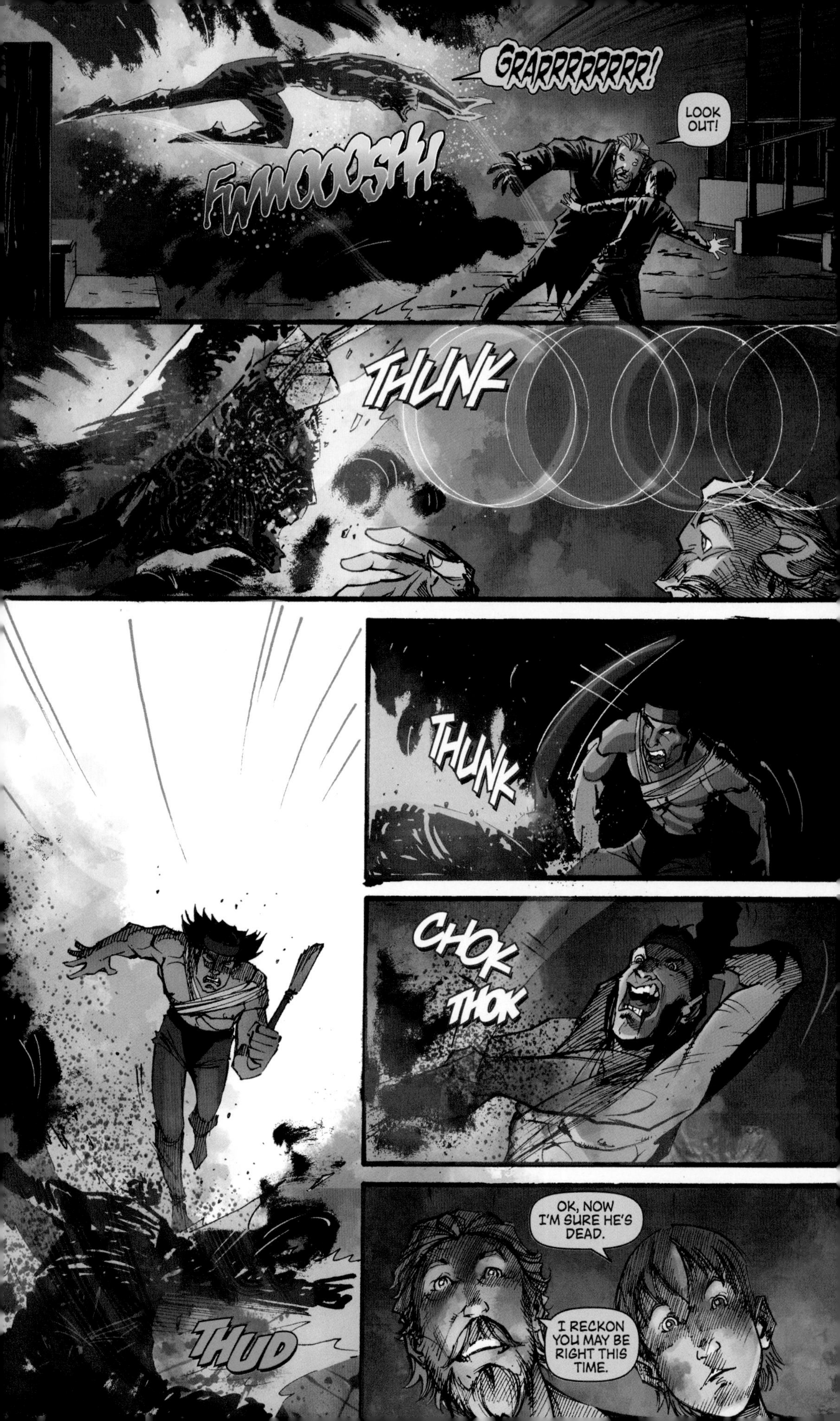
GRARRRRRRR!
LOOK OUT!
FWOOOSHH
THUNK
THUNK
CHOK
THOK
THUD
OK, NOW I'M SURE HE'S DEAD.
I RECKON YOU MAY BE RIGHT THIS TIME.

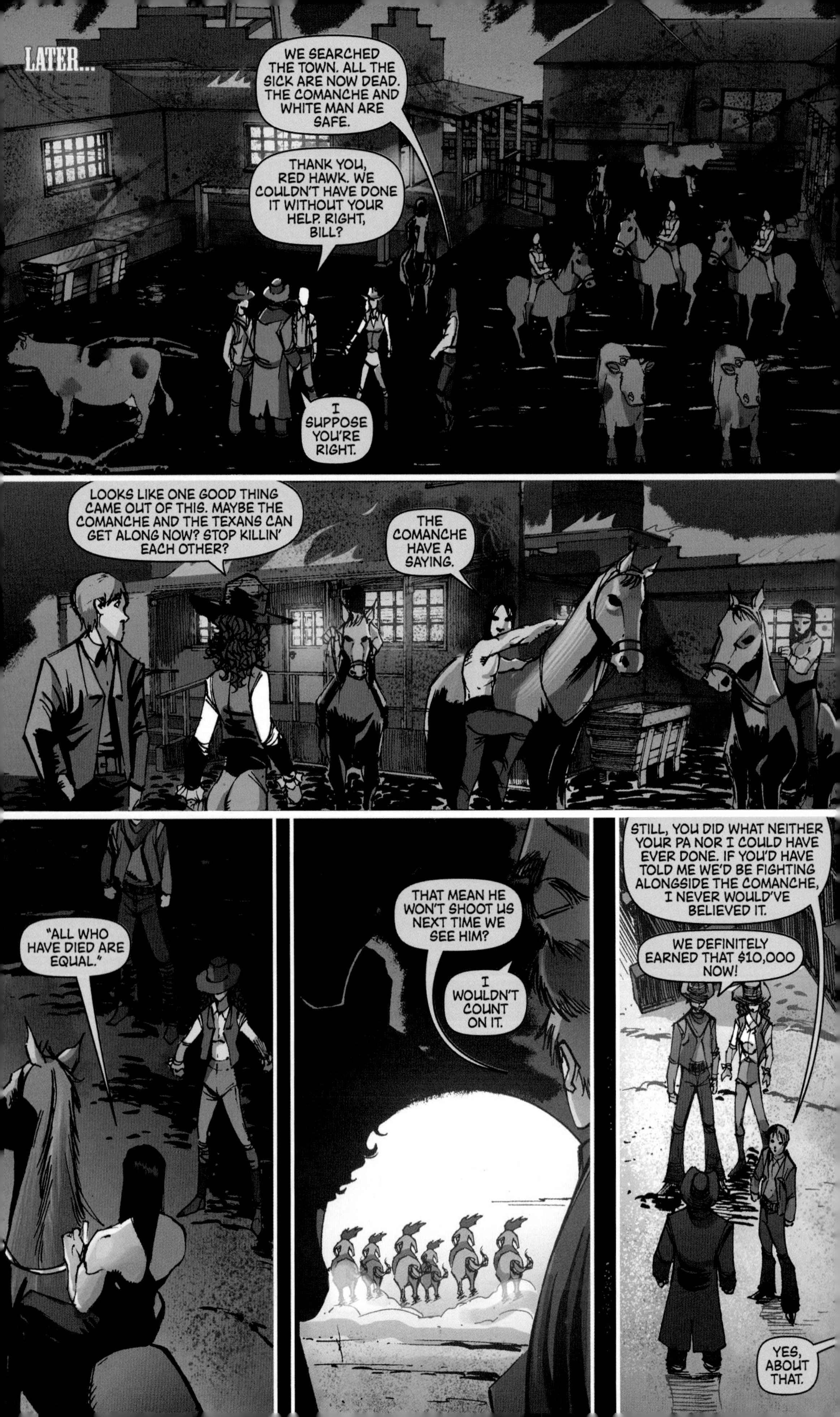
LATER...
WE SEARCHED THE TOWN. ALL THE SICK ARE NOW DEAD. THE COMANCHE AND WHITE MAN ARE SAFE.
THANK YOU, RED HAWK. WE COULDN'T HAVE DONE IT WITHOUT YOUR HELP. RIGHT, BILL?
I SUPPOSE YOU'RE RIGHT.
LOOKS LIKE ONE GOOD THING CAME OUT OF THIS. MAYBE THE COMANCHE AND THE TEXANS CAN GET ALONG NOW? STOP KILLIN' EACH OTHER?
THE COMANCHE HAVE A SAYING.
"ALL WHO HAVE DIED ARE EQUAL."
THAT MEAN HE WON'T SHOOT US NEXT TIME WE SEE HIM?
I WOULDN'T COUNT ON IT.
STILL, YOU DID WHAT NEITHER YOUR PA NOR I COULD HAVE EVER DONE. IF YOU'D HAVE TOLD ME WE'D BE FIGHTING ALONGSIDE THE COMANCHE, I NEVER WOULD'VE BELIEVED IT.
WE DEFINITELY EARNED THAT $10,000 NOW!
YES, ABOUT THAT.

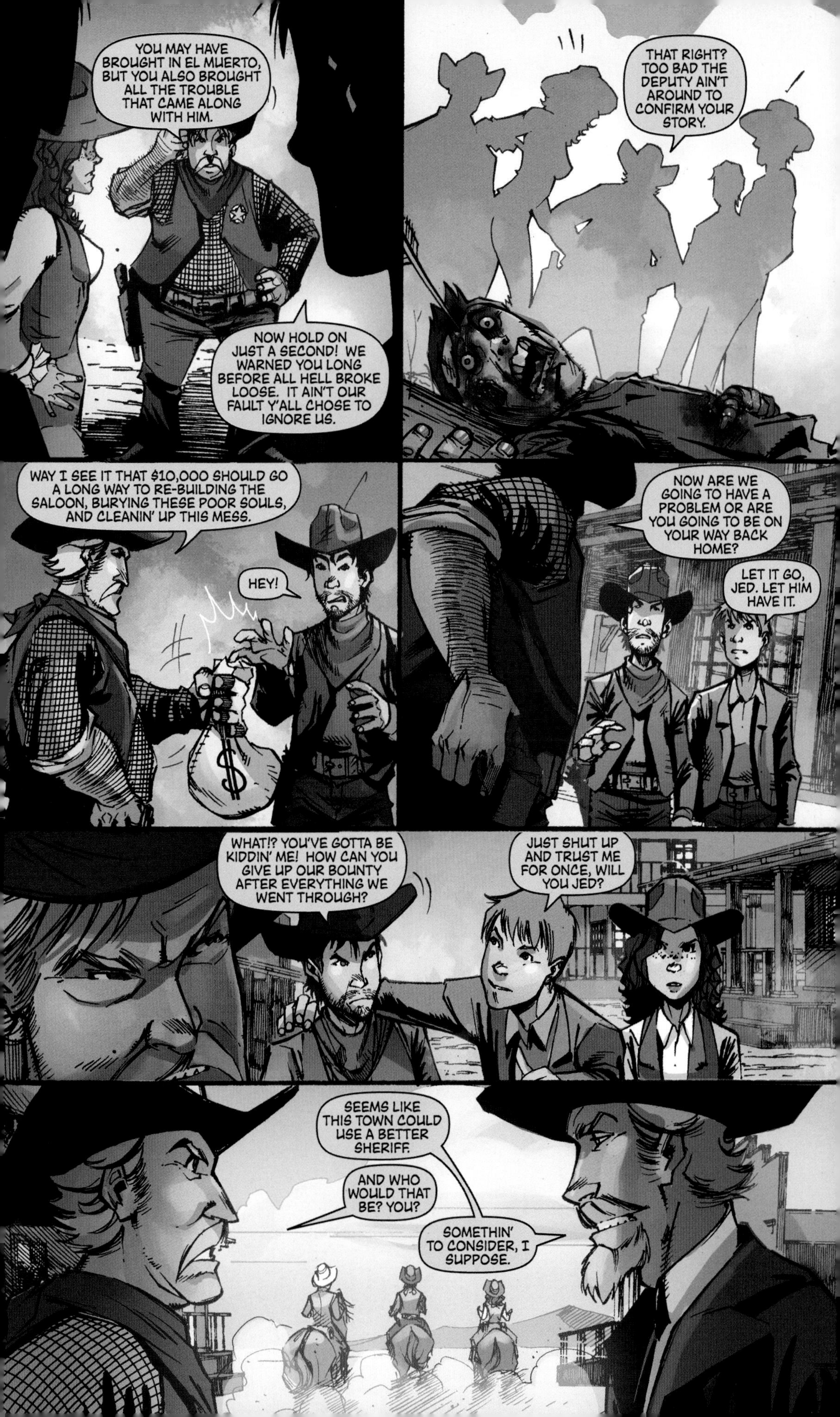
YOU MAY HAVE BROUGHT IN EL MUERTO, BUT YOU ALSO BROUGHT ALL THE TROUBLE THAT CAME ALONG WITH HIM.
NOW HOLD ON JUST A SECOND! WE WARNED YOU LONG BEFORE ALL HELL BROKE LOOSE. IT AIN'T OUR FAULT Y'ALL CHOSE TO IGNORE US.
THAT RIGHT? TOO BAD THE DEPUTY AIN'T AROUND TO CONFIRM YOUR STORY.
WAY I SEE IT THAT $10,000 SHOULD GO A LONG WAY TO RE-BUILDING THE SALOON, BURYING THESE POOR SOULS, AND CLEANIN' UP THIS MESS.
HEY!
NOW ARE WE GOING TO HAVE A PROBLEM OR ARE YOU GOING TO BE ON YOUR WAY BACK HOME?
LET IT GO, JED. LET HIM HAVE IT.
WHAT!? YOU'VE GOTTA BE KIDDIN' ME! HOW CAN YOU GIVE UP OUR BOUNTY AFTER EVERYTHING WE WENT THROUGH?
JUST SHUT UP AND TRUST ME FOR ONCE, WILL YOU JED?
SEEMS LIKE THIS TOWN COULD USE A BETTER SHERIFF.
AND WHO WOULD THAT BE? YOU?
SOMETHIN' TO CONSIDER, I SUPPOSE.

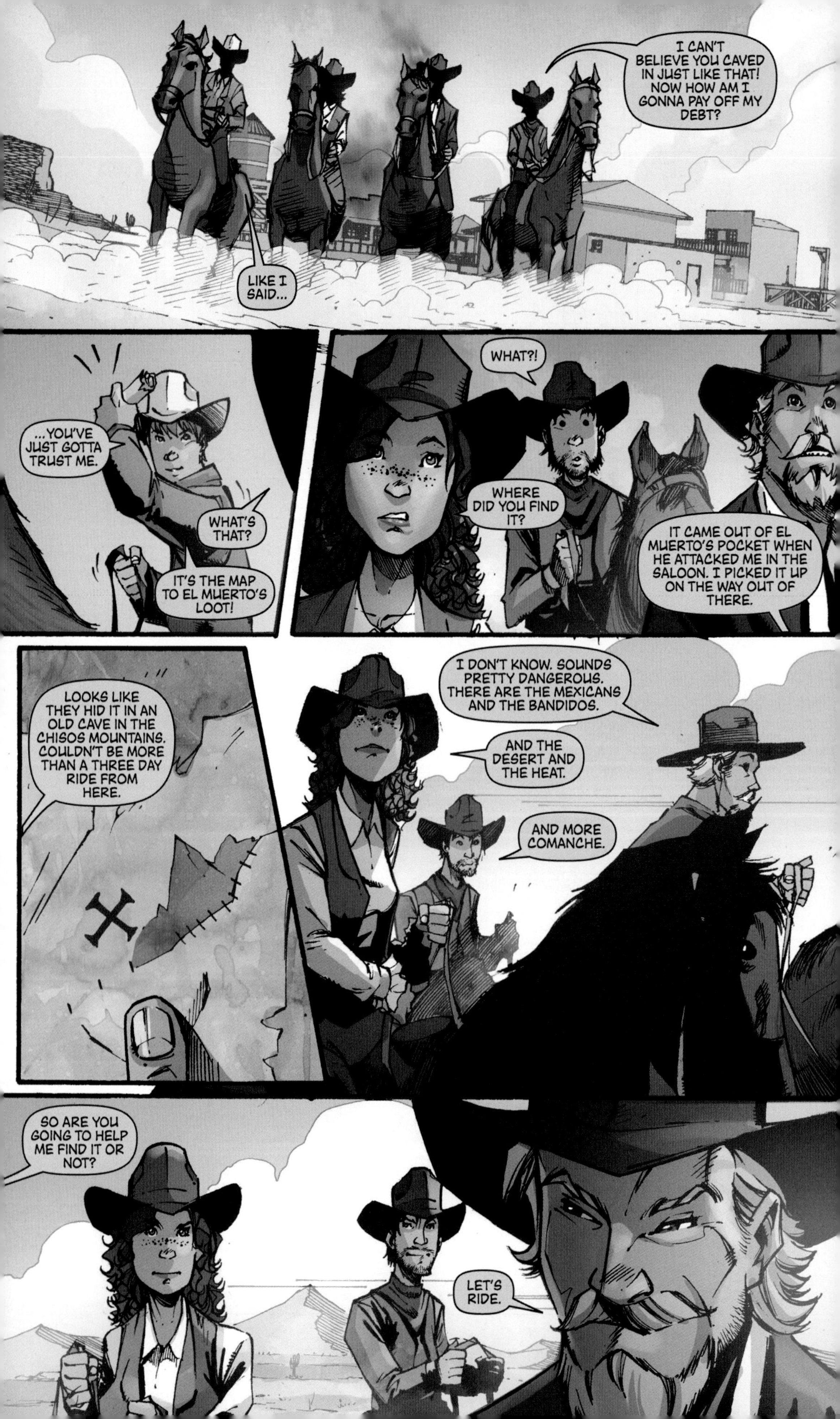
I CAN'T BELIEVE YOU CAVED IN JUST LIKE THAT! NOW HOW AM I GONNA PAY OFF MY DEBT?
LIKE I SAID...
...YOU'VE JUST GOTTA TRUST ME.
WHAT'S THAT?
IT'S THE MAP TO EL MUERTO'S LOOT!
WHAT?!
WHERE DID YOU FIND IT?
IT CAME OUT OF EL MUERTO'S POCKET WHEN HE ATTACKED ME IN THE SALOON. I PICKED IT UP ON THE WAY OUT OF THERE.
LOOKS LIKE THEY HID IT IN AN OLD CAVE IN THE CHISOS MOUNTAINS. COULDN'T BE MORE THAN A THREE DAY RIDE FROM HERE.
I DON'T KNOW. SOUNDS PRETTY DANGEROUS. THERE ARE THE MEXICANS AND THE BANDIDOS.
AND THE DESERT AND THE HEAT.
AND MORE COMANCHE.
SO ARE YOU GOING TO HELP ME FIND IT OR NOT?
LET'S RIDE.

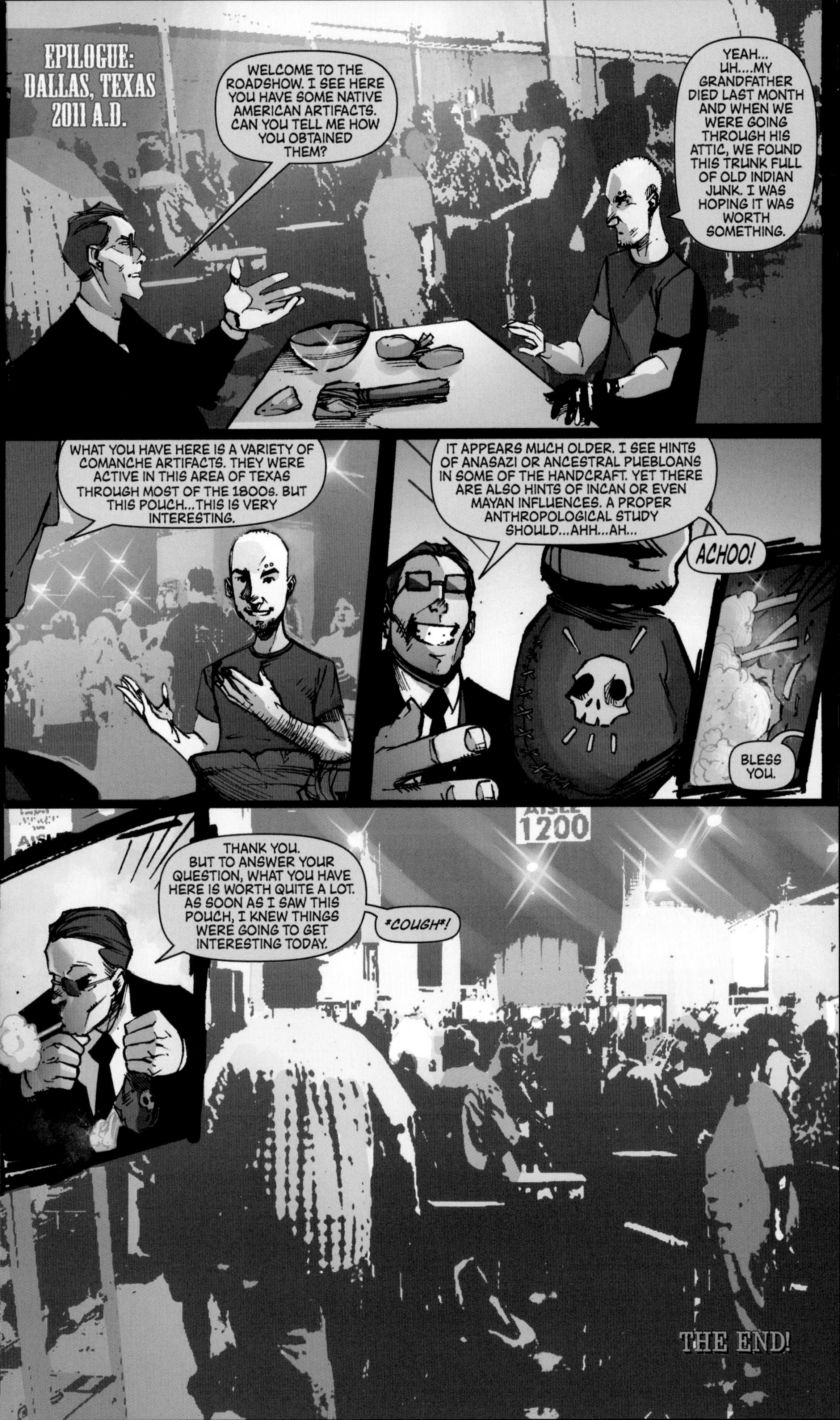
EPILOGUE: DALLAS, TEXAS 2011 A.D.
WELCOME TO THE ROADSHOW. I SEE HERE YOU HAVE SOME NATIVE AMERICAN ARTIFACTS. CAN YOU TELL ME HOW YOU OBTAINED THEM?
YEAH... UH....MY GRANDFATHER DIED LAST MONTH AND WHEN WE WERE GOING THROUGH HIS ATTIC, WE FOUND THIS TRUNK FULL OF OLD INDIAN JUNK. I WAS HOPING IT WAS WORTH SOMETHING.
WHAT YOU HAVE HERE IS A VARIETY OF COMANCHE ARTIFACTS. THEY WERE ACTIVE IN THIS AREA OF TEXAS THROUGH MOST OF THE 1800s. BUT THIS POUCH...THIS IS VERY INTERESTING.
IT APPEARS MUCH OLDER. I SEE HINTS OF ANASAZI OR ANCESTRAL PUEBLOANS IN SOME OF THE HANDCRAFT. YET THERE ARE ALSO HINTS OF INCAN OR EVEN MAYAN INFLUENCES. A PROPER ANTHROPOLOGICAL STUDY SHOULD...AHH...AH...
ACHOO!
BLESS YOU.
AISLE 1200
THANK YOU. BUT TO ANSWER YOUR QUESTION, WHAT YOU HAVE HERE IS WORTH QUITE A LOT. AS SOON AS I SAW THIS POUCH, I KNEW THINGS WERE GOING TO GET INTERESTING TODAY.
COUGH!
THE END!

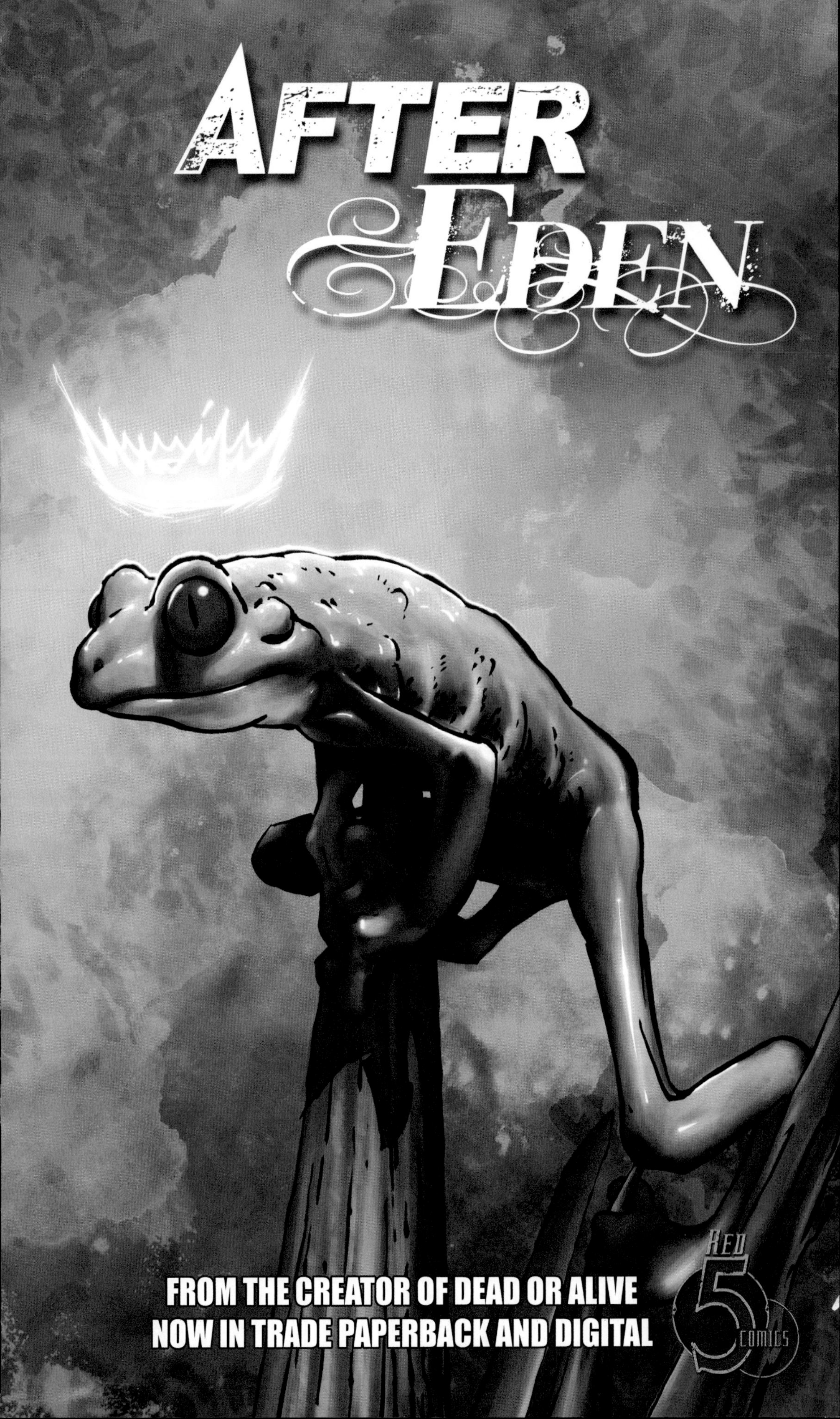
AFTER EDEN
FROM THE CREATOR OF DEAD OR ALIVE
NOW IN TRADE PAPERBACK AND DIGITAL
RED 5 COMICS

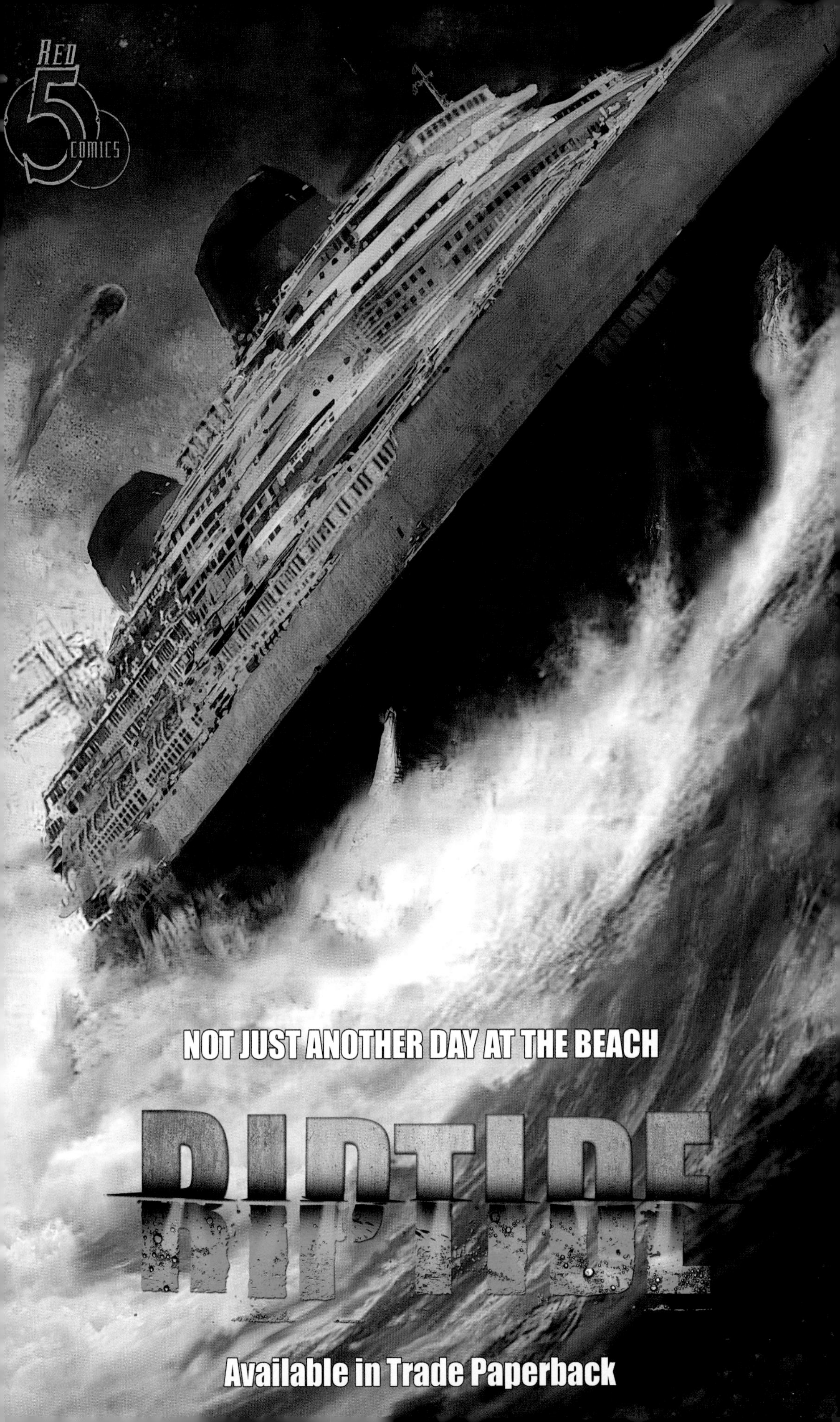
RED 5 COMICS
NOT JUST ANOTHER DAY AT THE BEACH
RIPTIDE
Available in Trade Paperback